THE GOOD, THE BAD,
AND THE UNCANNY

"A fast, intelligently written tale that is fun to read."
—*The Green Man Review*

JUST ANOTHER JUDGEMENT DAY

"Another unrestrained ride through the Nightside."
—*Monsters and Critics*

THE UNNATURAL INQUIRER

"Sam Spade meets Sirius Black . . . in the Case of the Cosmic MacGuffin . . . crabby wit and inventively gruesome set pieces."
—*Entertainment Weekly*

HELL TO PAY

"If you're looking for fast-paced, no-holds-barred dark urban fantasy, you need look no further: the Nightside is the place for you."
—*SFRevu*

SHARPER THAN A SERPENT'S TOOTH

"A captivating tale."
—*Midwest Book Review*

continued . . .

GHOST OF A CHANCE

SIMON R. GREEN

ACE BOOKS, NEW YORK

THE BERKLEY PUBLISHING GROUP
Published by the Penguin Group
Penguin Group (USA) Inc.
375 Hudson Street, New York, New York 10014, USA
Penguin Group (Canada), 90 Eglinton Avenue East, Suite 700, Toronto, Ontario M4P 2Y3, Canada
(a division of Pearson Penguin Canada Inc.)
Penguin Books Ltd., 80 Strand, London WC2R 0RL, England
Penguin Group Ireland, 25 St. Stephen's Green, Dublin 2, Ireland (a division of Penguin Books Ltd.)
Penguin Group (Australia), 250 Camberwell Road, Camberwell, Victoria 3124, Australia
(a division of Pearson Australia Group Pty. Ltd.)
Penguin Books India Pvt. Ltd., 11 Community Centre, Panchsheel Park, New Delhi—110 017, India
Penguin Group (NZ), 67 Apollo Drive, Rosedale, North Shore 0632, New Zealand
(a division of Pearson New Zealand Ltd.)
Penguin Books (South Africa) (Pty.) Ltd., 24 Sturdee Avenue, Rosebank, Johannesburg 2196,
South Africa

Penguin Books Ltd., Registered Offices: 80 Strand, London WC2R 0RL, England

This is a work of fiction. Names, characters, places, and incidents either are the product of the author's imagination or are used fictitiously, and any resemblance to actual persons, living or dead, business establishments, events, or locales is entirely coincidental. The publisher does not have any control over and does not assume any responsibility for author or third-party websites or their content.

GHOST OF A CHANCE

An Ace Book / published by arrangement with the author

PRINTING HISTORY
Ace mass-market edition / September 2010

Copyright © 2010 by Simon R. Green.
Cover art by Don Sipley.
Cover design by Judith Lagerman.
Interior text design by Laura K. Corless.

ISBN: 978-0-441-01916-8

ACE
Ace Books are published by The Berkley Publishing Group,
a division of Penguin Group (USA) Inc.,
375 Hudson Street, New York, New York 10014.
ACE and the "A" design are trademarks of Penguin Group (USA) Inc.

PRINTED IN THE UNITED STATES OF AMERICA

10 9 8 7 6 5 4 3 2 1

GHOST OF A CHANCE

||||||||||||||||||||||||||||

Everybody knows there are bad places in the world.

Houses that make you walk by on the other side of the street. Bedrooms that no-one in their right mind would try to sleep in. The television screen that isn't empty enough, the mirror with too many faces reflected in it, the voice in the night, and the dark at the top of the stairs. There are bad places everywhere, in crowded towns and empty fields. Places where there are no safety barriers, where the walls of the world have worn thin, places . . . where we know we're not safe. It's in these bad places that we see things we don't want to see.

As I was walking up the stair,
I met a man who wasn't there.
He wasn't there again today.
I wish that man would go away.

Ghosts. They've been around as long as we have, in one form or another. Strange sights and sounds, visitations and wonders, spirits of cold earth and empty graves come back to trouble the living. Things that won't lie down; and none of them bound by the laws of the living. The dead; and things that aren't dead enough.

There are bad places in the world, but it isn't ghosts that make these places bad; it's the bad places that make ghosts.

....

As the world changes, so do the ways in which we see ghosts. From dark shapes in the night and ancestral revenants to lovers separated too soon and thwarted enemies; from stone tape recordings and electromagnetic phenomena to men and women caught in repeating loops of Time, like insects trapped in amber. Ghosts have always been with us, like guests reluctant to leave the party, like bad memories that won't go away . . . Ghosts are nightmares of the Past, refusing to give way to the Present. Mankind's dark side, Humanity's unconscious.

England's dreaming . . .

And so, in this brave new twenty-first century, don't expect ghosts to be limited to old manor houses or abandoned rectories. The modern idea of the bad place, the genius loci, the setting that disturbs and troubles us, has moved on. These days you're more likely to see ghosts in empty car parks, in shut-down factories, or in an underpass with a bad reputation. Places where it can get very dark and very dangerous, and no-one with any sense goes there alone.

There *are* such things as ghosts whether you believe in them or not. Tapping on your window late at night, waiting patiently to be noticed at the foot of your bed, stubbornly refusing to lie down. And that's where the Carnacki Institute comes in. The Institute exists to investigate, interpret, and hopefully Do Something About all the many mysteries and strange supernatural events that flare up every year. All the things that shouldn't happen but unfortunately do. The Institute's field agents are trained to deal with spooks and spirits, poltergeists and demons, Timeslips and other-dimensional incursions. They are ghost finders, and when they find them . . . they step on them. Hard.

Of course, not all ghosts are dark forces, intent on Humanity's ruin. Some are poor lost souls, trying to find their way home. And they . . . can be the most dangerous of all.

ONE

''''''''''''''''''''''''''''''''''''

OUT OF TIME

These days, ghosts turn up in the damnedest places.

It was a cold night under a cold sky, in a supermarket car park a short distance outside the Georgian city of Bath. The supermarket was shut, the car park was deserted, and all the normal people had gone home to sleep the sleep of the just, or at least the weary. A great open space, now, with its carefully laid-out parking bays, half a dozen cars parked haphazardly across the asphalt. A dozen or so abandoned supermarket carts stood forlorn and forgotten in the night. Nothing moved in the surrounding empty fields, not even a breath of wind; and only the faintest of sounds made it all the way from the distant city. Nothing of interest here, nothing to see; except for the three figures standing together in the middle of the car park, looking expectantly about them like theatre patrons waiting for the play to begin.

No lights in the closed supermarket. There was only the harsh yellow glare of the car-park lights, left on as a favour to those who waited, and the blue-white glare of the full moon, sailing high in the star-speckled sky. A cold wind gusted suddenly out of the east, adding a distinct chill to the hour before dawn. Scattered litter tumbled end over end across the great open space, like mice suddenly disturbed in a dark basement. The two men and one woman ignored the wind and the chill as they waited for something to come out of the darkest part of the night and do its best to scare them.

"How much longer are we going to stand around here, freezing our nuts off?" said Happy Jack Palmer.

"Until something ghostly shows up and justifies our expense claims," JC Chance said cheerfully. "If not tonight, then perhaps tomorrow night, or the night after that. It is, after all, the suspense and uncertainty of things that makes life worth living."

"I'd hit you if I dared take my hands out of my pockets long enough," Happy said darkly. "What, exactly, are we supposed to be looking for?"

"I wish you'd, just once, read the briefing files, " said Melody Chambers, not looking up from the equipment she was casually assembling in a semicircle before her. "No-one's seen anything, as such, but there have been hundreds of reports from people using this car park after dark: feelings of unease, panic, even outright terror . . . and a very definite sense of being watched by unseen, malevolent eyes. People are afraid to come here any more, even in broad daylight."

"Ah," said JC. "The usual."

"Why can't ghosts manifest during working hours?" said Happy, a bit wistfully. "It's not as if there's any rule that says ghosts can't appear in daylight. I think they do it to be spiteful."

"That's right, Happy," said JC. "They're only doing it to annoy you."

Happy scowled fiercely. "I am not an early-morning person! I have been up for twenty-seven hours straight, and I'm not even getting overtime! Somewhere there is a hotel bed calling my name, and I wish I were in it."

"So do we," said Melody. "If only so we could get a little peace and quiet. I've known poltergeists that were less of a nuisance than you."

"Can't we at least order some pizza?" said Happy. "I'd kill for a meat feast with a stuffed crust."

"Hush, man," said JC, peering about him into the gloom with lively enthusiasm. "If you want to find ghosts, you have to go where ghosts are. Logic. You can't expect to find Jaws in a swimming pool."

"I want to go home," Happy said miserably.

"You always want to go home," said Melody. "How you ever got the nickname Happy is beyond me. I can only suppose your school was an absolute hotbed of irony."

"Listen," said Happy, "I am a Class Ten telepath. If you could see the world as clearly as I do, you'd be clinically depressed, too. I want some of my little pills."

"Not now," JC said immediately. "I need your head clear and your thoughts sharp."

"Spoil-sport." Happy sniffed loudly, sulking. "Come on, JC, we've been here almost five hours now, and nothing's happened. This place is as dead as my love life. Let's call it a night. My stomach's empty, my back is killing me, and my feet aren't talking to me. All to investigate a ghost that may not even be here. I mean, be fair: a sense of unease and of being watched? You can get that in a public toilet."

"Bear up," said JC. "All in a night's work for the intrepid heroes of the Carnacki Institute."

Happy grimaced. "God, I hate it when you're being this cheerful. It's not natural. Especially given the nature of what we do."

"Be strong!" urged JC, beaming even more brightly because he knew it got on Happy's nerves. "Remember . . . when the Ghostbusters have a headache; when the Scooby gang are having a panic attack; when Mulder and Scully don't want to know and the psychic commandos of the SAS are sitting in a corner crying their eyes out . . . Who do you send for? The specially trained field agents of the Carnacki Institute!"

"He's quite right, you know," Melody said coldly. "It isn't normal to be that cheerful, at this hour of the morning. You haven't been dipping into Happy's pills again, have you?"

"I do so love to see the sun come up!" said JC.

"They're not paying me enough for this," growled Happy. "In fact, they couldn't pay me enough for this. It's only the general gloom and the opportunities for self-pity that keep me going."

"Be quiet, you annoying little man, and let me concentrate on my instruments," said Melody. "Or I'll short-circuit your kirlian aura."

Josiah Charles (JC) Chance looked fondly on his bickering team-mates, then turned his attention back to the shadows and the dark. JC was tall, lean. Full of energy, and far too handsome for his own good. Well into his late twenties, he had pale, striking features, a great mane of dark, wavy hair, intense eyes, a proud nose, and a mouth whose constant smile would have been more reassuring if it had touched his piercing gaze a little more often. He wore a rich cream suit of quite striking style and elegance, and wore it well. A born adventurer, risk-taker, and experienced ghost finder, JC Chance was the rising star of the Carnacki Institute; and he knew it. He knew more about ghosts, hauntings, and paranormal phenomena than any man should who hoped to sleep soundly at night. Fortunately, he also knew a lot of things to do about them. Really quite unpleasant things, sometimes, but that came with the job.

Melody Chambers was the main brain and science geek of the team, and therefore strictly responsible for all the marvellous new technology supplied by the Carnacki Institute. In fact, Melody had been known to slap people's hands away if they even tried to touch her tech. She was very protective of her toys, even if she did tend to break them on a regular basis, usually by trying to get far more out of them than the design specs allowed. Pushing the very edge of her late twenties, Melody was pretty enough in a conventional way, short and gamine thin, and burned constantly with more nervous energy than was good for her. She had a disturbing tendency to rush headlong into any situation that looked like it might promise her something, anything, that she hadn't encountered before, armed with a complete willingness to kick the hell out of anything that proved even a bit stubborn. Melody Chambers wasn't nearly scared enough of the dark, considering what she did on nights like this.

She wore her auburn hair scraped back into a severe bun, serious glasses with black plastic frames, and clothes so anonymous they actually sidestepped fashion or style. In her spare time, she enjoyed a sex life that would have scared Casanova out of his jockstrap. It's always the quiet ones . . .

Then there was Happy Jack Palmer. Telepath, smart-arse, and full-time gloomy bugger. Closing fast on thirty, and resenting it bitterly, Happy was short and stocky, prematurely balding, and might have been handsome if he ever stopped scowling. He wore grubby jeans, a rude T-shirt, and a battered old jacket, and looked like you'd have to put him through a car wash to get the top layer of soil off him. He shaved when he remembered and enjoyed all the worst kinds of food, traces of which still showed on his jacket. He claimed to have a heart of gold. In a box, under his bed. The most reluctant hero ever accepted into the ranks of the Carnacki Institute, and owner of so many medical prescriptions he had to file them in alphabetical order to keep track, Happy had an unequalled talent for detecting the presence of things that most people wouldn't even admit existed.

He saw things and heard voices, and only the pills let him lead anything like a normal life.

Thrown together by fate, held together by repeated success, the three of them made a good team and did good work. And because they worked so well together, they got all the most difficult, dangerous, and demanding cases. Happy was always threatening to quit but never did. Partly because he enjoyed the company, mostly because he enjoyed the free medical benefits. JC made no secret of the fact that he was still looking for some solid proof on the fate of human consciousness after death. And Melody stayed because the Institute gave her access to the very latest tech, and because she couldn't hope to do nearly as much damage anywhere else.

She moved happily back and forth in front of her assorted computers, scanners, and certain arcane assemblies of her own design, arranged on a collapsible frame. Her fingers flashed across keyboards, adjusted dials, and administered the occasional warning slap to any piece of equipment that didn't do what it was supposed to do fast enough to suit her. Lights flared and flickered, monitor screens blazed, and information came flooding in from every direction at once. JC kept a watchful eye on it all, from a safe distance.

"Picking up anything interesting?" he ventured casually after a while.

"You wouldn't understand if I told you," said Melody, not looking round. "Everything's operating as it should, all the motion detectors and temperature tests are fine, and there's not a single energy spike across the board. Rest assured that if anything ectoplasmic should deign to show its face in what's left of tonight, I am ready and waiting to analyse it in any number of interesting ways. A ghost mouse couldn't fart around here without me knowing."

"And if our ghosties and ghoulies don't present any measurable activity?" said Happy, cunningly.

"Then that's why we have you," said Melody. "Though I often wish we didn't."

"Girl geek."

"Spice Girls fan."

"Children, children," JC murmured. "Play nicely, or there will be spankings."

"I hate it here," Happy said miserably. "It's cold, it's damp, and I think moss is starting to grow under my testicles."

"Eeew," said Melody. "There's a mental image I wasn't expecting to take home with me."

"Hold it," said Happy, his head coming up suddenly, like a hound catching a scent. "Hold everything. Did either of you feel that?"

"Feel what?" said JC, moving in close beside Happy and looking quickly around.

"We're not alone," said Happy, frowning, concentrating. "There's something here with us . . . No visible presence, can't say I actually heard or smelled anything . . . but there's definitely a sense of being observed. And not in a good way."

"Not friendly, then?" said JC.

"What do you think?" Happy said pityingly. "When was the last time we encountered a happy ghost? Very definitely not including the Laughing Ghoul of Leicester, bad cess to his mouldering bones. If you were hoping to meet Casper the Dead Baby, you're in the wrong team. We only get the bad-tempered ones."

"Let us remain optimistic," said JC. "If only out of a sense of perversity."

"Easy for you to say," growled Happy. "You're not a Class Eleven sensitive. Damn . . . the presence is so strong now it's almost overwhelming. My head is pounding."

"Take some of your pain-killers," said Melody. "You're so much more bearable when you're medicated."

"No," said JC. "No pills, Happy. Concentrate."

"Not even the little purple ones? You like those."

"Maybe later, Happy. Hang in there. Melody, anything showing up on your instruments?"

"Nothing. Not a damn thing anywhere. And no; I don't *feel* anything."

"You wouldn't," Happy said scathingly. "You have all the sensitivity of a night-club bouncer."

"Not listening, not listening," said Melody.

"According to the briefing files," said JC, "an old lady was knocked down and killed in this very parking lot a few months ago. A reversing car ran over her. Driver swore he never even saw her. Could she be our ghost? I do good work with little-old-lady ghosts. They trust me."

"No fool like a dead fool," Happy said absently. "This doesn't feel like any old lady, JC. I'm not even sure it's human. I'm getting images now, sounds, associations . . . None of them recent. This is old, and I mean really old. Centuries past . . . Dark, brutal, hungry. I don't like the feel of this at all."

"Where is it?" said JC, glaring about into the harsh light of the car park and the darkness beyond. "Can you narrow it down to a location, or even a direction?"

"It's everywhere!" said Happy, turning round and round in small, stumbling circles. "It's closing in on us, from every direction at once! The whole damn area's haunted, not only the car park . . . But this is the focus, all right. We're standing at ground zero."

"Melody?" said JC. "Tell me something, Melody. Anything."

"My instruments are lighting up like Christmas trees," said Melody, moving quickly from one screen to another. "But none of the readings make any sense. I'm getting sharp spikes in the upper electromagnetic range, massive energy surges almost overloading the sensors . . . Far too strong for any human revenant. Something's coming, JC. Something huge and powerful . . . Coming up out of the past, out of the deep past, the really long-ago . . . I've never seen readings like these, JC. We are off the scale here, people."

"It's been here all along," whispered Happy. "Waiting

for some poor damned fools to break its bonds and turn it loose . . ."

"Hold on," said Melody. "I'm getting something, on the radio station I keep detuned for Electronic Voice Phenomena. I can't tell where it's coming from, but . . . Listen to this. It's in the air, all around us . . ."

She cut in the main speakers, and a massive chorus of grunts and growls, sudden shrieks and deep coughing sounds, spilled out into the empty car park. Voices, the voices of men, but as much animal as human, the voice of the beast in all of us. There was rhythm in the sound, and definite traces of sense and meaning, but no recognisable words. Harsh, aggressive, and terribly exalted; but also deeply disturbing, on a primitive, almost atavistic level. Voices from out of the Deep Past, when we were still learning how to be human. JC shuddered as gooseflesh rose up all over him, and his scalp crawled. Melody clung desperately to her instruments like a drowning woman. Happy's face twisted as he shrank away from the sounds. JC put a calming hand on Happy's shoulder and gestured for Melody to shut off the sounds. She did so, and blessed silence returned to the car park. Nothing moved in the harsh glare of the electric lights or in the surrounding darkness. Even the wind had stopped blowing.

"What the hell kind of language was that?" said Happy, shaking his head slowly.

"I'm not sure it was a language," said Melody, giving all her attention to the monitor screens. "Or at least, not anything we would recognise as such. It's old, very old. Ancient. It may even predate language as we know it."

"So much for the little-old-lady theory," said JC. "I

have a strong suspicion we are in way over our heads, people, and sinking fast."

Happy sniffed loudly. "Situation entirely bloody normal then."

A car horn went off, the sudden sound shockingly loud in the quiet night. It blared viciously, aggressively, on and on as though some unseen hand were pressing hard on the horn. It sounded like some angry beast, roused suddenly from slumber with slaughter on its mind. More horns joined in, from every corner of the car park. The noise grew unbearably loud, the cars howling like a pack of wolves beneath the full moon, anticipating prey. And then the sound cut off abruptly, all the horns stopping simultaneously. The sudden quiet would have been a relief . . . if the night hadn't been so heavy with threat and menace. Happy slowly took his hands away from his ears.

"Well," he said, a bit shakily, "something wants us to know it's here."

"Don't make a big thing out of it," said JC, quietly, "But . . . take a look around."

The six cars left in the car park overnight weren't where they had been. Instead of being dispersed haphazardly across the open space, they were now arranged in a perfect circle around the three ghost finders. The cars hadn't moved in the usual way. Their engines hadn't started, and their wheels hadn't turned, but there they were, lying in wait, their turned-off headlights like terribly empty eyes, their grillework like snarling teeth. Keeping their distance for the moment, like so many junkyard dogs considering their attack. The driver's door on one car swung slowly open. The ghost finders held themselves still, holding their breath in anticipation of their first look at whoever was behind what was happening. But the door simply hung open . . . promising, teasing, taunting; and then slowly it closed itself again.

Out in the shadows at the very edge of the car park, where the harsh glare of the electric lights gave way to the heavy dark of the night, the supermarket carts were moving. They rolled silently along, as though pushed by unseen hands, forming a great circle around the outer limits of the car park. As though laying down a line that could not be crossed, cutting the ghost finders off from the safety and protections of the sane and rational everyday world. Simple shopping carts, nothing but wire and wheels, suddenly infused with real threat and menace by some unknown force.

JC realised that his hands had clenched into fists at his sides, and he made himself relax. Just looking at the cars and the carts made his flesh creep, but then, that was the idea. To unnerve them, to frighten them, to prepare them for what was coming. Something was playing mind games. JC smiled his widest smile. No-one played those games better than he.

One by one, the car park's electric lights started to go out. Fading away one after another like so many guttering candles, the lights disappeared. Starting at the outskirts, moving slowly but inexorably inwards, darkness crept across the car park. It closed in on the three ghost finders, cutting them off, until there was nothing left but the dark, surrounding a small circle of light produced by Melody's instruments. Her panels blinked and flickered, stubbornly holding out against a malign outside influence. The only other light now was the harsh blue-white glare of the full moon. What used to be called, in the old days, a hunter's moon.

"All right," said Happy. "This is not good. Officially, and very definitely, not good. Melody?"

"Don't look at me," she said immediately. "It's all I can do to keep my tech operating. There's so much power out there, in the night, in the dark—power off the scale. It's like we're in the eye of the hurricane, and I can't guarantee how long that's going to last."

"Wonderful," said Happy, bitterly. "Don't suppose there's any chance this supermarket was built over an old Indian burial ground, like in that movie?"

"In south-west England?" said Melody. "Roman burial site, maybe. But the one thing my instruments agree on is that we're facing something much older than that. What was here, before the Romans? History never was my strong point."

"Ah . . ." said JC.

"What?" said Happy, suspiciously. "That was your *I've just remembered something, and you're really not going to like it* voice. Ah *what*?"

"If either of you had taken the time to read the briefing files thoroughly, you'd know there are reports of Iron Age settlements all through this area," said JC, keeping a careful eye on the shopping carts as they slowed smoothly to a halt. They still looked like they were watching. "Even some Neolithic sites. Stone Age human settlements, thousands of years old. Back when we were still learning how to be people. Primitive people, with primitive but still-powerful beliefs. Melody, can your instruments confirm whether there is any such evidence here, right under our feet?"

"Easy-peasy," said Melody, her fingers moving rapidly over the keyboards. "Yes . . . Yes! Definite traces of some kind of ancient settlement; and not that far down, either. The evidence suggests it was recently disturbed, then covered over again."

"Of course," said JC. "It's all coming clear now."

"Is it?" said Happy. "If it did, it missed me completely. Spell it out, for the hard of thinking among us."

"The building contractors must have found the ancient site when they were laying the foundations for this new car park," JC said patiently. "Unknowingly, they uncovered a seat of power that hadn't been disturbed for thousands of years."

"Is it just me," said Melody, "or are those cars . . . a bit closer than they used to be?"

"The cars aren't the problem," said JC, staring out into the dark. "They're not part of the haunting. That's simply the ancient Power, stretching its muscles."

"Power?" said Happy. "What Power?"

Light blazed up all around them, hot and fierce, firelight thousands of years old. It jumped and leapt, and so did the men and women around it, as the Present was abruptly shouldered aside and replaced by the Past. The three ghost finders huddled together, hanging on to each other, as Time Past filled their eyes. Flames burned fiercely, leaping up from a huge banked bonfire, or bale-fire, around which the Tribe danced and howled, jumping and slashing at the air, brandishing roughly carved stone totems. Men, women, and children, shorter and stockier than their modern counterparts, hunched and distorted but still powerfully built; filthy dirty and wrapped in crudely tanned skins and furs. Primitive Man, Pre-civilisation Man, dancing and prancing and slamming bare feet against the bare ground, crude amulets of animal claws and human finger bones hanging round their throats. Shrieking faces, painted blue with woad and red with fresh blood.

And stretched out before the fire, naked and helpless, held down on the flat sacrificial stone by four elders of the Tribe—the sacrifice. Young, very young, little more than a child; with a stone blade held firmly over her frantically rising and falling chest. She wasn't screaming, she knew it would do no good, but her eyes were full of a terrible, hopeless dread.

The fire blazed up, throwing flames and cinders high into the night sky, under the malignant eye of the full moon. Drums pounded deafeningly loud, providing the only music for the dance. A powerful, demanding rhythm, driving the dancers on to further exertions and greater excesses, an endless thunder to madden their already deranged minds. And when the fury and the madness had reached its peak, the stone knife slammed down into the victim's chest; and everything stopped. She screamed, then, but the sound was lost in the great roar that went up from the rest of the Tribe. The shaman hacked roughly into the victim's chest, levering aside the bones to cut out the heart and tear it from its cavity. He held the still-beating heart up, and the Tribe howled again. It was still, horribly, a very human sound.

And then, just like that, it was gone. The fire, and the sacrifice, and the dancing primitive people worshipping Something, in their primitive way. The small circle of scientific light was back, bounded by watching cars and the feeling of a Presence, on the night.

Happy shook his head slowly. "Human sacrifice," he said thickly. "Death and horror and celebration, repeated so often it's imprinted on this place, like grooves cut in a record. Genius loci, the spirit of the place; a bad place, poisoned by the psychic stain of what happened here . . . Sacrifice, to ensure the sun will rise again, and that spring will follow winter, and that at least some of the babies will live. One life offered up freely for the greater good. In worship to some great Power."

"But what woke it up, after lying quiet for so long?" said Melody. "There's always a focal point to every haunting, some single trigger . . ."

"The fools," said JC. "The bloody fools . . . When the building contractors broke ground here, they must have dug down deep enough to uncover the ancient site. They stopped work and consulted the supermarket bosses, who were afraid that archaeologists might move in and bring operations to a halt, costing them millions. So they had the contractors cover over the disturbed site and built their new car park here anyway."

"Yeah," said Happy. "So far, so typical. So?"

"Don't you get it?" said JC, almost angrily. "First they disturb the energy stored in the old site, the ancient bad place with all its memories of long-forgotten Power. And then they held a big opening ceremony here, made a real celebration of it. Even then, they might have got away with it . . . If an old lady hadn't died here, killed by a man in a hurry. So—a ceremony, blood and death, calling across the centuries, like to like. A direct link between Past and Present, awakening . . . Something ancient and unspeakably powerful. All it needed to manifest fully was three poor damned fools who thought they knew what they were doing. A telepath, a woman with powerful technology, and a leader who should have known better. It's us. We did this. We woke it up."

All six cars started rocking back and forth in place, shaking wildly. Their headlights snapped on, burning bright like dragons' eyes. Their engines revved and roared like angry beasts, their horns bleating and blaring. Then they all surged forward. The three ghost finders scattered, and the cars ploughed right through Melody's stacked instruments. The comforting circle of light disappeared, replaced by the fierce, stabbing beams from the cars and the pitiless glare of the full moon. The cars screeched around in narrow turns and came back again, only to slam into each other in head-on collisions, like maddened stags going head to head in rut. They rocked to a halt, steam rising from the crumpled bonnets, their headlights slowly fading like the light going out of dying eyes. The three ghost finders came together again, breathing hard.

"Whatever it is, it doesn't know how to drive a car," said Happy. "Sorry about your toys, Melody."

"They'll give me some more," she said, but her heart wasn't in it.

JC glared at Happy. "Concentrate! That was only the overture, to throw us off-balance and remove the advantage Melody's tech gave us! What do you *feel*, Happy?"

"Something's here," Happy said slowly. "Something's right here, with us. The chain of events opened a door, and now Something from the Past is forcing its way through, into the Present!"

JC turned to Melody, scrabbling on her knees amid the wreckage of her instruments. "Anything still working that you can use to break the link between Past and Present, slam the door shut in its face?"

"Not a damned thing!" Melody rose suddenly, brandishing a very large machine-pistol. "On the other hand . . .

Any caveman with a club who turns up here is in for a nasty surprise."

"I want a gun," said Happy. "You never let me have a gun."

"Damn right," said Melody. "I am not having the words *friendly fire* on my death certificate."

"Hush," said JC, looking slowly around him. "It's here . . . I can feel it, like the gaze of a blind god, smell it, like the dragon's breath . . . the cold of the winter that never ends, the dark between the stars . . ."

"Nothing like imminent death to bring out the poet in you, JC," said Happy. "How about composing something really lyrical that we can retreat to? Because I'd really like to get the hell out of here . . ."

"Too late! Too late . . ." JC glared about him, searching for an answer he could sense but not pin down. "Think! Something big, Something powerful . . . What did those primitive people dance and sacrifice to, what did they believe in and worship, strong enough to make the sun rise and the winter end? They weren't ready for gods yet, nothing so civilised . . . But together, their massed minds and desperate need invoked a powerful Force from Outside . . . Created, or summoned, by the terrible brutal passion of their faith . . . A god with no name or singular nature; simply a Presence . . ."

"Could it be one of the Great Beasts?" said Melody. "The Hogge, or the Serpent?"

"No," Happy said immediately. "I know them. What I'm feeling . . . is even older than they. More primitive. Just a force. A Presence. And since its worshippers had no language to name it, to define it and limit its powers . . . We can't hope to control or dismiss it with any of the usual techniques or formulas. We don't have anything we can use against it!"

The dark was all around them now. The supermarket was gone, and most of the car park. Only a circle of moonlight remained, stabbing down like a spotlight, picking them out. No stars shone in that dark night, no distinction left between earth and sky. Just the three of them left, the only living things in the night, huddling together for comfort and warmth, adrift in an endless dark sea. And it was cold, so cold . . .

"Dark and cold," said JC, shuddering despite himself. "The dark before the sun rises, and the cold of the winter that never ends. It's threatening us, demanding our worship."

Suddenly, it was there with them. A vast, endless Presence hammering on the night, manifest but not material, enforcing its awful Presence on the world through an act of sheer malicious will. The monster in the dark that all children know and fear because they are so much closer to the primitive. An ancient Presence, powerful and pitiless, demanding worship and sacrifice, blood and horror. Out of the Past, out of Time, come to drag Humanity down to its own level again.

Happy fell to his knees, both hands pressed to his head. He was crying raggedly, his face distorted by strange passions as he fought to maintain his psychic shields and keep out the primordial demands beating against his thoughts. Melody stood close by him, swinging her machine-pistol back and forth, desperate for something definite she could fight. And JC . . . stood thoughtfully, frowning a little, as though considering some difficult but distasteful problem.

"It wants a sacrifice!" Happy cried out miserably. "A human sacrifice!"

"No," said JC. "We don't do that any more."

"If we don't give it what it wants, it'll take us!" said Happy. "And after us, it'll move on to the city!"

"Well," said JC, his voice carefully calm and composed, "we can't have that, can we? Consider the haunting, my friends; every manifestation has its heart, its focus, its specific link to Present Time. And in this case . . . that focus, that last link in the chain of events, has to be the poor little old lady who was killed during the opening ceremony. Find her for me, Happy."

"Are you crazy?" Happy glared at him through teary eyes. "I don't dare drop my shields! It'll eat me alive, I can't . . ."

JC looked at him, and Happy's babbling cut off immediately. JC could do that. One moment he was talking quite calmly and reasonably, and the next he was looking at you with eyes dark as the night and twice as cold. JC tried hard to be a good man, but you only had to look into his eyes at moments like that to know he had the potential to be something else entirely. Happy swallowed hard, sniffed back his tears, and concentrated.

"She's still here. Faint but definite trace. Lost, alone, walking up and down in the night, trying to find her way home."

"Bring her here," said JC. "Bring her to me."

Without looking down, Melody placed a comforting hand on Happy's shoulder. He stopped shaking and glared out into the dark as he concentrated.

The Presence was thundering in all their heads, a great demanding wordless Voice, but Happy fought through it to reach a much smaller presence, the tiniest motes of light, drifting through the dark. He called to it, and the light hesitated, then changed direction. She came walking slowly out of the dark, into the circle of light, a little old lady in a battered old coat, walking stiffly but steadily, her wrinkled face calm but puzzled. She stopped abruptly, her eyes slowly focusing on the three ghost finders. JC stepped forward.

"Hello," he said, his voice surprisingly kind. "Can you tell me your name?"

The ghost looked surprised for a moment, as though being asked to remember something that really wasn't important any more. "Muriel," she said finally. Her voice sounded perfectly normal. "Muriel Foster. Yes. I don't . . . I don't quite remember how I got here. My memory isn't what it was . . . Don't get old, young man. No-one ever tells you how much hard work it is, being old."

"Muriel . . ."

"I shouldn't be here, should I? There's somewhere else I ought to be. I feel . . . like I've been dreaming, and now it's time to wake up."

"That's right, Muriel," said JC. "It's time for you to go on. To the place appointed for you, where there is no old age, and all old things are made new again."

"Yes," said Muriel. "I'd like that."

"Can you hear the thunder all around us?"

"Of course; I'm not deaf, you know."

"All you have to do is walk towards the thunder," said JC. "Just . . . keep walking. And all of this will be over."

Muriel looked at him sharply. "There's something you're not telling me. I may be old, young man, but I'm not stupid. Tell me this; this thing you want me to do . . . Is it necessary? Does it matter?"

"Yes," said JC. "It will save a great many lives."

"Good," said Muriel, drawing herself up. "It's been a long time since I've had the opportunity to do something that mattered."

She nodded briefly to JC and walked steadily out of the light and into the dark. Happy and Melody looked disbelievingly at JC, but he merely looked after Muriel. There was a moment, as though something incredibly powerful was holding its breath; and then, instantaneously, the Presence was gone. The car park was back again, the lights shone brightly, the stars were back in the sky, and the moon was just a moon.

Happy made a sound, deep in his throat, and rose to his feet. JC turned to look at him.

"How are you feeling, Happy?"

"Never mind me; what did you just do? She trusted you, JC! And you sacrificed her to the Presence!"

"Of course I didn't," said JC. "What kind of person do you take me for?"

"Right now, we're not too sure," said Melody. "Perhaps you'd better explain it for us. Bearing in mind that if I don't like what I hear, I still have this gun."

"It's really quite simple," said JC, patiently. "The Presence depended on live sacrifices. They were the source of its power. And I fed it a ghost, a dead woman with not a spark of life left in her. Nothing actually there for the Presence to feed on. Essentially, we gave the Presence a really bad case of spiritual indigestion. It couldn't consume dear Muriel, so she passed on to her reward . . . and with her gone, the haunting's focal point was removed. The link between Past and Present was broken, and the Presence went home crying. An elegant solution to a tricky problem, I think you'll agree."

Happy and Melody looked at each other.

"I nearly had a coronary," said Happy.

"Me too," said Melody.

"You hit him first, you're closest," said Happy.

"After you," said Melody.

"Look," said JC. "The sun's coming up."

They looked. It was. Spreading out across the horizon, in long streamers of glowing red and gold, pushing back the dark, breathing life into the world.

"Come, children," said JC. "Back to the hotel, and breakfast is on me. Who's for a good fry-up?"

"Can I take some of my pills now?" said Happy.

"Why not?" said JC.

TWO
''

THE SCARIEST PLACE ON EARTH

Buckingham Palace is a big place, with a lot of rooms. State-rooms, living-rooms, exhibition rooms. Room for everyone and everything; including a few very specialised institutions that shouldn't need to exist but unfortunately do. Tucked away behind locked doors and closed-off corridors, the Carnacki Institute has been based in Buck House for many years, under many names. It has always been a Royal Prerogative, rather than a government department, because ghosts are far too important to be entrusted to the whims of transitory politicians. Hell, most of them don't even know the Carnacki Institute exists. Her Majesty the Queen decides whether or not to tell each new Prime Minister, as they come to office. Some cope better than others. No-one ever talks about the Missing Prime Minister of 1888, whose entire existence had to be removed from the history books.

The Carnacki Institute takes its responsibilities very

seriously, and sometimes, entirely ruthlessly. It comes with the job.

The Institute was first convened in 1587, the result of a Royal Charter from Queen Elizabeth I. Consequently, all operatives are answerable only to the head of the Institute and the reigning monarch. Either of whom can order any operative killed at any time. This ensures security, honesty, and integrity, and helps motivate everyone to do the very best.

The Carnacki Institute is a job for life, however long that might be.

....

JC, Happy, and Melody waited unhappily in a small room at the back of Buckingham Palace, at the end of a corridor that doesn't officially exist. They'd barely stepped off the train back from the West Country, exhausted and hollow-eyed and running on fumes, when all their mobile phones went off at once, summoning them to Buck House to meet with the Boss of the Carnacki Institute. Passing travellers were briefly disturbed by a flurry of foul language, not a little brandishing of fists, and a few bitter tears. Normally, it was understood that field agents were entitled to at least a month's downtime between missions, to prevent them burning out. To be called back in this abruptly meant something seriously bad was in the wind.

Either a new and very urgent case . . . or the Boss had finally found out what the three of them got up to between cases, and they were all in real trouble. The Boss tended to take a very dim view of those necessarily private pleasures and distractions that made a field agent's life bearable; so the agents went to great pains to make sure she never found out about them. They didn't want to worry her. JC and Happy and Melody made their way across London in silence, really hoping it was merely a dangerous new mission.

And now here they were, sitting in the outer office, waiting to be called in to what people in the know considered the scariest place on earth.

Like most of Buckingham Palace, the Boss's outer office was always kept that little bit warmer than it really needed to be; and the recirculated air in that small, windowless room was giving JC a headache and a seriously dry mouth. It was either that or the stark terror. JC had learned to deal with ghosts and revenants and demons; but the Boss was another matter. He looked around the office, hoping for something interesting to take his mind off the horrors to come, but there really wasn't much to look at. Only a brutally efficient desk for the Boss's secretary, typing happily away as though she didn't have a care in the world, the heartless cow, and a half a dozen visitors' chairs of such blatant discomfort that they had to have been designed that way to keep the visitors in a properly respectful frame of mind.

There were the portraits on the walls. Dozens of them, covering all four walls, no room even for a clock or a calendar. Portraits of past field agents who had covered themselves with glory, if not renown. Only the Institute knew what its agents did to protect Humanity from the Outer Forces, and it didn't even tell itself unless it needed to know. Officially, these portraits were always referred to as the Honoured Members. Field agents more usually referred to them as the Honoured Dead because no field agent ever expected to die of old age. Most didn't even make it to their midlife crises.

The oldest portraits on the walls were only that—paintings in various styles from various periods, often by artists with famous names and reputations. Which is why there are unexplained gaps in certain artists' careers. The clothes in the portraits changed with the passing fashions, but the faces all had the same look. Hard-used, heroic, haunted. Unsmiling faces, with eyes that had seen things they could never forget. After the paintings came photographs, from the first daguerreotypes to sepia prints, to the sharp digital images of today. Men and women who had gone down into Hell and kicked arse, for no other reward than knowing it was a job that needed doing. No medals, no honours, and sometimes not even a body for the funeral. The job was its own reward.

The faces in the portraits were different every time JC was summoned to the outer office. He didn't know who was in charge of rotating them, or even if there was any significance in the choices. He half suspected the portraits chose their own positions.

JC sat easily on his stiff-backed chair, his cream suit immaculate as always, and did his best to project an air of unconcerned nonchalance. With a touch of insolence. Never let your enemies think they've got you worried. And, having searched his conscience all across London, although the prospect of meeting the Boss in person frankly unnerved him, as it did everyone . . . he really wasn't that worried. He hadn't done anything too terrible, recently, and he was confident in his ability to talk his way out of any lesser charges.

Happy, on the other hand, was not looking at all well. He sat bolt upright on his inflexible chair, looking guilty and put-upon in equal measure. His hands were clasped tightly together in his lap, to keep them from trembling too obviously, sweat beaded on his high forehead, and he'd developed a small but definite twitch in one eye. At least he hadn't started whimpering yet. Typical of Happy; always convinced that the Universe was out to get him. Of course, in this job, sometimes it was. Or the Boss; which was just as bad.

The seriously heavy-duty wards preventing him from using his telepathic abilities probably weren't helping. Happy always described the experience as enduring the hangover without having first enjoyed the drunk.

Melody was playing the latest version of Doom on her phone and giving it her entire concentration, apparently completely impervious to the demands and dangers of the everyday world. Melody really didn't care much about the ordinary world, except when it interfered with her personal needs and interests. And she was never happier than when she had a new toy to play with. Only someone who knew her really well would have detected the sullen anger coiled and waiting in her tense muscles. Melody's first impulse was always to fight. With her tech, her knowledge, or a really big gun. She always played to win, or at the very least to go down with her teeth buried in an enemy's throat.

Happy cracked first. He turned abruptly in his seat and glared at JC. "This is all your fault!"

"Really?" said JC. He made a point of relaxing even further in his chair, so that he seemed positively boneless. "And how, pray, is this my fault? Considering that we haven't even been told what we've been called in for yet."

"Because it always is your fault!" said Happy.

"He has a point," said Melody, not looking up from her computer game. "Always first through the doors, always first into the thick of things, and dragging us along behind you. With us usually yelling *Can we please talk about this first?* Remember Harroby Hall?"

"I thought we'd all agreed that the Harroby Hall situation was not my fault," said JC, with quiet dignity. "Neither of you noticed anything out of the usual either. How were we supposed to know the house was the haunting, and not the people? That the extremely unfortunate Price family were in fact living in the ghost of a house that had burned down thirty years before? It's not as if any of your precious instruments detected anything, did they, Melody dear? Still, since we're so happily reminiscing, perhaps we could share some precious memories of the Case of the Glasgow Bogle? When you assured me that the Bogle was, in fact, *entirely harmless*? Hmm?"

"Well it was," Melody muttered defensively. "Right up until Happy provoked it."

"Oh right, blame me!" said Happy. "Why do I always get the blame?"

"Because you deserve it," snapped Melody, crushingly. "Remember the Phantom Bugler of Warwick-on-Sea?"

Happy sniffed, stuck out his lower lip sulkily, and wouldn't meet her eyes. "How was I supposed to know it wasn't a bugle? I've led a very sheltered life. Or at least, I did, right up until I got drafted into this bloody organisation. I can feel one of my heads coming on."

"Children, children," murmured JC. "Let us not discuss our personal failings while the enemy is listening."

They all looked across at the Boss's secretary, Heather. She smiled sweetly upon them without slowing her typing for a moment. Heather (if she had a last name no-one knew it, for all sorts of security reasons) was the perfect secretary. Knew everything, said nothing; or at least, nothing that mattered. Calm, professional, and pleasantly pretty, in a blonde curly-haired round-faced sort of way, Heather dressed neatly rather than fashionably; and as the Boss's last line of defence, she was probably the most-heavily-armed person in Buck House. Supposedly, Heather was equipped to take down a whole army of terrorists, if necessary, and certainly no-one felt like testing the rumour. You had to get past Heather to get to the Boss, and unless you had exactly the right kind of paperwork, signed and countersigned in all the right places, that wasn't going to happen. JC once saw Heather kick an overpresumptuous Parliamentary UnderSecretary so hard in the balls that half the faces in the portraits winced.

That JC was still prepared to try to charm and wheedle information out of her showed how nervous he really was.

"Heather, my darling . . . looking ravishing as always, of course; might I inquire . . . ?"

"No, JC, my darling, you might not," said Heather, kindly but immovably. "The Boss will see you when she is ready to see you and not one moment before. All I can tell you . . . is that the Boss is really not a happy bunny this morning."

JC raised an eyebrow. "Is she ever?"

"Sorry," said Heather. "That falls under Classified Information."

"Come on, Heather," said Happy, giving his best shot at an ingratiating smile. "Can't you at least tell us what we've done wrong this time? I mean, how deep in it are we?"

Heather smiled sweetly at him. "Do you possess a pair of waders? Or perhaps scuba gear?"

"Situation normal, then," said Melody, going back to her game.

"Oh God," said Happy, burying his face in his hands.

"Told you not to shoot that albatross," said JC. "Now brace up, man. We've been here before and made it out the other side. If we were in serious trouble, Heather would have shot us the moment we walked through the door."

"You might think that," Heather murmured, "I couldn't possibly comment."

Happy moaned briefly, then produced half a dozen bottles of pills from various pockets. He rolled them back and forth in his hands, considering the multi-coloured contents, and squinting at the handwritten labels.

"Now . . . These yellow ones are to remind me to take these red ones . . . And the blue ones are only for use in cases of possession. These stripey ones are for radiation exposure, the hundreds and thousands are for my mood swings, and these chequered ones . . . are to give me a better outlook on life."

"Trust me, those aren't working," said Melody. She glared at him sharply. "I thought we were weaning you off those things. So many pills can't be good for you. It's a wonder to me you don't rattle when you cough."

"I need a little something, now and again, to help keep me stable," Happy said defensively. "I've got to do something to keep the voices quiet."

Melody sniffed loudly. "If this is stable, I'd hate to see you when you weren't. Forget stable, Happy, that horse bolted long ago. Why not settle for coherent?"

"You're being mean now," said Happy. "I wonder what these violet ones are for . . . ?"

"You have no idea what half that stuff will do to you,

in the long term," insisted Melody. "Have you even considered the side effects, or the cumulative effects?"

"I read all the little leaflets that come with the pills, very thoroughly," said Happy.

"Yeah," said JC. "Looking for loopholes."

Happy knocked back a yellow and two reds. JC took a purple, just to keep him company.

The intercom on Heather's desk buzzed officiously. Heather stopped typing to listen to something only she could hear, then nodded briskly to JC, Happy, and Melody.

"In you go, 007, 8, and 9. The Boss is ready to see you now."

"How come no-one ever asks if we're ready to see her?" growled Happy. He hiccuped, then smiled suddenly. "Oooh . . . They're kicking in fast today . . ."

JC and Melody took a firm hold on his arms and headed him towards the heavily reinforced steel door that led to the Boss.

....

The current Boss of the Carnacki Institute was Catherine Latimer. She sat commandingly behind her Hepplewhite desk, while the three field agents arranged themselves untidily before her. She gestured sharply at the three chairs set out in front of the desk, and the trio immediately sat down, like school pupils called before their headmistress, for crimes not yet made clear. JC and Melody did their best to look contrite; Happy didn't have the knack.

Catherine Latimer had to be in her late seventies but was still almost unnaturally strong and vital. Medium height, stocky, grey hair cropped short in a bowl cut, her face was all hard edges and cold eyes. She wore a smartly tailored grey suit, without a flash of colour anywhere, and smoked black Turkish cigarettes in a long, ivory holder; an affectation from her student days in Cambridge. (There were long-standing rumours that she'd made some kind of Deal with Someone, in her college days, but no-one had ever been able to prove anything.)

Every day she sent agents out on missions that could lead to their deaths, or worse. If it bothered her, she hid it really well. But every agent knew that if they fell in the field, she would move heaven and earth to avenge them.

JC always thought of her as the last of the Bulldog Breed. But only to himself, and never in her presence. He didn't think she could actually read minds, but he didn't feel like taking the chance.

Rather than meet the Boss's unnerving gaze directly, JC looked around her office. It was not without interest. The Boss had been a field agent herself, back in the day, and she still kept souvenirs of that time around to brighten up her otherwise-coldly-efficient office. So, apart from the expected shelves crammed with books and files, and the necessary modern technology, there was also a large goldfish bowl, half-full of murky ectoplasm, in which the ghost of a goldfish swam calmly back and forth, flickering on and off like a faulty light bulb. An old Victrola wind-up gramophone, complete with curving brass horn, waited patiently in one corner. It played the memories of old 78 rpm recordings that didn't physically exist any more. JC had once heard it play a 1908 recording of the last English castrato, David Tennich. A beautiful, eerie, subtly inhuman sound. The Haunted Glove of Haversham, which had strangled seventeen young women in 1953, until the Boss figured out what was going on, and captured it, now resided under a glass display case. Very firmly nailed to its wooden stand, just in case. It looked like a very ordinary glove.

And, finally, there was a portrait of Her Majesty the Queen, taking pride of place behind the Boss's desk. The whole face seemed to follow you around the room.

Having run out of excuses not to meet the Boss's gaze, JC decided to get his retaliation in first. He arranged his crossed legs so casually it was practically an insult, leaned back in his chair, and looked down his long nose at the Boss.

"What is so important that we had to be summoned here, like peasants to the Great Hall, so soon after our last case?" he demanded. "We are entitled to sufficient downtime between cases. It would say so in our contracts if we were allowed contracts, which we aren't, and is another matter I'd like to discuss. Hold everything; don't tell me one of the Royal corgis has got possessed again . . . I keep telling you, they're too inbred these days. The corgis, not the . . . Look; we do all have lives, you know, outside the Institute . . ."

"I know all about your lives," said the Boss, in her usual calm, thoughtful tone. "I know everything there is to know about you and your team, Mr. Chance. Including all the things you think I don't know. You, for example, run a bookshop in Charing Cross Road; ostensibly antiquarian, but actually specialising in rare and dangerous volumes of forgotten lore, forbidden knowledge, and forsaken arts. The erudite scholar's equivalent of the backpack nuke. Merely opening some of those books was enough to set off alarms in organisations like this all over the world.

"You recently acquired a folio copy of that damned

and utterly poisonous play *The King in Yellow*. Reading it is enough to drive most men mad. On its one and only performance in Paris in 1898, the audience stormed the stage and killed and ate the entire cast. And I am here to tell you that those specially enchanted blast goggles you purchased on eBay will not be enough to protect you if you try to read it."

She switched her thoughtful gaze to Happy, who jumped in his chair and giggled nervously.

"You, Mr. Palmer, are an accountant. Because there's always good money in accounting, and because you find numbers soothing. You can make numbers make sense, unlike people. You work for us because I know what else you do with numbers . . . And as long as you continue to work for us, no-one else will ever have to know."

She turned to Melody, who glared right back at her. Melody was only ever impressed by technology.

"Miss Chambers, I believe you like to say you're Something in Publishing. In fact, you publish specialised erotica for the fetish community. Some of it so specialised I'm frankly hard-pressed to see where the erotica comes in."

"People have always liked to play dress-up," said Melody. "I just take it a bit further than most."

"How shall I love thee, let me count the ways," murmured JC. "I should come here more often; I learn the most intriguing things . . ."

"For once, the three of you are not here to be judged on your many and various misdeeds," said the Boss. She stopped to fit a new cigarette into her holder and lit it with a monogrammed gold Zippo. "Annoying though they frequently are. I have told you before, Mr. Chance; travel expenses do not extend to first class."

"Only way to get a little peace and quiet, these days," said JC.

The Boss glared at Happy. "Nor am I happy with your continuing demands for new medications. When you finally die, we'll have to bury you in a coffin with a child-proof lid."

Happy sniffed. "I only stay with the Institute for the free prescriptions and access to unstable chemicals. I am a medical miracle. Universities have been bidding against each other for years, for the rights to my body for scientific research. Some don't even want to wait till I'm dead."

"And I'm only here for the tech," Melody said firmly. "Can't do the job without the right equipment."

The Boss's nostrils flared slightly. "You just like to play with the latest toys. And break them."

JC realised, with something like wonder, that the Boss was only saying these things in order to avoid saying something else. She was distracting herself with familiar complaints so she could put off having to tell them about the new case. Which meant it had to be something really bad . . . He watched, impressed despite himself, as the Boss squared her shoulders and got down to business.

"All of this . . . is irrelevant. You are not here to receive the various dressing downs you so thoroughly deserve; you are here because the Institute is faced with a major emergency. Something bad has happened, down in the London Underground. Oxford Circus Tube Station is haunted. A Code One Haunting."

JC sat up sharply. "A Code One, right here in the heart of London? That's supposed to be impossible! The whole city's covered with overlapping layers of pacts and protections, laid down ever since Roman times."

"The unprecedented nature of the haunting is what makes this such an emergency," said the Boss. "If what we suspect is true, all hell is about to break loose in the Underground."

"What's happened?" said JC. "Tell us everything."

"It started slowly, sneaking in around the edges, almost unnoticed," said the Boss, leaning back in her chair and watching the shapes her cigarette smoke made in the air. "Stories of odd-looking people on overcrowded platforms, who never seemed to get on any train. Uneasy presences, felt rather than seen, on deserted platforms late at night. Lights that flickered on and off, or changed in intensity, for no reason anyone could explain. Strange announcements, by unauthorised voices, saying awful, disturbing things. People travelling up the escalators who never arrived at the top. Horrid laughter in the tunnels, and never anybody there.

"Then things got worse in a hurry. Indistinct figures were seen throwing themselves in front of approaching trains; but after each train had been stopped and the tracks inspected, no body was ever found. Men and women claimed to have been pushed violently from behind, just as a train was coming in, but when they turned and looked, no-one was anywhere near them. More and more travellers were reported missing—seen going down into the Underground system, then never heard from again.

"And people came and went . . . who didn't look entirely like people.

"It all came to a head at Oxford Circus Station, at eight thirty-five this morning. We've had to stop all the trains going in and out and shut the whole place down; no-one in or out, until further notice. I have a few witness statements, recordings, for you to take a look at. No comments, please, until you've seen them all."

She spun her desk-computer screen around so they could all see it and stabbed at her keyboard with two fingers, her cigarette-holder jutting grimly from one corner of her mouth. The first witness was a man in his late forties, neat City suit, respectable. You'd have believed anything he said in a court of law. But his face was grey and shocked, and his mouth was slack, as though he'd just been hit. His eyes were frightened, desperate.

"Trains were running when none were scheduled," he said, in a voice that sounded on the edge of tears. "Bad trains. They didn't stop, only slowed down as they passed by, so everyone on the platform could get a good look. Strange trains with strange markings, in the kinds of writing you see in dreams. The metal of the cars steamed, blazing with unbearable heat, and inside . . . there were things, terrible things . . . awful shapes, not human . . . beating fiercely against the closed doors and windows, fighting to get out, to get at everyone waiting on the platform. We all screamed. Some turned and ran. The things in the cars laughed at us and beat on the windows with their fists. They would have killed us all if they could. I won't go back into the Underground again. It's not ours any more."

The next witness was a woman in her mid thirties. Her face was calm and relaxed, and her voice was quite steady, and entirely reasonable. But blood had dried all down one side of her face from where she'd yanked out a chunk of her own hair. She played with the bloody mess while she talked.

"I was on the northbound platform when the train came in. It was pretending to be an ordinary train, but it wasn't. There were people trapped inside. As the cars rolled to a halt, we could see men and women, screaming soundlessly, as they tried desperately to escape; but the cars wouldn't let them out. Some of us tried to help, but the doors wouldn't budge. Up close, we could see the bloody trails left on the windows by broken fingers and torn-away nails. The train moved off again and took them all away. And I know . . . it would have taken us, too, if it could. It wanted to, but it was already full. That downbound train, bearing them off to Hell . . ."

The third witness was a child. Maybe eight or nine years old, in a pretty party dress. She laughed at the camera, but it was an adult's laugh, not a child's. And all she would say was *Look who's come to see you!* over and over again.

The Boss turned off her screen and fixed the three field agents with a steady stare. "So far, we've studied three hundred and seventeen witness statements. Those were the most . . . representative. We've had to section many of them under the Mental Health Act, for everyone's safety. Hopefully, we'll be able to do something for them once this nasty business has been dealt with. For the moment, the official version is that the Underground has been the subject of a terrorist attack, involving a new nerve gas that induces nightmare hallucinations. That should keep the press out, for a while. Understand me; this has to be cleared up fast."

"And that's why you called us in," JC said happily. "Because we're the best you've got."

"No," said the Boss. "You're just the best available. Everyone else is busy, or too far away to be called in quickly enough. So you get the case. Don't drop the ball on this one, people, or I will have yours off with a blunt spoon. I want this dealt with, whatever it takes."

"You always do," said JC. "Do we get any backup?"

"No," said the Boss. "Too risky. You're on your own."

"Oh joy," said Happy.

"Deep joy," said JC.

"Happy happy joy joy," said Melody, unexpectedly.

"Get out," said the Boss. "Shut this down hard, and fast, and all your many sins will be forgiven, if not forgotten. And try not to get yourselves killed. It's expensive replacing good field agents."

"Would this be a good time to talk about a raise?" said Happy.

THREE

::::::::::::::::::::::::::::::::::::::

GOING UNDERGROUND

In the old days, in the really old days, when people had to go in search of the dead, they went underground. They left the sunlight behind them and went down, all the way down, into the Underworld, there to parlay with gods and demons for the right to talk with the departed. Never an easy journey, and always a price to be paid, for a chance to talk to the dead. Gods come and go, civilisations rise and fall, belief systems prosper and fail; but still, even in this day and age, if you have business with the dead, you often have no choice but to go down, all the way down, into the dark places under the world.

• ::::::::::::::::::::::::

JC Chance, Melody Chambers, and Happy Jack Palmer went down into the London Underground, into Oxford Circus Tube Station; and the police locked them in, then retreated swiftly to what they had been told were safe positions. The three ghost finders stood close together in the entrance lobby, instinctively drawing together for strength and comfort. The lobby was brightly lit and completely deserted. The ticket barriers were firmly closed, along with all the narrow enquiry windows; and nothing moved anywhere. The white-tiled walls, the brightly coloured posters, the sane and sensible lists of destinations . . . everything was as it should be. Except that nothing and nobody moved anywhere in all that sharp, merciless light.

Two men and a woman, standing on the set of a movie that hadn't started filming yet. Waiting for someone, or something, to shout *Action!*

The first thing that struck JC was how complete the quiet was. Silence hung heavily on the air, reluctant to be broken or disturbed. It had no place in a busy station like this. It should be alive with sound, with the clatter and clamour of people rushing back and forth, and the distant thunder of trains coming and going, and the endless self-important announcements. But here, and now, there was nothing. Only the eerie quiet of an empty place, from which people had been driven, screaming.

Happy's first reaction to Oxford Circus Station was to flinch sharply, as though he'd been hit. He barely stifled a groan of pain. For a telepath of his class, the station wasn't empty at all. It was packed from wall to wall with faces and voices and any number of conflicting emotions, all the ingrained psychic traces of the millions of passengers who'd passed though the place, leaving a little of themselves behind, forever. Layer upon layer of them, falling away into the past, and beyond. Happy's stomach muscles clenched, and sweat popped out all over his face. It was like everyone was shouting in his head at once, plucking viciously at his sleeve, jostling him from all sides. He blindly fished a bottle of pills out of an inner pocket; and then JC's hand came sharply forward out of nowhere and clamped firmly, mercilessly, onto his wrist.

"No pills, Happy," said JC, as kindly as he could. "I need you to be sharp, and focused."

"I know, I know!" said Happy, jerking his wrist free. "I can handle it. I can."

Reluctantly, he put the pills away, then scowled fiercely as he concentrated, painstakingly rebuilding and reinforcing the mental shields that let him live among Humanity without being overwhelmed by them. It wasn't easy, and it got harder every year, perhaps because every year he grew a little more tired, at making sure the only voice inside his head was his. He was shaking and muttering and sweating profusely by the time he'd finished. He nodded curtly to JC, who nodded calmly back in return.

"Better now?" said JC.

"You have no idea," said Happy, mopping roughly at his face with a surprisingly clean handkerchief. "One of these days, the strain of doing that will kill me, and maybe then I'll get some rest."

"We couldn't do this without you," said JC.

It was as close to an apology as Happy was going to get, and he knew it. He sniffed loudly and looked around him.

"Ugly place, this, in more ways than one. I mean, did they have a competition, and this colour scheme won? I've been locked up in cheerier institutions than this. And they had piped music."

Happy grinned suddenly. "Anyone want to say *It's quiet, too quiet*? I mean, it is traditional."

JC laughed briefly and went striding around the empty lobby, looking closely at everything and running his hands over the silent ticket machines. He paced back and forth, on the trail of something only he could sense, his head up like a hound on the scent, sniffing for invisible clues. His eyes gleamed, and he grinned widely. JC was on the job and having the time of his life, as always.

Melody, meanwhile, ignored them both with the ease of long practice. She was only interested in the various pieces of high-tech equipment she'd brought with her, piled precariously high onto an unsteady trolley. She just knew the Institute technicians had damaged something when they loaded the trolley up; they always did. No-one understood or appreciated her precious machines like she did. She wouldn't be happy until she'd set up base somewhere and could reassure herself that everything was working properly. She ran through her checklist again, making sure nothing had been left behind.

She paid no attention to what JC and Happy were doing. She trusted them to hold up their end. Inasmuch as she trusted anything that wasn't a machine. You could fix machines when they went wrong . . . She dimly realised they'd stopped bickering, and she looked around, fists on her hips.

"Yes, fine," she said. "Don't do anything to help, will you? I can handle all this vitally important and extremely heavy equipment myself. Unaided."

JC shot her an amused glance. "You know very well you don't like us touching your toys, Melody. In fact, you have been known to stab at our hands with pointy things if you even think we're going to touch something."

"That's because you always break them! You two

could break an anvil merely by looking at it! You break more of my things than the things we go after. What I meant was, I need your help to get this trolley up and over the closed ticket barriers. Unless you have some clever trick to get us past them."

JC smiled at her pityingly, took out his travel card, and slapped it against the clearly indicated contact point. The barriers sprang open.

"Very good!" said Melody. "Now consider the sheer amount of equipment packed onto this trolley and tell me how you're planning to squeeze it all through that narrow gap."

"You're so sharp you'll cut yourself one of these days," said JC. "But it's not going anywhere yet."

"Why not?" said Melody, immediately suspicious. "What still needs doing?"

"Listen," said JC. He stood very still, his head cocked slightly to one side, a single finger held up, as though testing for some spiritual breeze. "*Listen* . . . Get a feel for the place. It's 5:07 P.M. Well into the city rush hour. There should be crowds of people flowing through this station, heading home after a hard day's work or shopping. Men and women and children, workers and families—the city's human lifeblood—chasing headlong through its arteries. They should be filling this place, loud and raucous and determined to be on their way."

"God, you do love the sound of your own voice," said Melody.

"It's always worse when he gets like this," Happy said gloomily. "It means he's moved into full smug mode because he thinks he's spotted something we haven't."

"All right, I get it, it's quiet," said Melody. "Can we move on now, please?"

JC looked at Happy, smiling his most superior smile. "Do you get it, Happy?"

"Maybe," said Happy, reluctantly. "It's the wrong kind of quiet. Not only the absence of noise but the actual suppression of all sound, of everything that's alive and natural. As though something else has replaced the sound of people. An unwanted Presence, like a weight on the air, pressing down on the world. This light is all wrong, too. It's too bright, too stark . . . merciless and forensic, like a dissecting lab. We are very definitely not alone down here."

"Well," said Melody, after a moment, "that was very nicely spoken, Happy. All very fab and groovy, splendidly atmospheric and ominous; but you're as bad as he is. Feelings are useless until I can get my lovely machines set up, and we can start analysing the data! So suck it up, brain boy, and help JC and me lift this bloody trolley over the bloody ticket barriers. Preferably without dropping anything fragile."

"Your vibrator broke down again last night, didn't it?" said Happy.

"Stay out of my head!"

"Lucky guess, lucky guess," said Happy, holding up both hands and trying not to grin. "Let's shift the trolley and get this show on the road."

"God loves a volunteer," said JC. "Come, children, lift that barge and tote that bale; the ghosts are waiting."

····················

The three of them man-handled the trolley over the barriers without too much trouble, Melody alternately coaxing and bullying the equipment to stay in place. They then had to carry it down the escalator to the tunnels and platforms below, as none of the metal stairways was moving. Apparently the main computers were down. Personally, JC thought they were lucky to still have the lights, but he had enough sense to keep the comment to himself. There was such a thing as tempting fate. JC, Happy, and Melody bumped and clattered the trolley all the way down the unmoving metal steps, accompanied by a certain amount of bruised limbs, trapped fingers, and really foul language, before they finally reached the bottom.

Happy gave the trolley a good kick, on general principles, then stopped suddenly and stood very still, one hand upraised to ward off questions from the others. He frowned thoughtfully, listening with more than his ears. JC and Melody looked at him, then at each other, shrugged pretty much simultaneously, and listened, too. The continuing quiet didn't seem any different.

"Well?" said JC, after a while.

"I've got a bad feeling," said Happy.

"You've always got a bad feeling," said Melody. "It's your standard default position. You probably had a bad feeling as you left the womb behind and headed for the light."

"Something's down here with us," said Happy, not listening to her at all. "And it's not anything I expected. This isn't like anything we've ever encountered before, people. This is something new. Or maybe something very old, come round again. Big and powerful and utterly different."

"Dangerous?" JC said quietly.

Happy came out of his trance and shot JC a disgusted look. "What do you think?"

"Moving on, moving on," said JC, heading for the nearest platform. "Do feel free to share your feelings with us at any time, Happy, you know how I value your contributions; but do it on the move, please. I can feel a clock ticking, somewhere."

"Bully," muttered Happy.

"Will somebody please help me with this trolley!" said Melody.

....

They finally established themselves on a southbound platform, deep under the surface. The light was as sharp and fierce as ever, the silence still heavy and unrelenting; and nothing moved anywhere. The three ghost finders bustled around, helping set up Melody's equipment on a semicircular standing frame. Making rather more noise than was necessary, as though to impose their presence on the quiet. Melody oversaw the installation of every piece of equipment, cooing over some of them in a disturbingly maternal way. Their separate power source was a small black box that sat happily on its own, on the platform floor, tucked under the frame. JC really wanted to ask what it was, and how it worked, and how such a small box could power so much equipment . . . but he knew he wouldn't understand any of the answers, so he didn't bother. Melody looked a lot happier as, one by one, her instrument panels and monitor screens lit up, along with any number of flashing brightly coloured lights. Though he would never admit it, JC found the lights comforting. It wasn't real equipment unless it had bright flashing lights.

But the moment they hit the platform, all three of them had to fight a constant irrational urge to stop, turn sharply, and look behind them. Even though they knew there wasn't anything there. Something was watching them. They all felt it, in their various ways. JC glared at the dead platform surveillance cameras, Happy kept a careful watch on the shadows, and Melody worked even harder to get her sensor arrays up and working. They were all of them, after all, professionals.

Melody fired up her various computers and smiled happily as, one by one, they came on-line and muttered busily to themselves, reaching out through state-of-the-art short- and long-range sensors to test the situation on more levels than anyone but Melody could comfortably handle. Her fingers flew across one keyboard after another as she darted back and forth before the flickering monitor screens, eyes bright, teeth worrying at her full lower lip as she drank in rivers of information as though it were the finest wine. Melody was in her element and on the job, and as far as she was concerned, all was right with the world.

Melody wanted to be the first scientist to put a ghost under the microscope and find out how it worked.

JC and Happy wandered the length of the southbound platform, looking about them, taking their time. They didn't know what they were looking for; only that they'd know it when they saw it. The sound of their footsteps was strangely muffled, hardly echoing at all in the quiet. And yet it all seemed normal enough. The huge posters on the walls advertised recent and forthcoming movies, along with all the usual ads for expensive products and services, and even the descending list of destinations on the far wall seemed reassuringly sane and definite. The two men stopped at the end of the platform and peered dubiously into the great dark maw of the tunnel-mouth; but nothing looked back.

"I don't see anyone," said JC. "Can't say I feel anything much, either."

"Feel the air," said Happy. "It's colder than it should be, and . . . brittle. I'm getting a definite feeling of anticipation. Of something *about* to happen. And even though lights are still on . . . doesn't it still *feel* dark, to you?"

"Go on," said JC. "What else?"

"Eyes," said Happy. "A constant feeling of being observed, by unseen eyes. Not human. Nature . . . unknown. But I can feel them, digging into my back. Whatever it is that's down here, that terrified and traumatised all those people . . . it knows we're here."

"Good," JC said briskly. "At least now we can be sure we're not down here on a wild ghost chase. Melody? Do you have anything interesting to tell us yet?"

"Don't shout! I can hear you perfectly." Melody concentrated on what her instrument panels were telling her, not even glancing round at JC and Happy. "Short- and long-range sensors are all on-line and reporting in, but so far all they're giving me is a headache. Information's coming in faster than the computers can deal with it, and none of it makes any sense. I'm getting readings all across the board: temperature spikes, radiation surges, electromagnetic fluctuations I would have said were impossible under normal conditions; and a whole bunch of weird energy signatures are popping up all over the place."

"Purpose?" said JC.

"Beats the hell out of me," said Melody, stabbing viciously at various keyboards with both hands. "I'm getting definite indications of Time shifts. Intrusions from the Past. Some recent, some not. And underneath all that . . . I'm reading Deep Time, JC. From long before this station even existed. This is bad, JC, seriously bad. I've never seen so many extreme readings in one place before."

"Go on," JC urged. "Throw caution to the winds and give me your best guess as to what's happening here."

"I do not guess!" snapped Melody. "I am a scientist! I study data and draw logical conclusions. Only . . . there's nothing sane or logical about any of this. I can't make head nor tail of what my computers are telling me. If I didn't know better, I'd say they were scared. All I can tell you is that whatever it is we've got down here, it's spread itself through the whole station. There isn't a single platform or tunnel here that hasn't been touched, and changed."

"But is it still confined to the station?" JC said carefully.

"Maybe. Probably. My long-range sensors get confused, the further out they reach. And before you ask: no, I can't locate any heart or central core to this haunting. It's all over the place."

"It's bad," said Happy. He was wringing his hands together, unconsciously. "I need a pill, JC, I really do. A little something, to take the edge off."

"No you don't," said JC.

"Come on, JC! You're feeling this, too; I can tell. Like ice in your blood, and knives at your throat. Like something really bad could come charging out of that tunnel-mouth at any moment. And for everything you feel, it's a thousand times worse for me. Who's afraid of the big bad wolf, JC? I am. I am."

"You're no use to me with your brains shut down," said JC. "There'll be time for pills later. Now come on; concentrate. You're stronger than you think. What exactly is it that you're picking up?"

Happy slumped down onto the nearest metal seat and looked down at his hands squirming together in his lap.

He stopped them moving with an effort. He was breathing hard, sucking the air in as though he couldn't get enough of it. JC studied the telepath carefully, trying not to let his concern show. He'd never seen Happy this upset.

"Something awful happened down here," Happy said softly, his words so quiet JC had to lean forward to hear them. "And I think it's still happening. Something really nasty has set up home here, and it has plans, JC, big plans. Some strange intelligence, not human, not human at all. It feels . . . like the end of the world."

JC nodded slowly. "Then it's official. Oxford Circus Tube Station has become a bad place, the kind of place that makes ghosts and maintains hauntings. But why? Nothing's happened here to justify such a change. No train crash, no terrorist bombing . . . No disaster of any kind, man-made or natural. So what was the triggering event?"

Happy shrugged. He was breathing a little more easily though he didn't look one bit less miserable.

"Sometimes," he said heavily, "bad places just happen. That's life for you. And death."

"Oh come on; there's always something," Melody insisted. "Just because we can't detect it, or recognise it, doesn't mean it isn't there. We need to run some experiments, collect some new data."

"Spoken like a true scientist," said Happy. "Remember that time when you wanted to stick a thermometer up that ghost's behind, so you could measure its core temperature?"

"That would have worked if you hadn't stopped me."

"Yeah, right," said Happy.

"You want a slap?" said Melody. "I'm sure I've got one here somewhere."

JC left them to it and walked up and down the platform for a while, listening to the flat sound of his footsteps, trying to pin down exactly what it was that so bothered him about the place. They'd been there for some time, making all kinds of noise, more than enough to draw anyone's attention, but . . . No ghosts, no manifestations, not even a black cat with a bad attitude. Still, there was no doubt that he was looking very cool and elegant in his smart cream suit, and that was a comfort.

JC liked to remind himself, now and again, of what was really important.

He looked back at his team. Melody was busy with her equipment, doing things only she understood. Happy was sulking quietly on his metal seat. So, when in doubt, keep them busy and keep them occupied, and they won't have time to be scared. It always worked for JC. He clapped his hands sharply to get their attention. The sound hardly echoed at all.

"Talk to me, Melody," he said cheerfully. "Tell me things of importance and interest."

"Getting definite readings now, of a single great intrusion from the Past," said Melody. "Deep Past. And I do mean really Deep Past."

JC looked at her thoughtfully. "The same kind of entity we encountered in the car park?"

"I said Deep Time, and I meant it," said Melody. "We are talking ancient, maybe even primordial. So powerful it's like a gravity well, without the well, a spiritual maelstrom . . . only pushing out, not in. Something so powerful it distorts and transforms its whole environment merely by being here. But I'm also getting a whole bunch of more recent readings, from what are quite definitely contemporary phenomena. People and events imprinted on Time, hauntings only days or weeks old. Ghosts, JC. Lots and lots of ghosts."

"A new energy source, reinvigorating lesser patterns," JC said thoughtfully. "But what kind of energy source?"

"I hate to say it," said Melody, turning to look directly at JC for the first time, "but I think we have to consider the possibility of an other-dimensional intrusion. That something from a higher dimension has descended into our world and made itself at home here."

"That's it," said Happy, surging to his feet. "We are now officially way out of our depth. I think I'll bolt for the exit now. Try and keep up."

"Stand still, man," said JC. "Melody, can you track this intrusion down, pinpoint its location?"

"Let's not," Happy said immediately. "Really really bad idea, people."

"I can point you in the right direction," said Melody. "Go and find it with my blessing, give it a good kicking, then drag it back here so I can poke it with a stick."

"Love to," said JC.

"I have fallen among mad people," said Happy. "*Am I the only sane person here?* We are not trained, equipped, or armed enough to deal with Great Beasts or Outer Monstrosities, or any of the Abominations! We are ghost finders, not god killers! Being in the same place as . . . whatever this thing is, is playing hell with my head. I can feel it, out there, waiting for us. Waiting for us to come to it, so it can do terrible things to us! Please, JC, trust me; we are not ready for this."

"Happy, you heard the Boss," said JC, not unkindly. "There's no-one else. Or at least, no-one else who can get here in time. We can't let this spread, Happy. We have to stop it here."

"How?" said Happy. All the anger had gone out of him, leaving only fatigue and bitterness. "What can we do?"

"What we always do," said JC. "Hit hard, move fast, improvise wildly, and snatch victory from the jaws of defeat at the very last moment through superior gamesmanship and blatant cheating."

"Oh, that's what we do, is it?" said Melody. "I've often wondered."

Happy turned his back on both of them, staring determinedly off into the distance. He would have liked to indulge in a sulk, but upset as he was, he still knew that JC was right. He had to do something. Because he was there. Because there wasn't anybody else. Story of his life, such as it was.

"Ghosts," he said loudly. "I can sense ghosts everywhere. All kinds, too. But most of them are irrelevant. Old stone tapes, stirred up by the arrival of the Intruder. No connection to what's really going on. There is a purpose to all this. An intelligent purpose, with a definite end in mind."

"It's always the same with you," Melody said cuttingly. "Every case we work, you always have to bring up the *big picture*, look for some sinister hidden intent, so you can fit it into your Grand Conspiracy of Absolutely Everything."

"She does have a point," said JC.

"The dead are at war with the living," said Happy, spinning round to glare at JC and Melody. "Or some of them, anyway. Abhuman creatures are constantly trying to get to us, to force their way into our world from their strange outer dimensions, to eat us, or rule us, or replace us. It isn't only me that thinks this, you know. Most of the big thinkers at the Carnacki Institute are convinced that something is happening, behind the walls of reality, beyond the fields we know. That certain Powers and Forces are working constantly to weaken the barriers between our worlds and the afterworlds, for reasons of their own."

"Have you stopped taking your antipsychotic medication again?" said JC.

"It's not only the Institute that believes this!" Happy insisted. "The Crowley Project are just as concerned."

"Those bastards," said Melody, giving a recalcitrant computer a good slap, so it knew she was serious. "I wouldn't put anything past them."

"The Project are undoubtedly a bunch of complete and utter evil bastards, with an unhealthy interest in world domination," said JC. "But it doesn't necessarily mean they're any more clued in as to what's really Going On than anyone else." He stopped and considered the matter for a moment. "Do you suppose the Project know about Oxford Circus yet?"

"Wouldn't surprise me," said Happy. "They hear about everything, eventually. Word is, they have more field agents out in the world than we do." It was his turn to look thoughtful as he considered possibilities. "Do you suppose . . . Could they be responsible for what's happened here? Could this be some experiment of theirs, gone horribly wrong? And they've got the hell out of Dodge and left us to clean up their mess? Wouldn't be the first time."

"Maybe," said JC. "And maybe not. Who knows anything, where the Crowley Project are concerned? Still, I have to wonder if we can expect interference on this mission from some of their field agents."

"Oh, this gets better all the time," said Happy. "I can feel one of my funny turns coming on."

"The Boss would have warned us if there was any danger of confrontation," said Melody. She stopped and looked up from her precious instruments, a new concern in her face. "Wouldn't she?"

"You know the Boss," said JC. "She only ever tells us what she thinks we need to know. So we can concentrate our minds on the matter at hand. But . . . I'm pretty sure she would have told us if there'd been any indication the Crowley Project were involved in the creation of this particular mess. Because it could have a bearing on what we might have to do, to shut it down. So, no . . . I think we can rule out bumping into any Project agents down here, on the grounds that no-one with any working brain-cells would come down here, into the middle of all this, unless they absolutely had to."

"Good point," said Happy. "Suddenly, I feel so much more secure. I may even do my happy dance."

"Please don't," said Melody. "Some things are an affront to nature."

"So, children, let us bend our talents to the matter at hand," said JC. "All hauntings, no matter how extreme they may become, are the result of a single triggering event. Something specific happens to set everything else in motion. Identify, remove, or defuse that unfortunate beginning, disrupt the pattern, and the haunting will collapse. I don't see why this mess should be any different, for all its apparent scale. So let's find the starting point and shut it down; and then we can all go home."

"You make it sound so simple, and so easy," said Happy. "And you know perfectly well it never is."

"Right," said Melody. "Save the pep talk for newcomers. We know better."

"Remember when we trapped the Hammersmith Soul Thief in a mirror, last year, then smashed it?" JC said patiently. "That worked out fine, didn't it? We never heard from him again."

"Well, yes," said Happy. "But it still took me ages before I could look into my mirror without expecting to see him standing behind me, peering over my shoulder, and *smiling*."

"But it worked," JC said firmly. "Just like my brilliant gambit at the supermarket, this morning. We can do this, people."

Happy wouldn't look at him. "I wish it was that simple, JC. I really do. But there's something down here with us, and I don't think we've ever met anything like it before. There are . . . Things, Powers, at work in the afterworlds. Some Good, some Bad, some so far beyond us we can't even hope to understand their motivations and purposes. Sometimes they help us, sometimes they interfere, and sometimes they send us down to Hell with a nudge and a laugh. It isn't the ghosts we have to fear; it's the things that make ghosts."

"Happy, you really are a first-class gloomy bugger," JC said affectionately. "You could gloom for the Olympics, and still take a Bronze in existential paranoia."

"Everyone has to be good at something," said Happy, smiling a little in spite of himself. "But don't change the subject . . ."

"Happy, you can believe in whatever you want," said JC, cutting him off with an upraised hand. "As long as it doesn't get in the way of doing the job. We are not here to take part in some mystic war between Absolute Powers from the Outer Realms. We are here to solve a haunting and put everyone and everything to rest again. That's what we do."

"I swear, you two argue like an old married couple," said Melody. "And it's interfering with some of my more sensitive instruments. Go take a walk around, check out the other platforms, look for clues or something, and leave me in peace to get on with my work. Stick your phones in your ears, and I'll give you a yell when I have something definite to tell you."

JC looked at her carefully. "Are you sure, Melody?"

"Of course I'm sure. Off you go. I can cope."

JC nodded. "We won't be long." He grinned at Happy. "Exploring time! We need to take a look at the other platforms, see if they all feel the same as this. You check out the rest of the southbound lines, and I'll take the northbound. Keep in touch, and report back here in an hour, whether you've found anything or not."

Happy's eyes got really big. "Are you kidding? Are you out of your mind? You want me to go wandering around this place *on my own*?"

"Yes," said JC. "What's the matter? You want someone to hold your hand?"

"Yes!" said Happy. "Preferably someone I know."

"Go," JC said sternly. "Be a big brave ghost finder, and there'll be honey for tea."

He waved one elegant hand around and strolled away, humming a merry tune. Happy made a really vile gesture at JC's immaculate back, produced a bottle of pills from nowhere, and defiantly dry swallowed three of mother's little helpers, one after the other. He looked at

Melody, but she was making a point of giving all her attention to the equipment ranged before her. Happy sighed, and his shoulders slumped. He shuffled towards the exit arch, like a small boy on his way to school, knowing that the school bully was waiting.

They thought he was scared all the time because he was a coward. The truth was, only he could see the world clearly enough to know how truly scary it was. He saw things and heard things, and every single one of them was real. Horribly real. If Humanity knew what they shared the world with, what walked their streets by day and snuggled up beside them at night; if they could see it all, just for a moment . . . they'd all go stark staring mad. Happy had learned long ago not to talk about it. People didn't want to know. But he had no choice. If the Boss knew what he faced every day, she'd give him a medal. Or, if she was really feeling kind, a lobotomy. And maybe then he'd get some peace at last.

Ghosts are the only ones who never have to feel scared. Because the worst thing in the world has already happened to them.

""""""""""""""""""""""

It didn't take JC long to decide that the whole of the Oxford Circus Tube Station was infected. Everywhere he looked, something looked disturbed, subtly alien. It was hard to judge distances in the unrelentingly fierce light. He walked down one platform for ages, without reaching its end. Eventually he had no choice but to turn around and go back; and there was the exit he'd come in by, waiting for him. Directions become treacherous and signs untrustworthy. The same archway took him to a dozen different places, including one painfully over-bright corridor that twisted and turned like a maze. The angles between floor and wall seemed subtly *wrong*, and his head ached trying to figure out why. And what shadows there were were very dark.

He particularly didn't like one tunnel-mouth, at the end of a certain platform. Its interior was too dark, too deep, as though it might go on forever. There was no sound, and not a trace of movement, but still he kept expecting something to come crashing out of the tunnel-mouth at any moment and sweep him helplessly away to somewhere unbearably awful. He made himself stare into the darkness until his breathing steadied and his hands stopped shaking, then he very deliberately turned his back on the tunnel-mouth and walked away, head held high.

Everywhere he went, the tunnels and platforms were full of odd sounds and weird smells, and things glimpsed out of the corner of his eye that were never there when he turned to look at them directly. He kept thinking he caught glimpses of people, turning the corner ahead of him, or peering briefly out of open archways, but they were never there when he arrived. And though he couldn't quite put his finger on it, there was something subtly *wrong* about these people that disturbed him strangely on some deep unconscious level.

As though there was something obscurely loathsome about them that he ought to know, ought to recognise. While he still had time.

JC strode up and down the white-tiled corridors, investigated every platform, and made a point of peering into every single tunnel-mouth. The adrenaline was really buzzing now, and he was grinning widely. He was walking alone, into the face of danger and the heart of the unknown, and he couldn't have been happier. On every case, he couldn't wait for the overture to begin, for a chance to come face-to-face with something he'd never seen before. It was the only reason he stayed with the Institute. He couldn't wait for the supernatural to start its act, reveal its hidden hand, for good or bad, so he could roll up his sleeves and get stuck in. Because once he was actually doing something, he'd be too busy to feel scared.

For all his studiedly calm exterior, JC knew enough about his job to be sensibly cautious. But he also knew, or thought he knew, enough about the situations he faced every day . . . to be pretty sure of what needed doing to put things right. He knew things, had taught himself things, that the rest of his team never knew about, and that the Boss would almost certainly not approve of. JC believed in being prepared, and very heavily armed, at all times; and some of the things he carried in the inner pockets of his marvellous cream suit were officially banned by the Geneva Convention. (Supernatural and Weird Happenings Section.)

He stopped abruptly, half-way down a platform, and looked around. He was almost certain he'd been there before; but everywhere he looked, things seemed subtly *different*. As though certain details were changing, in slow and sneaky ways, right before his eyes. Someone was playing tricks on him. He walked slowly forward, and the posters on the wall beside him stirred lazily, the details seeming to blur and shimmer, rearranging themselves before his eyes. An ad for the new James Bond movie was suddenly an old propaganda poster from World War II, when whole families huddled together deep in the Underground, sheltering from the bombs of the Blitz. A simple cartoon, backed up by a government admonition to keep your mouth shut in case of spies: *Be Like Dad; Keep Mum.* The cartoon father-figure turned its simple head and winked an eye at JC. Blood ran from its mouth.

JC reached out to touch the poster, then pulled his hand back again. He had a sudden horrible intuition that it might plunge on into the poster, as though into a deep pool. He made himself walk on, as outwardly casual and unconcerned as ever. The next poster shouted the wares for some new overblown sci-fi epic. As JC watched, the improbable starships, with their blazing energy beams stabbing across the starry night, faded slowly away, revealing instead a stark and brutal poster entitled: *What You Should Do in the Case of Sonic Attack.* It made scary reading. At the top was a date: 35 October, 2118.

JC kept walking, increasing his pace slightly, glancing at the posters he passed. Scenes seemed to slip and slide, slyly re-creating themselves. Disturbing images clung to the wall, becoming strange windows into unsettling alien worlds and strange dimensions, all of them accompanied by unfamiliar text—the kind of writing you see in dreams, rich and meaningful, packed with a terrible significance and urgent warnings you can't quite seem to grasp. JC walked faster and faster, wanting to see as much as possible while he could. He was fascinated. What would have unnerved and disturbed lesser men was meat and drink to him.

And yet, at the same time, a small but very real voice insisted on being heard, informing him that the only reason he was so immersed in his work . . . was because he had nothing else in his life he cared about. He never allowed himself to think that out loud. Not even when he lay awake in his single bed, in the early hours of the morning when the dawn seems furthest away . . . when a man's thoughts turn almost against his will to what he's made of his life as opposed to what he meant to make of it. When he looks back at his past, and sees nothing to value, or into his future . . . and sees nothing but more of the same. JC had always been a loner, even before the Carnacki Institute found him; and if his work was all he had, it was more than most people had.

He could never have a love in his life, only lovers. Ships that passed in the night and never called afterwards. Because JC could never even hint at what he really did for a living without scaring the other party away. So most of the women who passed through JC's life said little, kept themselves to themselves, and left no trace behind. There hadn't been anyone for months . . . but JC couldn't seem to bring himself to care, much. You can still be lonely even when there's someone else in the room if she's not the right kind of someone.

He couldn't connect with any of the Institute's female field agents. They were too competitive, or too traumatised, or too haunted . . . there was always something. So JC lived alone and told himself he preferred it that way. He kept himself as busy as possible, so he wouldn't have to tell himself that too often.

He did love his work. It was fascinating. Always something new.

Genuinely intrigued and delighted, he watched the posters change. His work never let him down.

························

Further away from JC than simple distance could account for, Happy went bouncing through empty white-tiled corridors, peering this way and that with wide, wondering eyes. He'd dosed himself with a wide variety of pills, and he was really rocking and rolling by then. There was a spring in his step and iron in his spine, and his thoughts were racing at a thousand miles a second. His experienced brain could handle a dozen conflicting chemistries at once and still know which way was up. Happy was grinning fiercely, his eyes barely blinking at all, and he was waiting for something nasty to show itself, so he could leap on it with loud cries and wrestle it to the ground before giving it a good kicking.

A properly medicated Happy could walk up to a banshee and ask if it knew any show tunes.

His psychic shields were still firmly in place, not even touched by the various chemicals fighting it out for supremacy in his battered grey cells. Happy took drugs to give him an edge, not to hide behind. Or at least, that was what he told himself.

He stopped at an intersection and spun round and round on his toes, his head up as though testing the air, listening for sounds only he could hear. He'd been nagged for some time by a constant feeling there was someone behind him; but no matter how quickly he turned around, there was never anyone there. Happy reined in his raging thoughts with an iron will unsuspected by the rest of his team and stood very still. There was definitely someone, or something, down in the corridors with him. He didn't need his telepathy to tell him that. He sniffed loudly, giggled briefly, and rubbed his dry hands together. It was times like this he wished he carried a really big gun. Or even a really big stick. With nails in it.

Many people asked, and not a few demanded to know,

why Happy needed to take so many pills. A few, with some experience of telepathy, said they understood; but they didn't, really. Happy only ever took what he needed to make himself brave, smart, or strong enough to be able to do his job properly, so he could strike back at those aspects of the world that had made his life such a misery from an early age.

Revenge is always the best comfort.

At home he ate, slept, and watched television, just like anybody else. Drugged himself with the routine and the ordinary and the everyday. He couldn't afford to be doped up all the time. Couldn't afford to bliss out and dream his life away. Because Happy knew what else lived in the world alongside the rest of us. He needed to be prepared. Because you never knew when something might be sneaking up on you from behind.

No friends, no lovers, no love. Because he could never share his world with anyone. It wouldn't be fair.

Happy looked around, and the corridors stretched away in every direction, impossibly long, openly threatening. Happy laughed out loud and clapped his hands together, the sound almost shockingly loud in the quiet.

"You can't get me!" said Happy, in a loud breathy voice. "You can't even touch me because I'm not really here. I'm armoured up, and ninety degrees from reality, far beyond your reach. So come on out and give me your best shot; and I'll laugh right in your face. How do you like them apples, Casper?"

The corridors lay open and silent before him, but Happy knew someone was listening. Checking him out, from a distance. Happy wondered what it made of him and his altered state of consciousness. Maybe it was scared of him. That would be fun. Ghosts were quite simple things, really; if they couldn't scare you, they were usually lost for an alternative. So Happy set off down the nearest corridor, full of chemical good cheer and hardly shaking at all, medicinally armed against anything the unknown could throw at him.

Happy liked to think of himself as the last of the Untouchables.

,,,,,,,,,,,,,,,,,,,,,,,,,,,,,

Back on the southbound platform, Melody struggled with her precious equipment, trying through expert intimidation and sheer force of personality to make the damned things do what they were supposed to. She bent over the computer keyboards, staring right into the monitor screens, coaxing and cursing them in the same half-conscious murmur. Melody dealt in hard facts and felt helpless and vulnerable without them. She'd approached the Carnacki Institute in the first place because all her researches had convinced her that only the Institute could provide her with answers to questions no-one else would even discuss. She'd hoped for a nice quiet life in some nice quiet Institute Library; instead, they made her a field agent and sent her out into the world to find her own answers. Typically, her experiences in the field had only provided her with a whole new set of questions.

Still, her position did give her access to cutting-edge, state-of-the-art technology, and that made up for a lot. The instruments ranged before her could break down and analyse events and energies that most scientists wouldn't even admit existed. Of course, that wasn't enough for Melody Chambers. She didn't only want to know what existed in the hidden corners of the world; she wanted, needed, to understand how they worked and why. Melody hated a mystery.

Some nights, lying on her back in the dark with an exhausted lover slumbering beside her, Melody dreamed of a special Nobel Prize, just for her, awarded for her unprecedented advances in the field of the so-called supernatural. The first woman to make the unseen world make sense.

She worked furiously, her fierce gaze tracking impatiently from one screen to another, following the flow of information with quick jerky movements of her head. Although she'd never admit it, she always hated this part of the mission, where the other two went off on their own to see what there was to see and left her behind, on her own, to see things second hand through her instruments. She didn't like being left on her own. Like the girl who tags around after a boys' gang, and always gets dumped at the first opportunity. She felt better when there was someone else around. Someone close at hand. They didn't have to be right there with her; just . . . around. So she could call on them for . . . assistance, if she wanted to.

She felt the same way sometimes when she was alone in her little flat. No matter how many other people had been through it.

∷∷∷∷∷∷∷∷∷∷∷

Happy and JC returned at the end of the agreed hour, making a certain amount of noise so Melody could be sure it was them coming and not get over-eager with her machine-pistol. None of them had anything specific to report, and the more closely Melody questioned the men about what they'd seen and encountered, the more vague their answers became. And when they questioned her, Melody was forced to admit that while her machines were providing her with more sensor readings than she could keep track of, she had nothing useful to contribute either.

"I'm picking up ghosts everywhere," she said quickly, in self-defence. "I've never seen so many hauntings in one place. No actual personality or surviving intent in most of them; only images from the Past, impressed on Time by the extreme conditions of their creation. Snapshots of what was, repeating loops of history, preserved like insects trapped in amber. Presumably drawing energy from our other-dimensional Intruder. Unless they've been stirred up by our presence. Or my machines."

"She doesn't know what's going on either," Happy said to JC, smiling widely.

JC looked at the state of Happy's pupils and sighed audibly. "Tell me at least you haven't touched the little yellow pills, Happy. You know what happens when you take the little yellow ones."

"Not yet," Happy said cheerfully. "But it's probably only a matter of time. I always get a bit jumpy when the ghosts start manifesting. In case one of them takes a fancy to me and follows me home like a stray dog. I'm probably the only ghost finder in the Carnacki Institute with his own exorcist on speed dial."

"I wouldn't worry," said Melody. "They'd soon leave, once they got to know you."

"How very unkind," said Happy, trying for wounded dignity, then ruining it with a sudden hiccup.

"Never get personally involved with a ghost," JC said sternly. "No matter how tragic its story. Nothing good can ever come of it."

"Damn, I'm peckish," Happy said abruptly. "I'd kill for a curry and chips."

He wandered over to a nearby vending machine, studied the display of snacks on offer with owlish eyes, and made his selection. He forced money into the slot, then bounced up and down before the machine, humming an old Smiths' song. The machine chuntered quietly to itself for a while, then a slot opened in the front and the food shot out. Happy actually had the thing half-way to his mouth before he realised something was wrong. He stopped at the last moment, his eyes widened, and his mouth pursed up in disgust as he saw what he was holding. The pastry slip was hot and steaming, but the meat oozing out of it was rotten and decaying. Maggots burst out of the pastry, writhing and roiling. Happy cried out and threw the stinking mess on the floor. It hit with a wet, slapping sound, and Happy stamped on it again and again, making shrill distressed noises, until all the maggots were crushed and dead, and nothing was moving. Then he scraped the bottom of his shoe against the platform and rubbed both hands hard on his jeans.

"Okay, that was interesting," said Melody. "There's no way that could have happened naturally."

"No!" said Happy. "Really? You do amaze me. *Of course it didn't happen naturally!* Oh, my comfortable glow is all shot to hell now. My anus has puckered itself all the way up to my chest bone."

"Far too much information, Happy," murmured JC.

"There's no way the food could have decayed that quickly inside the machine, under normal conditions," said Melody. "Whatever it is that's down here, it's drain-ing the living energy out of everything within reach. Pre-sumably our Intruder needs help in maintaining its hold on our dimension."

"You're going to try and explain entropy to me again, aren't you?" said Happy. "Please, JC, don't let her ex-plain entropy to me again. My head still hurts from the last time."

"Hush, man," said JC. "It would seem our Intruder is accumulating power and adjusting local conditions to suit its own needs. But to what end, what purpose? Why does it need a physical presence in our world? What's it all about?"

"My name is not Alfie," Happy said sternly.

Melody checked her instrument panels again. "I can tell you this; there's more than one centre down here, more than one power source. The energy readings are off the scale in a dozen different locations. If I'm interpreting these data correctly . . . we've got ghosts, demons, and abhuman creatures swarming all over this station. Drawn here, like moths to a flame . . . or tourists to a disaster site. Something very big, and very bad, is slowly coming into focus here. Once it's fully manifested in our material plane, it will have established a beachhead, a door be-tween its dimension and ours . . . one we might not be able to force shut again. In which case, the haunting would spread, and the whole of London would get hit by the psychic fall-out."

"Damn," said JC. "And I thought Happy was the gloomy one."

"And," said Melody, "I'm pretty sure . . . we're not the only living people down here. Someone else is down here with us."

FOUR

....

TWO MONSTERS AND A GHOST

Whereas the Carnacki Institute is concerned with gathering knowledge of the unseen world in order to protect Humanity, the Crowley Project doesn't give a damn. All they care about is amassing knowledge and power for the sake of the Project. They only investigate hauntings so they can take advantage of the situation and exploit it for their own ends. Some say they want to rule the world, and some say they already do. The Crowley Project loot and brutalise all the manifestations of the unseen world because they want to know the secrets of Life and Death. They want to rule not only this world but the afterworlds, too. They want it all.

Some of them eat ghosts, consuming their energies and absorbing their knowledge and memories. Some of them create bad places on purpose, poisoning the psychic wells of the world with awful technologies and bad intent, dropping bloody bait into the waters to attract otherworldly monsters. For the fun of it, and the sport.

They create disasters and glory in destruction, and dance in the aisles of crashing planes. Just because they can. *Do what thou wilt* is the whole of their law. They are the main rivals and deadly enemies of the Carnacki Institute, and so it has been for centuries. Because the Light must always be at war with the Dark, or because Good and Evil simply cannot abide each other; or maybe because every coin must have two sides. Two organisations, forever at each other's throats; two small fish in a pond that is so much bigger than either of them have ever realised.

Field agents Natasha Chang and Erik Grossman have come to Oxford Circus Tube Station on behalf of the Crowley Project. And they're not there for the ghosts.

                    ,,,,,,,,,,,,,,,,,,,,,,,,,,,

Natasha Chang was a self-made femme fatale, her bright eyes and merry smile a cover for a cutting edge and a concealed agenda. A beautiful creature in her late twenties, she had artfully bobbed dark hair, dark, slanted eyes, and an even darker heart. Daddy was a corrupt Hong Kong businessman with a thing for the English aristocracy, who fled Hong Kong in a hurry, one step ahead of the police and all the people he'd cheated and betrayed. He brought his considerable fortune to the United Kingdom and married a very minor member of a very old family, who needed the money. Daughter Natasha grew up half-Chinese, half-English rose, privileged and cosseted but still looked down on as a half-breed by all her peers at school. She emerged from that venerable institution driven to win at any cost. The coldly ruthless child of cold and ruthless parents, Natasha struck out for freedom and an independent income at an early age. By helping Mummy murder Daddy when she was fourteen years old. She could have spent the rest of her life partying, pampering and indulging herself; but that wasn't enough for Natasha. There were slights to be avenged. She ached to be out in the world, doing things. Bad things, preferably. Because every femme fatale needs more-and-more-difficult objectives to test herself against, to reassure herself that no-one runs her life but her.

Natasha cultivated an arrogant aristocratic poise that never failed to fascinate and intimidate those around her, and she strode through the world as though she fully intended to walk right over anyone who didn't get out of her way fast enough. A lot of men found that attractive, and a challenge, as they were supposed to, the fools. Natasha's mixed-race background gave her an exotic air that she exploited mercilessly in affairs of the heart. She'd been married three times and widowed four. (That last one took a lot of killing.) She wore the very best clothes by the very best designers and never looked less than stunning. Because for Natasha, her beauty was another weapon she could use. Currently, her make-up was bold and striking, with subtle Egyptian touches around the eyes; her long, sharp fingernails were painted with real gold leaf; and she wore enough heavy rings on both hands for them to qualify as knuckle-dusters. She was wearing a pink leather cat suit, her favourite, because she had seen Eleanor Bron wear one in the Beatles movie *Help!* at an impressionable age.

She was also a gifted telepath. She'd won that ability in the divorce settlement from her first husband.

Erik Grossman couldn't have passed for a beautiful creature in a dark room during a total eclipse of the sun.

A rogue scientist and self-made mad doctor in his early thirties, Erik had been banned from universities all over Europe for his unorthodox and unethical medical experiments. At the last count, Interpol had arrest warrants out for him under eleven different names. Erik had his own private gallery of Wanted posters with his face on them, the one touch of personal vanity he allowed himself. Erik's problem was that he saw the human body as a series of fascinating but inherently flawed and inefficient mechanisms; and he couldn't resist the urge to tinker and try to improve them. To begin with, he cut bodies open and committed terrible, ruthless surgeries on what he found there. When that didn't work, or didn't work well enough to satisfy him, he moved on to cybernetics and the brutal introduction of technology into living bodies. And, occasionally, vice versa.

Erik's other problem was that he couldn't always be bothered to find properly willing subjects. So he used stray animals and homeless people, along with drugs and machines and techniques he was forced to create in his own very private laboratories because they didn't exist anywhere else. He had his successes and his failures, but he wasn't nearly as efficient as he should have been in disposing of the remains. Erik was on the run, hunted across Europe by a dozen different organisations, when the Crowley Project found him and lured him to its cold bosom with the offer of well-stocked laboratories, cutting-edge technology, and more untraceable animal and human test subjects than he could shake a scalpel at. In return, of course, for his exclusive services.

Erik wasn't cruel, as such—unlike Natasha. He didn't care enough about his subjects to feel anything for them. They were only raw materials. For him, the end was everything.

He wasn't much to look at. Medium height, a bit podgy, with flat blond hair and pale blue eyes. People found his presence disturbing because on some level they could sense they meant nothing to him. There was less human feeling in Erik than in many of the ghosts he pursued. He tended to slide and shuffle along, head down, as though always half-expecting to be shouted at, or struck. But when his eyes came up, they were always fierce and angry, a man rehearsing his revenges against an indifferent and ungrateful world. He did have feelings. But typically, he only wanted the things and people he couldn't have, to justify his doing terrible things to those who denied him what he wanted. This was obvious to many people, but no-one had ever been foolish enough to tell him. It wouldn't have been safe.

Erik wore a good suit, badly. Grace and elegance were not in him, only a brute, stubborn persistence. There was always a general air of untidiness and grime about him, and nearly always a few spots of blood down his shirt front. In the field, he carried the bare minimum of useful technology, in a pack on his back.

Erik didn't give much of a damn about ghosts or hauntings. But helping investigate them was part of the price he paid for the Crowley Project's indulgence and protection. They only called on him when they absolutely had to, not least because most other agents wouldn't work with him, no matter what they were promised or threatened with. Natasha Chang was the first field agent they'd found who'd put up with him, because she found tormenting him amusing. Erik put up with Natasha for his own, very private reasons.

Natasha strode around the Oxford Circus entrance lobby like the Queen on a state visit, giving every impression that she was slumming just by being there. She took a keen interest in everything but didn't touch anything; that would have been beneath her. She studied the ticket machines and the closed ticket barriers closely, frowning a bit. Erik leaned back against the closed and locked iron gates and smiled smugly.

"Would I be right in assuming that you have never travelled on the Tube, Natasha dear?"

"Of course not," snapped Natasha, looking at everything except him. "I don't do anything the common herd does."

"Heh-heh," said Erik, in his low, breathy voice. He pushed himself away from the gates and shuffled around the lobby, his eyes darting back and forth, taking in everything. Including Natasha. She caught him eyeing her covertly, spun round, and surged towards him like an attack dog let off the leash. She grabbed his crumpled shirt front with both hands and slammed him back against the nearest wall. She supported his weight easily, his feet kicking helplessly a good distance above the floor. His arms hung down at his sides; he knew better than to try to grab her wrists. She thrust her face right into his.

"Don't look at me like that, Erik. Never look at me like that, or I'll rip your eyes out and make you eat them. We are partners in the field, nothing more. You are less to me than the filth beneath my feet, and if you even dare to dream about me, I'll give you nightmares you'll never forget."

"I love it when you talk dirty," said Erik. And his tongue shot out to lick the tip of her nose.

Natasha dropped him onto his feet and backed quickly away, rubbing hard at her nose with the back of her hand. Erik readjusted his shirt and sniggered loudly.

"You're big and strong and scary, and I love you for it, Natasha dear, but always remember . . . I'm as dangerous as you are."

"You think you can threaten me, you little worm?" said Natasha, glaring at him from a safe distance.

"Heh-heh," said Eric. "Save the sweet talk for another time. We have work to do here, remember?"

Natasha gave him her best dismissive sniff, and he ignored it with magnificent disdain. He eased over to the closed ticket barriers, produced a length of wire from somewhere about his person, and stuck it into the gate mechanism. He jiggled the wire for a moment, and the barriers sprang smartly open. Erik made his piece of wire disappear with a somewhat overdone conjurer's gesture, then stood back and indicated for Natasha to go through ahead of him. On anyone else it would have been a charming gesture, but on Erik it looked sleazy and opportunistic. Natasha stuck her aristocratic nose in the air and stalked right past him. Erik considered goosing her as she passed but decided that on the whole he rather preferred having his testicles where they were. He glided through the barriers after her, and they both stopped at the top of the frozen escalator, looking down the motionless steps. Erik moved in close beside Natasha, and she made a point of moving away. The light was very bright, the silence very deep, and down below, nothing moved at all.

"JC, Melody, and Happy are down there," Natasha announced coolly. "I can feel them. Already hard at work, the industrious little souls. I do hope they turn up something interesting. If only so we can have the fun of taking it away from them."

"We're not only here for the haunting," Erik reminded her diffidently. "We're here for them. Oh, I have been looking forward to this. They think they're so smart, so good . . . I'll show them what smart really is. Can I kill the girl? I'd really like to kill the girl. I have a brand-new really unpleasant technique I've been dying to try out on someone."

"JC is our main target," said Natasha. "He goes first. He's the dangerous one. Ever since he took charge of this team, they've enjoyed success after success. And we can't have that, can we? Their progress threatens the Project's intentions. So JC has to die. Once he's been taken care of, we can amuse ourselves with the junkie telepath and the girl geek."

"Vivienne MacAbre seemed very impressed with the whole team," ventured Erik. "Don't think I've ever seen her so . . . vehement before."

"I felt the threats and menaces were quite unnecessary," Natasha said primly. "I am an experienced field agent. I mean, *Come back with their heads or don't bother coming back*? When have we ever needed threats to motivate us? When have we ever failed the Project?"

"Vivienne scares me," said Erik. "I like that in a woman."

Natasha gave him her best withering glance, but he didn't care. He was already thinking about things she didn't like to think about.

Vivienne MacAbre was the current Head of the Crowley Project. That wasn't her real name, of course. In the kinds of circles Project people moved, to know the true name of a thing was to have power over it. Vivienne was

a tall, willowy woman in her early forties, with olive
skin and dark ethnic features, and a great mane of curly
dark hair. Of Greek origin, supposedly, though of course
no-one knew anything for sure. She became the current
Head of the Project in the usual way, by assassinating
her predecessor. If you couldn't protect yourself from
your own underlings, you weren't fit to be Head of the
Project . . . Which have always believed very firmly in
survival of the fittest. Certainly no-one had tried to as-
sassinate Vivienne since she became Head. Though
Natasha did sometimes allow herself to dream a little, of
what might be possible in the future . . . as long as she
was careful to only dream such things a safe distance
away from Project Headquarters, in its bland anonymous
tower block in the middle of London.

People were always very cautious about what they
said or thought around Vivienne MacAbre. Because
those who weren't had a disturbing tendency to disappear. Sometimes right in front of people.

At the briefing, Natasha and Erik had sat stiffly to
attention on hard-backed chairs, while Vivienne gave
them the terms of their mission in her usual calm and
subtly chilling voice. Apparently something important
was happening down in Oxford Circus Tube Station, and
the Crowley Project wanted it. Whatever it was. So
Natasha and Erik were tasked with the destruction of
JC and his team and the retrieval of anything of interest the team might have uncovered. Both Natasha and
Erik got the distinct impression there was rather more
to the situation than that; but they knew better than to
ask questions. The Crowley Project operated on a very
strict Need To Know basis. And as Natasha said to Erik
afterwards, safely outside Vivienne MacAbre's office,

whatever was going on at Oxford Circus, it couldn't be that important, or the Carnacki Institute would have sent one of their A teams. JC and his people were good, but they barely qualified as a B team.

Natasha and Erik stood at the top of the unmoving escalator, considering the still-life scene before them. The intensity of the silence and the stillness intrigued them. They looked at each other. Natasha smiled suddenly at Erik.

"I'll show you mine if you'll show me yours. What marvellous toys did you bring with you this time, you awful little man?"

Erik smiled smugly in return and fished in the bulging pockets of his jacket. He avoided Natasha's eyes. Moments like this were the nearest they ever got to a real relationship, and they made him nervous. He produced with a flourish a 375 Magnum pistol so big it shouldn't even have fitted into his pocket. He considered trying the famous monologue from *Dirty Harry* but knew he didn't have the voice to bring it off successfully.

"How typical," Natasha murmured sweetly. "A big gun for a small man. It's all about compensation, you know."

"How typical of a woman," countered Erik, "to think it's always about size."

He put the Magnum away and produced from his other pocket a piece of yellowed bone, barely three inches long. Carved deep into the bone were strange, curving patterns that seemed to seethe and swirl if you looked at them long enough.

"Aboriginal pointing bone," said Erik proudly. "And not just any bone—carved from the thigh-bone of the great naval explorer and map-maker, Captain Cook himself. Soaked for three years in the semen of a dozen hanged men, the first transported convicts to be hanged in Australia. I could point this at an elephant, and it would drop dead on the spot."

"They don't have elephants in the London Underground," said Natasha, crushingly.

"They might have," said Erik. "You don't know. You never travel on the Tube."

The next object out of his pockets was a flat metal box with two steel horns protruding. Natasha looked at it, then at Erik.

"Taser," he said proudly. "Of my own design. Press the button, and this little box will produce actual lightning bolts. If my pointing bone doesn't finish off the elephant, I can fry it with this."

"What is this sudden obsession with elephants?" said Natasha. "It's not more compensation, is it?"

Erik didn't deign to answer. The last object out of his pockets was a simple monocle. He showed it to Natasha but made no attempt actually to screw it into his eye.

"This specially treated lens can see through all illusions and reveal hidden traps. It can also show what's happening in deepest dark and brightest light. It can even, theoretically, reveal the true nature of any given object or person though I haven't actually tested that function under field conditions, as yet." He considered Natasha thoughtfully. "What would I see, I wonder, if I were to look at you through this marvellous monocle, Natasha dear?"

"Don't even think about it," said Natasha. "Now, my turn."

She started off by pulling two heavy punch daggers from the tops of her tall pink leather boots. The wide leaf-shaped blades had long oval holes in their centres.

"So when you thrust the blades deep into someone's body, bits of their organs or intestines will fall through the holes and be trapped there," Natasha explained. "When you pull the blades out again, the trapped body parts are pulled out with them. Note also the serrated edges, so the blades can cut through bone. I've never understood this modern fascination with flick-knives. Decorative, yes, but I want a blade that can do real damage."

"Of course you do," murmured Erik. "It's never about the kill with you; it's the suffering. And given the size of those knives, I could make a remark or two about compensation myself."

"Don't start with the elephant again," said Natasha. She thrust the knives back into the concealed sheaths in her boots with a casualness that made Erik wince, and produced from a concealed holster a small but perfectly formed 9mm pistol, silver-plated, with real pearl handles.

"Mummy gave it to me on my thirteenth birthday," Natasha said happily. "She had a feeling it might come in handy someday."

"That's boarding-school for you," said Erik.

"Well, quite," said Natasha, making the pistol disappear about her person. She pulled a small leather pouch from an inside pocket. "I had this made from the stretched and tanned testicles of an old lover," she said casually. Opening the drawstrings carefully, she spilled out onto her hand a dull red withered object that Erik couldn't identify at first. Natasha smiled. "This is the mummified heart of dear dead Daddy, gone and not missed in the least. Frankly, Mummy and I were somewhat surprised to find he actually had a heart when we opened him up. It's been treated in many special ways, by the Seven Sisters of Stepney Underneath, and now I can use it to call up the dead and make them answer to me. Not for long, admittedly, and it's a hard job getting anything useful out of them; but then, the dead always have their own agenda."

"Do I smell cardamom?" said Erik.

"Well, we had to preserve it with something," said Natasha.

Next up were two chicken legs, tied together with brass wire and several strands of human hair with complicated knots tied in them.

"I didn't know you were bringing lunch," said Erik.

"Don't show your ignorance, you common little man," said Natasha. "This is Old School voodoo, a powerful juju guaranteed to make a curse stick and fester, right down to the soul. You wouldn't believe some of the elements that went into making this."

"Were elephants involved?" said Erik, hopefully.

"Shut up." Natasha put the chicken legs away and produced a small plastic phial full of liquid, in which floated a single silicon chip. "Now this is special," Natasha said proudly. "This chip was programmed by a rogue technomancer and removed from a possessed computer. It's floating in debased holy water, mixed with burned mandrake ashes to give it a bit of a kick. Use the right Words, and this little chip can override any computer within a mile and a half."

"I thought they turned off all this station's computers?" said Erik.

Natasha gave him her very best glare, put the chip in a bottle away, and took out her iPod. Erik looked at it.

"This iPod contains over two hundred pre-recorded spells and rituals!" said Natasha, a little more loudly than she'd intended. "A good agent needs to be prepared for all eventualities!"

"I think I'll stick to my 375 Magnum and take my chances with the elephants," said Erik.

Natasha sniffed loudly and put her iPod away. "I don't need toys to succeed, unlike some people. I am a Class Ten telepath and a fully trained psychic assassin! I'm the one who got us in here, remember; broadcasting *Don't See Us* to all the security guards!"

"You really are getting a little loud, Natasha dear," said Erik. "For the sake of peace and quiet, I will freely acknowledge that you have the best toys, this time. But I really don't think we're going to need them. JC and his team are good, but we're better."

"You didn't spend enough time reading the briefing reports," said Natasha, forcing her voice back down to a normal level. "I've been studying JC and what he's accomplished with his team. They've come a long way in a short time. They're sharp, they're fast, and they come at you from unexpected directions. JC is quite possibly the best agent they've got working in the field at the moment. Taking him down isn't going to be easy."

Erik smirked and stabbed a podgy finger at her. "You fancy him! You do! He's your special Institute friend!"

Natasha grabbed Erik's finger and twisted it cruelly. He yelped and tried to pull free but couldn't. Natasha smiled.

"You need to remember who's in charge here, little man. I don't need your help to take down JC and his team. If you make yourself a distraction or a liability, I will drop you in your tracks and go on without you. Understood?"

Erik nodded frantically, and Natasha released his finger. Erik nursed his throbbing hand against his chest. "You play rough, Natasha. I've always liked that about you."

"If you're thinking what I think you're thinking," said Natasha, "you're a dead man."

Erik smirked. "Good thing I augmented my brain, to make it immune to telepaths, then."

"Don't underestimate JC," insisted Natasha. "He has skill and experience far beyond his years. He's a prodigy and a marvel, and quite possibly the next Head of the Carnacki Institute. Why else do you think Vivienne was so eager to sign his death warrant? She knows competition when she sees it. Remember the Case of the Horse Invisible, last year? JC. Did you even read what he did last night, face-to-face with a primal-god thing? No; JC is a better field agent than we'll ever be." She smiled suddenly. "Which is what will make killing him so much fun."

"This is a woman thing, isn't it?" said Erik.

"I could just eat him up," Natasha said dreamily. "I'm sure his ghost will prove to be particularly tasty."

Erik said nothing. There were some things about his companion that freaked even him out.

They stood together at the top of the escalator, looking down. All was still, and quiet.

"Time to go to work," Natasha said abruptly. "Time to ambush the good and virtuous, throw them down, and trample them underfoot."

"I don't know," said Erik. "I'm getting a really bad feeling about this. Something bad has come to Oxford

Circus. Something far worse than we'll ever be. Don't tell me you can't feel it, too, oh mighty Class Ten."

"Whatever it is, we can handle it," said Natasha.

"Probably," said Erik. "But why should we? Why not let JC and his people take the risks and soak up the punishment? Then we can move in afterwards, while they're weakened and off guard, kill them, and take the captured prize for ourselves."

"Every now and again you justify your presence as my partner," said Natasha. "Set up your equipment, little man, and let's take a peek at what our good friends and rivals are doing down there."

"You'd be lost without me," said Erik. "Heh-heh."

He took off his back-pack and lowered it carefully to the ground, as though it contained something breakable and highly explosive. He untied the heavy restraining straps, one by one, and carefully lifted out his latest creation. It wasn't in the least aesthetic, a brutally functional transparent cube containing rapidly moving parts, with a living cat's head jammed on the top. Wires sprouted from shaved points on its skull. The cube was an intricate clock-work mechanism, in which all the swiftly moving pieces were made of solid light and shaped energy, blazing fiercely with more colours than the human eye could cope with. The movements alone could make your brain hurt if you looked at them too long, as they rotated through more than three spatial dimensions. The cube ticked and tocked, but not regularly. It raced and paused and speeded up again, like a clock driven mad by seeing too much of the wrong kind of Time. Erik had put a lot of work into crafting the world's first far-seeing computer, and he was very proud of it. He patted the living cat head fondly, and it hissed and spat at him. Its unblinking slit-pupilled eyes were full of rage. Its thoughts enlarged and expanded through its intimate connection with the computer; it knew what had been done to it but was helpless to do anything about it. Natasha watched Erik make small, careful changes to the control panel on one side of the cube and turned up her aristocratic nose.

"Even by your standards, that is a seriously ugly object. Are you sure this . . . thing, will do what it's supposed to?"

"Of course," said Erik, bristling at the implied slight on his abilities. "The computer augments the cat's natural psychic abilities, and together they can See and Hear whatever is going on for miles in every direction. They can even peek a short way into the Past and the Future. Theoretically. Ignore the spitting and the hissing and the occasional squalling; the cat's head will do what I want, when I want it to. I plugged a wire directly into its little catty pleasure/pain centre, and a few volts can give it unbearable pain or incredible pleasure. I am its god. Though I still can't get it to purr for me." He leered at Natasha. "Think of it: absolute pleasure, at the touch of a button. I could perform a similar operation on you if you wanted. If you asked me nicely."

"And leave the button in your hands?" said Natasha. "I think not. Ask your cat what's happening down in the tunnels."

Erik reached for the control panel, then had to snatch his hand back again as the cat head tried to bite it. He giggled happily, tried again, and made a few small adjustments. The blazing mechanisms jumped and danced, pieces of solid light interacting on many levels, moving irrevocably towards one terrible configuration. The cat head howled, a long, rising sound that continued long after lungs would have given out. And then the cat's jaws snapped together, its whiskers twitched, and its eyes locked on to something only they could see. The cat head spoke, but there was nothing human in its harsh yowling voice.

"Something new has come to Oxford Circus," it said. "Or something very old. Something from the afterworlds has manifested in the tunnels, deep down in the dark. And it's not alone, down there. Its mere presence is enough to stir up ghosts and demons and monsters. The darkness is alive. And it's hungry."

Erik looked at Natasha. "See? I told you!"

"Shut up. We already knew there was a powerful force loose in the station."

"Still, something from the afterworlds, made flesh and therefore vulnerable . . ." Erik rubbed his hands gleefully. "Now that's a prize worth having."

"It's cold, and it burns," said the cat head. "It's wild and fierce and free, and it will kill you."

"You wish," said Erik absently, and turned off the cube. The cat's head fell silent, but its unblinking eyes still burned with hate.

"I'm hungry," said Natasha.

"Eat your chicken legs," said Erik.

"Hungry for ghosts," said Natasha. "There's nothing quite like them, nothing so . . . satisfying. I might even leave a few for you, this time."

"You know I don't indulge," Erik said primly. "Nasty habit, and dangerous to your mental health. If you ever had any."

"Prude," said Natasha. "Scaredy-cat."

Erik sniffed loudly but wouldn't meet her eyes. "I value the integrity of my mind far too much to risk contaminating it with inferior thoughts and memories." He gave in to curiosity and looked almost defiantly at Natasha. "I simply do not see what you people get out of it. Don't you ever get . . . confused, with other people's memories and identities suddenly crashing about inside your head?"

"Darling," said Natasha, "that's the good part. That's the rush. That's what makes them so very *tasty*."

"You're disgusting."

"I know you are, but what am I?"

And then they broke off and looked around sharply, as every ticket machine in the lobby suddenly spat up all the coins it had taken. Pound coins and assorted change jumped and clattered across the floor as they were ejected with force, bouncing and rolling everywhere, shining and shimmering in the over-bright light. Some of them rolled right up to Erik's feet, and he reached down to grab a handful; but Natasha stopped him with a harsh command. One by one the machines ran out of money and fell silent. Coins lay scattered all over the floor. Natasha watched the ticket machines carefully for a while, to see if they'd do anything else, but they remained still and silent. She turned her back on them and the money with studied insolence and returned to the top of the escalator. Erik carefully packed his cat-head computer back into its pack, then casually scooped up a handy two-pound coin. Only to yell and throw it away again.

"Hot!" he said. "Hot hot hot!"

"Did it burn you?" said Natasha, not looking around.

"Yes!"

"Good."

Erik scowled. "Damned thing was hot enough to have been coughed up from Hell itself. What was that for?"

"Someone is playing games with us," said Natasha.

"Could it be JC and his people?" said Erik, immediately forgetting the pain in his fingertips. "Could they know we're here?"

"No," said Natasha. "I'd know . . . if they knew. I think this is something else . . ."

She left the elevators, made her way back through the open ticket barriers, and strolled unhurriedly around the entrance lobby, frowning as she forced her telepathy into every psychic nook and cranny. Her gaze shot suddenly to one side, and she advanced remorselessly on one corner. And then she stopped as Erik hissed her name, and a ragged man appeared suddenly in the lobby with them. He shuffled slowly around, ignoring the coins on the floor as though they weren't there, and perhaps for him they weren't. He looked like one of the homeless, tall but stooped, a ragged man in ragged clothes, wrapped up in a long coat stained with damp and mould. He had long, matted hair and a filthy beard, and his eyes were dull, preoccupied with cold and hunger and memories that wouldn't go away. He slowly made a full circle of the lobby, shuffling right past Natasha and Erik without even seeing them. Until, slowly, he seemed to become aware that he was not alone. His head came up, and his dull eyes fixed on Natasha. He didn't seem at all surprised to see her, or even to care that much. He held out one filthy hand, mutely asking for money.

"He's not real," said Erik. "He's a ghost."

"Thank you, I had worked that out for myself," said Natasha.

"Is he aware?" said Erik, professionally interested. "Or is this only a stone tape, a psychic recording?"

"Oh no," said Natasha. "There's still some of him

here. I can pick up some of his thoughts, rattling around inside his head. He had a name once, and a family and a job; but he lost them all. He ended up on the streets, begging for small change, but he was never very good at it. He died here, in that corner, locked in overnight and overlooked by everyone. Would you like to know his name?"

"No," said Erik. "It doesn't matter. He doesn't matter. This is a simple haunting, stirred up by our presence, or perhaps the workings of my little computer. He isn't what we're here for."

"Hush," said Natasha. "I told you I was hungry."

She advanced slowly on the homeless ghost, which stood there, staring at her dully like an animal that had been beaten into submission. It wasn't until she was right before him that he seemed to become aware of the danger he was in. He looked at Natasha with growing horror but couldn't seem to move. Natasha licked her lips.

"You don't even know you're dead, do you? How . . . delicious."

She locked his gaze with hers, reaching out with her mind, forcing him to see her clearly through sheer force of will. The ghost's face twisted with horror, and he began to howl, a wordless scream of helpless dread. The cry of someone who knows no-one will come to save him. The ghost could see Natasha for what she was; and it terrified him. He drifted slowly backwards, not even moving his feet, and Natasha went after him. She stalked him all around the lobby, for the fun of it.

Until, finally, she lunged forward and locked her mouth on his, blocking off his howl. Living lips clamped down on a dead mouth, and he hung helpless before her as she sucked him dry, eating up every last trace of energy and consciousness that remained to him, and savouring it all. Bit by bit he faded away, becoming increasingly insubstantial as there was less and less of him, until not even a trace of the ghost remained. Natasha straightened up, licked her lips slowly, and laughed almost drunkenly. She looked sideways at Erik, backed up against the far wall, and sniggered at him.

"You don't know what you're missing, little man. You must learn to develop a taste for the good things in life. Ooh . . . I'm Daddy's bad little girl . . . Such a little terror. Are you excited, Erik? Did that turn you on? It did, didn't it? You'd love me to do that to you, wouldn't you, Erik? And maybe one day, I will. But I guarantee you won't like it one little bit."

FIVE

....

THE HORROR SHOW

"If we're not alone down here," said JC, "it's got to be field agents from the Crowley Project. Has to be. There aren't many people brave enough or crazy enough to go chasing after ghosts in the dark heart of a Code One Haunting unless they expected to get something out of it. Project agents would brave the fires of Hell itself to snatch away a single burning coal if they thought there was money or power or one-upmanship in it."

Typically, Melody didn't want to believe it.

"It could be commuters, travellers, left over from this morning," she said. "Couldn't it? Trapped down here and overlooked when the station was sealed off by our security people?"

"No," said JC as kindly as he could. "I read all the reports; security were very thorough. They checked every corridor, every platform, all the maintenance ducts and crawl spaces . . . They brought out the living and carried out the dead; no-one was left behind."

"What about the people trapped and carried off in the hell trains?" said Happy. "Some of them might have escaped."

"Those were downbound trains," said JC. "All the way down. I don't think we'll be seeing any of those people again."

None of them said anything for a while after that. None of them liked to admit there were some things even trained Institute field agents couldn't put right. One of Melody's instrument panels began chiming urgently, and she leaned forward to check its monitor screen.

"Hold everything," she said. "Long-range sensors are picking up something interesting . . . Someone is using very powerful and very nasty technology not far from here. These readings are . . . Damn. I'm getting definite traces of biotech—cutting-edge science with fully integrated organic components. Cybernetics' dark and unnatural cousin. Strictly illegal, banned in every civilised country and a few that aren't."

"Are you sure?" said JC. "I don't know anyone who's actually encountered Frankenstein tech in the field before."

"I'm telling you!" said Melody. "It's here . . . and it's operating. My machines can hear it screaming. If these readings are right, it's screaming all the time. JC, we have to do something about this!"

"We will," said JC. "Could this be Crowley Project tech?"

"Has to be," said Melody. "They're the only bastards hard-hearted enough to use it."

"I want a gun," Happy said immediately. "A really big gun. I want a fully functioning Death Star gun."

"Not even if Godzilla himself were to show up," said JC.

"Well, how about a big stick with a nail in it, to wave at them, then?"

"Brace up, man," said JC. "Odds are they'll be eaten alive by whatever's down here long before they can cause us any trouble."

"Strangely, I don't find that at all comforting," said Happy.

"Whatever is going on down here," said JC thoughtfully, "it must be really important, or the Project wouldn't risk sending agents into a site already under the control of Institute agents."

"We have this site under control?" said Melody. "When did that happen, exactly? I must have missed it."

"Normally, the Institute and the Project go out of their way to avoid direct conflict," JC said patiently. "Because retaliations have a way of escalating. Neither side wants all-out war. So whatever we have down here, it isn't simply another haunting gone bad. Not even another Code One Haunting. This has got to be something really special."

"He's getting enthusiastic," Happy said darkly to Melody. "Never a good sign, when he starts getting enthusiastic."

JC looked at Happy thoughtfully.

"Don't look at me!" said Happy. "I was engaged for telepathy and light housecleaning. Nothing was ever said about hand-to-hand conflict with trained Project agents."

"It's your telepathy I want," said JC, giving Happy his best persuasive smile. "Nothing too difficult, or too dangerous. Reach out and see if you can get a sense of who they've sent down here. You can back off if you even think they know you're listening in."

Happy sighed dramatically, but they all knew he was going to do it. He never could resist a challenge, especially if it involved being sneaky and underhanded. His face went blank, and his eyes became lost and far-away as he let his thoughts drift up and out, spreading silently and invisibly through the abandoned station. His mind was a cool, deep pool, calm and collected, entirely untroubled by all the pills he'd taken earlier. His hardened metabolism burned them up almost as fast as he could take them. His thoughts rose through the layers of stone and concrete and metal, slipping through the dark spaces, searching out the flaring lights of human thought. And then he winced abruptly, his hands curling unconsciously into fists at his sides.

"Oh, that feels bad. Really bad. Melody was right. They've made a computer out of a cat's brain. Its thoughts are like razor wire . . . It's been forced to See things the living should never have to know about. It keeps going insane, but the tech drags it back . . . Poor thing. Poor thing . . . Hold it; I'm getting human presences now. Two of them, a man and a woman. Very strong presences; the woman has a mind like a perfumed steel trap, and the man . . . Damn . . . His emotions run so deep they're almost primal. Ow! Ow, that hurt!"

Happy clapped both hands to his head and shook it hard. When he looked at JC and Melody again, his eyes were back to normal.

"The woman's a trained telepath—kicked me right out of there the moment she detected me." He cocked his head slightly, as though listening. "No . . . That's it.

Can't pick up anything now; she's got major psychic shields in place. And, unfortunately, now they know we know they're there."

"I hate sentences like that," said Melody. "You never know where they're going to end up."

"This new female telepath," said JC. "Could she be interfering with your mind, Happy? Stopping you from picking up what's really going on here?"

"No," Happy said immediately. "I'd know. She's good, but she's not that good."

"Did you get any names?" said Melody. "Knowing who they sent would give us some idea of how important they think this haunting is. Can't be Red McCoy; he's banned from the British mainland till 2018. And the Animal only operates out of Paris these days."

"That still leaves Janus Scott, Meredith DeLancie, and Tetsuo Darque," said JC. "All major players, all with previous experience of London hauntings, and all of them very much out of our league. Real A team people. And that's only the usual suspects."

"If that was a real A team telepath, she'd have fried my brains on contact," said Happy. "I told you; she's good, but I'm better."

"Maybe all of the Project's main players are busy somewhere else," said Melody. "Like ours. And they sent the best they had available. Like us."

"We can but hope," said JC. "I've never actually gone head to head with a Project field agent before, and I think I'd like to keep it that way. I mean, yes, I've had all the proper Institute training, for physical and psychic combat; but I'm really not a rough-and-tumble kind of guy."

"I've always been quite fond of a bit of rough-and-tumble," Melody said demurely. "But I take your point. Project agents are trained killers and psychic assassins. I'm just tech support."

"While I am a clinically depressed telepath and not at all a fighter," said Happy. "I do not do confrontations. It's in my contract."

"We don't have contracts," said JC.

"Well, it would be in my contract if I had one," said Happy. "God, we have got to get unionised. You know, I don't think I've ever actually met a Project agent in the flesh."

"Few do and survive," said JC. "They're nothing like us. The Crowley Project are supposed to be nearly as old as the Carnacki Institute, though they have gone through hundreds of different names down the years. The Project have always been very vulnerable to the cult of personality, to the Great Leader who wants to put his or her stamp on everything, including the organisation's name. Like a dog marking its territory."

"They're bad people," Happy said flatly. "There are lots of us in the Institute who believe the Project manipulate and even create hauntings, and bad places, for their own reasons. So they can take advantage of them. Sometimes what they're after is obvious: Objects of Power, or Forces that can be captured and put to use. But sometimes . . . what they're doing makes no sense at all, from the outside."

"I've heard things, too," said Melody. "Some of them eat ghosts. Don't look at me like that . . . It's what I've heard. They eat ghosts: memories, identities, maybe even souls for all I know. I never wanted to look into it that closely. People in the Institute don't eat souls. Do they?"

"No," said JC. "We still hang people for that. There are a lot of things Project agents do that we don't. They have no morals, no scruples, no inhibitions, and less restraint. They know a lot of things we don't because we won't do what's necessary to acquire such awful skills. The Crowley Project follow their own path, pursue their own ends, and all we ever need to know is which side they're on, so we can safely take the other. They are the bad guys in any given situation. They don't care about the dead or the living; they go after what they want, and to hell with whoever gets hurt or killed in the process."

"Well, yes, but there's more to them than that," said Happy.

"No there isn't," JC said flatly. "You think there is because all those pills you take make you paranoid. Not to mention seriously weird."

"All right then, tell me this," Happy said defiantly. "Why are new bad places appearing so frequently these days? Why are there always more, no matter how many we defuse or shut down? I hear things; and I don't just mean telepathically."

"Go on," said Melody. "Tell us, Happy. You always know the best gossip. And not because you're a first-class telepath with no scruples and no life."

"I shall rise above that," said Happy. "Look; this is me, rising."

"Get on with it," said JC.

"Hey; I'm not the only one who thinks this! There are a lot of people at the Institute, really high-up and seriously connected people, who worry about what the Crowley Project are really all about. Some of us have been wondering whether the Project might have . . . *done something* to weaken the barriers between this world and the

afterworlds. Either deliberately or by accident. Did they
try something that backfired or went badly wrong? Did
they try to make some kind of alliance with one of the
Outer Forces, try to bring something like that through into
our world? And then lost control over it? Is that why everything's going to hell in a hand-cart these days?"

"Maybe you should be taking more pills, not less,"
said JC.

"Or," said Happy, leaning forward, his voice dropping
into a conspiratorial whisper, "could it actually be even
worse than that? Could it be that the highest levels of the
Carnacki Institute have been doing things they shouldn't?
There are rumours . . . There are those who say that, possibly, there are people in the Institute on a much higher
level than we have access to who approved an operation
they shouldn't have; and as a result, something really
bad has happened, something that those very people are
desperately trying to put right before anyone finds out . . .
before the whole world falls apart. Could this whole
situation, this unprecedented Code One Haunting right
in the heart of London, be the result of a Major Working
gone terribly wrong? And that's why we're here, rather
than one of the A teams, because the Boss wants this
handled quietly, by entirely expendable agents?"

"Okay," said JC. "You're really starting to worry
me now."

"Good," said Happy. "Join the club. We've got our
own badges and everything. Now take it a step further.
What if there's another group? Some third organisation
that's so secret even we don't know about them, working in the shadows of the world for their own dark
reasons?"

"Stop that," JC said firmly. "Stop that right now before my brains start to leak out my ears. That way paranoia lies."

"Welcome to my world," said Happy.

"You've given me a headache now," said Melody, accusingly.

"I've got a pill for that," said Happy.

Melody let out a sudden bark of laughter. "Like I'd ever touch anything you use. I take my consciousness straight, not altered, thank you very much."

Happy sniffed. "Don't know what you're missing."

And then all three of them looked round sharply, staring into the right-hand tunnel-mouth. From out of the impenetrable darkness came the sound of an approaching train. A low, muted roar, drawing steadily closer. Except that this part of the Tube network had been shut down, all regular trains diverted to other lines and other stations. The three ghost finders moved instinctively closer to each other, staring into the dark tunnel-mouth as the sound of the train grew steadily louder.

"Is it coming here?" said JC. "To this platform?"

Melody looked quickly across her sensor readings. "Coming right at us, JC. Damn, it's moving fast."

Happy stepped reluctantly away from the others, as though drawn to the dark tunnel-mouth. He moved slowly forward, step by step, listening rather than looking. JC gestured for Melody to be quiet. Happy stopped at the very end of the platform, a few feet short of the gaping darkness.

"It's almost here. I can see a light, coming this way. The rail tracks are vibrating. I'd say this is almost certainly a real train. But it . . . *feels* wrong."

"Then get the hell back here with the rest of us!" said JC.

Happy seemed to suddenly realise where he was. He sprinted back down the platform, not stopping until he was safely past JC and Melody, and had put the rack of instruments between him and the on-coming train. "Sorry about that," he said breathlessly. "You can't take as many pills as I do to make you brave and fearless without losing some of your self-preservation instincts. And they turn your piss orange."

He broke off as the sound of the train grew suddenly louder—painfully, deafeningly loud. It filled their heads and shuddered in their bones, a far louder sound than any train should ever make. Like the roar of a great beast, it filled the station, harsh and threatening. JC realised he could feel it as much as hear it, a terrible presence that triggered a recognition in the darkest and most primitive levels of his mind, where the lizard brain had never forgotten how it felt to be hunted, to be prey. The whole platform shook, as though it was afraid of what was coming.

JC stuck his head right next to Melody's and shouted in her ear. "Is this *real*? Is that a real train coming, or some kind of psychic projection?"

"Are you crazy?" she yelled back. "Listen to it! Doesn't it sound real?"

"It's too loud! It's too loud, and I don't trust it! What do your instruments say? Is it *real*?"

Melody checked her instruments, clinging to them for support. "It's real enough! It's showing up on all the sensors as a real moving physical object!"

"Of course it's real!" yelled Happy, glaring at the tunnel-mouth. "I can hear screaming! I can feel real pain and horror and death! It's real! It's real! God help us all, it's real!"

A burst of compressed air slammed out of the tunnel-mouth ahead of the on-coming train, sweeping through the station, hitting the three ghost finders like a blow in the face. They all rocked back on their feet as the air wave hit them, then the train roared into the station at impossible speed, brakes squealing painfully as the cars shuddered and skidded to a halt. Clouds of steam bil-lowed up around the train and its long row of cars, thick creamy steam that stank of brimstone and blood, spoiled meat and sour milk. JC turned his head away from it. Melody bent over her instruments as though she could protect them with her body. Happy gazed into the slowly dispersing cloud of steam with an awful fascination, his face twisted with horror and disgust. JC made him-self look back at the train. The steam died away, reveal-ing a line of cars that stretched the whole length of the platform.

Every car was packed full of people, men and women from earlier in the day, caught and trapped, then taken away, not to be seen again, until that moment. They'd been in there for hours, travelling God alone knew where, in the dark places under the earth. Driven mad, they had turned on each other. JC and Happy and Mel-ody watched helplessly as the trapped passengers went at each other with their bare hands. Half-naked, clothes torn and tattered, they fought and tore at each other like animals, their faces distorted by savage, primal emotions. They murdered and raped and ate each other, laughing and crying and howling like the damned things they were. Blood and shit and piss, and other liquids from torn-out organs, had been spattered and smeared across the car-windows, but not enough to hide the hor-ror within. The uproar from inside the cars was almost unbearable, a horrible mixture of sounds that should never have come from human mouths.

JC and Happy and Melody saw it all, like glimpses into Hell.

JC grabbed Melody by the shoulders and physically turned her away from the sight, making her concentrate on her instrument panels instead. It helped to steady her, a little. She stopped shuddering and shaking and fought to understand what the readings were telling her. Happy was lying on the platform, curled up into a ball, both hands over his ears, while tears coursed down his face from behind clenched-shut eyes. JC shook Happy's shoulder hard, and even kicked him a few times, but Happy was beyond reaching. JC reluctantly left him to his misery. There was nothing he could do to help Happy, but he had to believe there was still something he could do for the people trapped in the cars.

He strode over to the nearest doors and tried to force them open; but they wouldn't budge, no matter how much strength he threw against them. He strained until his fingers cried out with the pain, and his back muscles ached fiercely. None of it did any good. He ran down the whole length of the train, trying door after door, and couldn't move any of them. The train wasn't going to give up its prey that easily. JC lurched back up the platform, breathing hard, his face slightly crazed, beating at the car-windows with his fists and shouting hoarsely, trying to reach the people within. To get them to acknowledge his presence, to stop them mutilating each other, if only for a moment. But none of them so much as noticed him, intent on the awful things they were doing and their own torment. JC wasn't even sure they knew the train had stopped.

He tried the front doors, nearest the engine, struggling to force his aching fingers into the gap between the doors.

"You really think that's a good idea?" said Melody, raising her voice over the bedlam. "You really want to let those animals loose, out here with us? Listen to them!"

"They're the victims here!" JC said savagely. "It's not their fault! They've been driven to this. Maybe if we can get them out . . . they'll be themselves again. We have to try! We have to try to save some of them . . ."

But he couldn't open the doors. He fell back from the train, breathing harshly, desperate to do . . . something. He spotted Happy still curled up on the platform and lurched over to him. He bent over the telepath, pulled the man's hands away from his ears, and shook him viciously until Happy's eyes opened and focused on JC.

"Leave me alone," Happy said pitifully. "I can't stand it. I can't."

"What are you picking up from the train?" demanded JC.

"Are you mad?" said Happy. "I'm doing all I can to shut it out! But it's too strong, too powerful . . . my shields are nothing to it! Fear and horror and suffering, that's what I'm getting! I'm not picking up a single coherent human thought from anyone on the whole bloody train!"

"Can you make them hear you?" said JC.

"They're beyond that," Happy said miserably. "They're trapped in the eternal moment. Damned to a single time and place, forever. Only aware of themselves and each other; and the awful things they're doing. They don't even know we're here."

JC turned to Melody. "Talk to me! What are your instruments showing? Anything we can use?"

"Massive energy readings," said Melody, concentrating on her instrument panels so she wouldn't have to look at the train. Her eyes were wild, and she looked like she might be sick at any moment, but she kept her voice steady. "Definite traces of other-dimensional energies, but not from the train, or the poor bastards inside it. There's something here in the station with us, deep in the system. In the tunnels, or maybe even underneath them. It's powering the train, making it possible. It's responsible for everything that's happening."

JC looked back at the long line of cars, packed with blood and horror and endless carnage. Bodies slamming together, teeth and fingers sinking into flesh; men and women driven out of their minds by base and brutal urges and appetites. They clung to life with a terrible tenacity; in the face of murder and rape and cannibalism, they would not lie down and die. Broken and bloodied, with gaping holes in them where flesh and organs had been torn away and eaten, still they fought on. A woman's screaming face was slammed against the car-window right in front of JC. Slammed again and again and again, till her features disappeared into a pulped and bloody mess. And still she screamed, and struggled . . .

He turned back to Melody, his voice shaking with shock and frustrated rage. "Do something! There must be something you can do! What good are your precious instruments if they can't do anything! Stop this! At least . . . open a door so I can get to them!"

"I can't!" Melody yelled back at him. "It's too big, too powerful! Just by being here, this train is overwhelming all my sensors. Something like this shouldn't even exist in our dimension. The material plane isn't strong enough to contain it. I think . . . the train itself is alive, and aware, and gorging itself on the suffering."

And then the engine revved up, the sound painfully loud, and the cars jerked forward as the hell train pulled out of the station, gathering speed impossibly quickly. Then it disappeared into the far tunnel-mouth and was gone, taking its cargo of the damned with it. That dreadful, downbound train.

Suddenly, the station was still and silent and sane again. Melody slumped over her instruments, sweat running down her face. Happy leaned against the wall, pressing his face against the cool tiles, his eyes wide open because he couldn't stand to see what he saw when he closed them. JC stood helplessly in the middle of the platform, trying to find something to say, and failing.

Happy tried to pull a bottle of pills out of his pocket, but his hands were shaking too much. He finally jerked the bottle out, only to watch it fall from his hands as he tried and failed to open the child-proofed lid. The plastic bottle hit the platform hard but bounced without breaking and rolled back and forth at his feet. Happy started to cry.

JC moved over and stood close beside him. He knew better than to touch the telepath but did his best to comfort Happy with his presence. JC had finally got his breathing under control, but he still looked like he'd been in a fight, and lost.

"We're all shaking," JC said finally. "How about that. We've faced worse than this, in our time. I have to say, I thought we were stronger than this."

"Normally, we are," said Melody. "But this was different. We deal with hauntings, echoes, memories of the

past. We're not used to dealing with real blood and vio-
lence and death, right there in front of us. Most of the
things we experience . . . actually happened long ago.
Done and finished, years before. There was nothing we
could do about them, nothing we could do to save the
people involved. We came in afterwards, to clean up
the mess they'd left behind."

"This is different," said JC slowly. "We have to stop
this happening, before it gets any worse. Before it has a
chance to spread . . ."

"Don't," said Happy. "Just . . . don't, okay?"

"Buck up, man," said JC, in something very like his
normal voice. He made himself stand up straight and
moved over to stand beside Melody, so he could pretend
to study the monitor displays. "We need more information. Hard information that we can rely on. Particularly,
we need to locate the source for all this. Can you give
me anything, Melody?"

She shook her head. "Whatever it is, it's unnaturally powerful and really well hidden. Defended by energies of a kind I've never encountered before. We're
way beyond this world's science, JC. We're in other-
dimensional territory now. It's confusing the hell out of
my computers; they can't tell me what it is, only what it
isn't. But if you're ready for some more bad news . . .
From the way its defensive shields reacted to my sensor
probes, I'm pretty sure it knows we're here and looking
for it."

"Wonderful," Happy said bitterly. "Can things get
any worse?"

"Hold it," said Melody. "I've got energy spikes all
across my boards! Something's coming!"

"Not another train," said Happy. "Please say it's not another train. I couldn't stand it."

"No," said Melody. "Nothing like the hell train. Nothing so brutal. This is more . . . subtle."

All three of them looked around, but there was nothing to see. The dark tunnel-mouth was empty, and the rail tracks were still. There was a subtle tension in the air, a feeling of imminence, of something about to happen. The light seemed even fiercer, the shadows deeper. And then webbing began to form, appearing out of nowhere all down the length of the platform. Thick grey spider-webs, forming like mist out of the brittle air. They crawled across the high ceiling, spreading in patterns like frost, shooting this way and that in sudden spurts. More of the stuff dropped from the ceiling, floating down in sheets of silver-grey gauze. Thick clumps of webbing formed in the angles and intersections between platform and wall, and shot up over the metal seats and the vending machines, cocooning them in moments. Long strands drifted on the air, undulating slowly on unfelt gusts of wind.

The webbing smelled of dust, and dead things, and the fading past. Both tunnel-mouths were blocked off with a single huge web, far beyond the ability of any earthly spider. Thick strands of webbing, like dull grey cables, drawn in intricate, jagged patterns. Both of the huge webs billowed slowly here and there, as though pressed from the other side by something large trying to get through. Long streamers drifted towards JC and his people, light as gossamer but full of purpose.

Heavy clumps of webbing fell in sudden jerks from the ceiling, hanging down like grey stalactites. JC's breath caught in his throat as he realised there were shapes inside the webbing. Human bodies, wrapped and cocooned, with blank, staring faces barely visible through the dull grey shrouds. The bodies didn't move. They were dead. They had to be dead. JC made himself study what he could make out of the faces; but he didn't recognise anyone from the missing persons files he'd studied earlier. He wasn't sure what he could have done if he had recognised anyone. And then a thought struck him . . .

"Happy," JC said carefully, "I don't think I trust this. Any of this. It's . . . too sudden to be anything natural. Is any of this real?"

"Not even close," said Happy. He was standing up straight now and was actually smiling. Now he had something he could recognise and deal with. "It's all a projected image."

Melody scowled as she tried to scrape thick masses of webbing off her precious instruments. It clung tenaciously to her hand as she tried to shake it off, and she had to rub her hand hard against her hip to shift it. "Bloody well feels real enough . . ."

"Of course it feels real, that's the point," said Happy. "But it's all nothing but a telepathically broadcast image designed to prey on standard fears and discomforts." He snapped his fingers dismissively, and every bit of webbing disappeared from the station. Happy smiled, smugly. "Kid's stuff. They must think they're dealing with amateurs."

"'They'?" said Melody, still surreptitiously rubbing her hand against her hip. "What they? Are you saying those images didn't come from whatever was running the hell train?"

"Exactly," said Happy. "Something that powerful doesn't need to deal in images. No; we underwent a psychic attack, one of the first things my Institute trainers taught me to defend myself against. It's the Project telepath. She knows where we are."

"Okay," said JC. "This we can deal with."

"And the other-dimensional nasty?" said Melody.

"We'll get to it," said JC. "After we've kicked the Project agents out of here."

"I love it when he gets all confident," Happy said to Melody. "Don't you just love it when he gets all confident? Doesn't it make you feel all safe and protected?"

"The hell train was sent to break our nerve, undermine our confidence," JC said patiently. "But in the end, it doesn't matter what's behind this haunting. If it's come into our world, it has to obey our rules. It can't operate here unless it's taken on a material form; and if it's material, we can kick its arse."

"I knew it," said Happy, rolling his eyes. "He's going to walk up to an other-dimensional entity and look for an arse to kick. I want a transfer to another team. Do you know if the Foreign Legion's hiring?"

"You don't speak French," said Melody.

"I'll learn!"

"Hush, man," said JC imperiously. "Your leader and commander is talking. Even if we are dealing with some Force or Power from the afterworlds, whatever it is must be using someone or something from our dimension as a focus, an entry point into our plane of existence. Some original event that roots the haunting in this station. So all we have to do is identify and locate the focal point, deal with it, and we can shut this whole mess down. Melody?"

"I'm working on it," said Melody. She felt rather better, now that she had a definite goal to pursue. "I'm getting so many readings, it's hard to tell what's significant and what isn't . . . I've never seen so many manifestations in one location. This place must be lousy with ghosts at the best of times."

JC looked at Happy. "Well?"

"Don't push me!" he snapped. "I'm trying! But the aether's so full of psychic information it's practically saturated. There's too much going on; it's like a thousand signals all broadcasting at once and bouncing around inside my head."

"Try," said JC.

"Bully! I need my pills."

"Then take some," said JC. "Do whatever you have to, to put your thoughts in order. Because you're no use to me like this."

"JC!" said Melody, turning away from her keyboards to glare at him. "You know what too much of that stuff does to him! Those pills are killing him by inches!"

"Yes," said JC. "I know. But we all do what we have to. Needs must when the Devil drives, and all that. A few for now, Happy. Just enough to let you function."

"You ruthless little shit," said Melody. And she turned her back on both of them and concentrated on her machines.

"You're a good man, JC," said Happy, fumbling a handful of bottles from out of his pockets and peering myopically at the handwritten labels. "I don't care what anyone else says."

He finally selected one particular bottle, smiled cheerily in anticipation, got the cap off with only a little effort, and knocked back two little green pills. He dry swallowed hard, considered, then took one more before replacing the cap and making the bottle disappear. He stood very still, contemplating what was going on inside him, then his lips widened into a smile like a death's-head grin.

"Oh yes . . . This is the stuff to give the boys! It's bad down here, but I'm the baddest thing in this station! Yes yes yes!" He broke into a soft-shoe routine, lost interest, realised JC was looking at him steadily, and giggled briefly. "On the job, JC! Oh yes! I'm getting something. I'm picking up all kinds of psychic traces, but only one original to this location that's recent enough to qualify as a probable focal point. God, I feel lucid. Something happened right here, on this platform, within the last few days."

"Are you . . . all right, Happy?" said Melody. "You don't look too good."

"I feel fine! Fine!"

"The sweat is pouring off your face, Happy," said JC. "And your eyes . . ."

"I am in the groove!" said Happy. "Now shut up and let me work. Oh, I'm on fire now! Someone died here. Murdered. A young woman . . . robbed of so many years, so much future life. That's a great source of power for whoever was responsible, all those potential years. Murder magic. Necromancy. Bad stuff."

"Can you reach her?" said JC. "Can you contact her? Bring her here, make her manifest for us?"

"She's coming," said Happy. His face was flushed, he couldn't stop grinning, and his eyes were fever bright. "Our life energies are drawing the murdered girl here. We blaze so brightly to her dead eyes, and so she comes to us out of the dark like a moth to a flame, or a child to a familiar, once-loved place. She's almost here. Be gentle with her, JC. She doesn't understand that she's dead. She's trapped in a half-way state, caught up in a dream that never ends. Never really aware of where she is, or what's happening. Don't try to wake her, JC. That would be cruel."

He'd barely finished speaking when a young woman appeared suddenly out of nowhere, right there on the platform before them, standing with her back to them as though waiting for a train. She stood on the very edge of the platform, lost in her own thoughts, occasionally looking down the tracks at the tunnel-mouth, waiting for a train that would never come. She didn't seem to notice JC or Happy or Melody. JC moved slowly, cautiously, forward until he was standing beside her, a polite distance away. She didn't look at him. JC looked at her.

His first thought was how beautiful she was. A pre-Raphaelite dream of a woman in her late twenties, with a huge mane of glorious red hair tumbling down around a high-boned, sharply defined face. Her eyes were a vivid green, and her mouth was a bright red dream, with a smile tucked away in one corner. She wore a long white dress that clung tightly here and there to show off a magnificent figure. She seemed calm enough, real enough . . . so full of life, with so much still to live for. All the things she might have done, all the things she might have achieved . . . For a moment, JC couldn't speak, overwhelmed with pain and rage at what had been done to her, at what she'd been so cruelly deprived of. He made himself look away and glanced back at Melody.

"Use the database of missing persons," he said quietly. "Find her. I need to know her name, and exactly what happened. I need to know everything about her."

"Way ahead of you," said Melody. "I'm looking at the

police report now, but there's not much in it. Only the bare facts of her murder, death from a single stab wound . . . no witnesses, no suspects. Nothing here to suggest she was anyone important."

"They're all important," said JC. "All the people, all the victims, who end up as ghosts. That's why we do this."

"This is an unusually strong manifestation," said Happy. "Try talking to her, JC. See if she'll answer you."

"What's her name?" said JC. "Do we at least have a name for her?"

"Kim Sterling," said Melody.

JC moved in close beside the ghost, and she turned her head slowly to look at him with her lost, dreamy eyes.

"Kim," said JC. "Kim, what are you doing here?"

"I'm an actress," she said, in a warm sweet contralto voice. "On my way to an audition. It's a good part, come right out of the blue; and I have a good feeling about it. This could be my big break, at last. I could really shine, in a role like this. I wish the train would come. It feels like I've been standing here for ages."

JC didn't have the heart to tell her that the train would never come, for her. Kim smiled at him suddenly.

"Do I know you? You look nice. Kind."

"I try to be," said JC. "But it's not always easy. I'm here to help."

"That's nice," said Kim. "But I don't need any help. I'm fine." She looked directly at him, and some of the dreaminess went out of her eyes. "Except . . . I have this feeling, that there's somewhere else I ought to be."

"Yes," said JC.

"I feel so cold . . . and alone . . ."

"You're not alone any more," said JC. "I'm here. We're all here, to help you. I'm JC."

"I'm Kim. I shouldn't be here, should I?"

"No."

"Why are you crying, JC?"

He hadn't realised he was.

"Are those tears for me, JC? No-one ever shed a tear for me before. No-one ever cared that much. I've been so alone since I came to London, despite all the people . . . I wish I'd met you before, JC."

"Yes," he said. "I wish I'd met you before, Kim."

She reached out a hand to him to wipe away the tears on his cheek. But her fingers were already transparent by the time they reached his face; and when he put up a hand to hold hers, his fingers passed right through her ghostly hand. Kim Sterling faded slowly away and was gone, and JC was left standing alone on the edge of the platform, reaching out to no-one. And then Kim re-appeared, standing at the end of the platform, next to the tunnel-mouth from which the hell train had appeared. She looked entreatingly at JC, then faded away again. JC turned savagely to Happy and Melody.

"That's it! She's the key, the focal point, the start of this haunting! Solve her murder, and we solve this case."

"Slow down, slow down," said Melody. "We don't *know* anything of the sort. Yes, her murder might be the instigating factor, but . . ."

"But nothing. Grab what you need; we're going after her."

"Are you sure about this, JC?" said Happy. "I could feel what you were feeling. And this is very definitely not the time to fall for a pretty face."

JC glared at Happy. "Stay out of my head!"

"It's not my fault! In my current, well-medicated state, it's like you're shouting the whole contents of your head at the top of your voice, and I do wish you wouldn't."

"She's the key," JC said stubbornly. "And we are going after her. Right now."

"Going where?" said Melody.

"We follow her! She's leading us somewhere."

"I'm not leaving my machines here, unguarded!" said Melody. "Anything might happen to them!"

"Your machines can look after themselves; you've said so often enough," said JC. "We have to go now; we can't risk losing her!"

"It'll all end in tears," said Happy. But as usual, no-one was listening to him.

JC was already off and running down the platform, heading towards where he'd last seen the ghost. Happy and Melody looked at each other, shrugged pretty much in unison, and went chasing after JC and the ghost of Kim Sterling.

''''''''''''''''''''''''

The three ghost finders ran full tilt through Oxford Circus Station, chasing the ghost as she receded endlessly before them, appearing and disappearing and reappearing. JC led the way, pursuing Kim down the endless white-tiled corridors, dashing in and out of low-arched entrances and exits, onto station platforms and off again; and still she hung on the air before him, drawing him on like some ghostly will-o'-the-wisp. Sometimes she was directly ahead of him, so close he could almost reach out and touch her, sometimes so far ahead she was only a pale figure in the distance. She wasn't moving of

her own accord. He knew that. He could see it in her
face, and in her eyes. Sometimes she called out to him,
but her voice only came to him as the barest whisper.
Something was using her as bait, drawing him like a
fish on a line. JC knew that, but he kept going anyway,
running as fast and as hard as he could drive himself.
Because this was his job, because he had to stop the
haunting from spreading . . . and because he couldn't,
wouldn't, let Kim down.

Happy and Melody pounded doggedly along behind
him, keeping up as best they could. Happy's face was an
unhealthy red, and already he was labouring for every
breath. Melody's arms pumped at her sides like a sprint-
er's though it didn't seem to be helping her much. They
both knew the ghost was bait, luring them on into some
kind of trap, but they trusted JC. Just as he trusted them
to have his back. They were a team, and they were professionals, and God help whatever was behind all this
when they finally caught up with it.

Howling winds came blasting out of nowhere, hitting
JC like a hammer, slamming him in the face hard enough
to blow harsh tears from his eyes. The wind came roar-
ing out of several side tunnels at once, bringing JC to a
sudden halt and buffeting him this way and that. He
fought it savagely, forcing himself on into the face of the
bitter-cold gale-force winds. He dug his feet in, leaned
forward with his head well down, and drove himself on,
step by step. Happy and Melody were right behind him;
using him as a wind-break and urging him on. In the face
of such stubborn resistance, the wind itself seemed to
lose heart, and all at once it fell away and was gone. JC
saw Kim floating not far ahead, and was off and running
again, followed by the others.

Blasts of almost lethal heat hit them next—a vicious heat-wave that came at JC from all sides at once, as though he'd been thrown into a blast-furnace. His exposed skin reddened and smarted painfully, and his cream-white suit started to smoulder. JC put his head down and kept going. The heat vanished, replaced by a vicious, bitter cold. JC almost cried out but was damned if he'd give his attacker the satisfaction. He pressed on, shaking and shuddering, grinding his teeth together to stop them chattering. He could sense Happy and Melody, still close behind him, but didn't dare break his concentration long enough to stop and look back.

He wouldn't let Kim down. He was damned if he'd let her down.

Psychic attacks came next: nameless dreads and anxiety attacks, illogical aversions and paranoias that jerked through his head like razor wire. The thought of going on became impossible, intolerable, unthinkable. But JC did it anyway. He snarled into the face of the attacks, shouldering aside his fears through sheer stubborn willpower. He didn't look back for Happy and Melody. He knew they'd still be there.

And that was when Natasha Chang and Erik Grossman launched their attack from ambush. At the last moment, Happy sensed somebody's presence and yelled a warning, and that was enough to save JC and his team. One word of warning, and their training kicked in. They all threw themselves in different directions, as a fusillade of bullets ripped through the air where they'd been. Puffs of pulverised stone and plaster flew on the air as bullets punched long lines of ragged holes across the corridor walls, and the occasional ricochet screamed through the still air. But not one bullet hit its intended target. JC and Happy and Melody had gone to ground, tucked away in convenient hiding-places. Natasha and Erik were forced to leave their own hiding-places in search of targets. Natasha stalked down the empty corridor, gun held out professionally before her, while Erik scurried along behind, clutching his gun with both podgy hands.

Happy hit them both with a telepathic blast, his chemically enhanced brain shouldering Natasha's defences aside long enough to undermine her thoughts and disrupt Erik's. Both Project agents yelled aloud as their guns seemed to become blisteringly hot, and instinctively they threw their weapons away. The guns were still in mid air when JC and Melody and Happy erupted out of their hiding-places and threw themselves at Natasha and Erik.

Natasha realised immediately what had happened, pulled her mental shields back into place, and hit Happy with a telepathic onslaught that stopped him dead in his tracks. The two most powerful minds went head to head, while their bodies stood perfectly still, staring unblinkingly into each other's eyes. Natasha had intended to go after JC, as the most powerful member of the Institute team, and because she ached to test herself against him; but Happy had proved himself the biggest immediate threat, so she had to kill him first. Happy caught that thought and laughed breathlessly at her.

Erik drew his Aboriginal pointing bone and stabbed it at Melody as she ran towards him. She changed direction immediately, and the tiles on the walls behind her cracked and exploded one after the other as the bone's influence moved in an arc across them. Erik raked the pointing bone back and forth increasingly wildly, spit-

ting out a series of baby swear-words, but Melody
jumped and spun and ducked with unexpected acrobatic
grace, always one step ahead of him.

JC hesitated, caught between helping his team and
needing to pursue Kim. And in that moment of indeci-
sion, Natasha hit Happy with a mental blast of pure rage
that rocked him back on his feet. Natasha seized the moment and threw her thoughts at the ghost of Kim, hanging on the air at the end of the corridor; and Kim screamed
shrilly as streams of blue-grey ectoplasm burst out of
her ghostly form, torn from her by the sheer force of
Natasha's will. The ectoplasm quickly formed itself into
solid bars under Natasha's urging, imprisoning Kim inside a spirit cage. Kim screamed again, caught between
two implacable forces, both of which had power over her
while she had none. But summon as it would, the unseen
force could not pull Kim through bars made from her
own ghostly form. The spirit cage held her.

By then, Happy had recovered, and he lashed out at
Natasha with his own rage. Natasha met the attack easily. She knew all about rage and its uses. Happy quickly
brought himself back under control, knowing he faced a
mind easily as powerful as his own and that if he didn't
fight with all the strength and subtlety at his command,
he was a dead man. He met Natasha's cold gaze and held
it, attacking her shields on a dozen different levels at
once, and Natasha was forced to give him her full attention. They stood face-to-face, totally absorbed in each
other, like two gun-slingers on an old Western street.
There was a war going on inside their heads.

The station disappeared for them, replaced by a psychic battle-field of their own creation, a desolate plain,
cracked dry earth under a night sky, full of pale, fading

stars. It was cold and silent, an empty place, with no help or distractions, fit only for battle and slaughter. Happy concentrated, and great stone golems burst up out of the earth, dry soil falling away from their brute heads and wide shoulders as they levered themselves up out of the broken ground. Crude, misshapen, only nominally human in form, they lurched and lumbered towards Natasha, to break and crush her with their heavy hands. She laughed at Happy, a brief, cold sound rich with contempt; and lightning bolts slammed down from the empty heavens to shatter the golems and reduce them to rubble.

Then Natasha had the advantage, and the battle-ground changed. The two telepaths stood in the ruins of a city, in the dark time of an apocalyptic future. Tall buildings had been thrown down and lay half-buried under crawling alien plants and weeds. A pale sun hung low on a sickly green sky. Natasha shot up suddenly, growing in size until her giant form towered over Happy. She raised a pink leather boot to stamp on him. But Happy immediately increased his size, shooting up past Natasha until it was his turn to tower over her. She grew again in size, then him, then her again—two incredible giants blasting up out of the ruins of a dead city, each of them trying to outdo the other. They became vast and colossal, leaving the world behind, until they were the size of gods, and threw planets and comets and worlds at each other.

Battles and battle-fields came and went increasingly quickly, there and gone in a moment, flashing like kaleidoscopes as two minds fought it out for dominance. They tore at each other like tygers, burning bright in the forests of their nights.

Back in the real world, in the station corridor, strange things were occurring in the vicinity of the two motionless telepaths, psychic fall-out from the mental wars. A rain of fish fell out of nowhere, slapping against the walls and flopping helplessly on the floor, drowning in fresh air. Rose petals fell, in twisting patterns of strange significance, then humped slowly across the floor like so many flat red slugs. And a slow, terrible pressure built upon the air, as two minds slammed together, and neither would give an inch.

Melody forced Erik back step by step, dodging his increasingly wild attacks with contemptuous ease. She was right on top of him, and enjoying the chance to try out for real the shokotan karate she'd only ever practiced in the gym. But though she danced and punched and kicked with dazzling speed, somehow Erik continued to evade her, constantly backing away, staying just out of reach. He didn't have any fighting skills of his own, but sheer terror had given him amazing speed and reflexes. He kept stabbing at her with his pointing bone, but Melody never gave him a chance to draw a bead. Behind her, posters on the walls burst into flames or exploded into multi-coloured confetti under the bone's malign influence. Melody spun and kicked, and Erik retreated, and neither dared break off long enough to try something else.

Erik was outraged. There'd been nothing about this in the briefings. Girl geeks weren't supposed to suddenly turn into warrior women. It wasn't fair. The blows and kicks got even closer, and he backed away even more frantically.

Neither Happy nor Melody could break off from what they were doing to help JC, so it was up to him to break

Kim free from her spirit cage. He stood before her, careful not to get too close to the shimmering blue-grey bars,
and spoke gently to Kim, calming her. She'd been shocked
right out of her deathly trance and, for the first time,
seemed fully awake and aware. Her vivid green eyes fixed
on JC, seeing him as real, and right before her. She looked
at the bars of the cage, then past them at the world beyond, and fear and panic surged up in her as she realised
she wasn't where and when she thought she was. She
started to fade away, retreating back inside, denying herself to deny the world; and only JC's calm, coaxing, caring voice brought her back again. She clung to his
presence like a lifeline, and he stood firm and steady before her.

"Trust me," he said. "I won't let you down. I can get
you out of the trap that holds you; but you have to work
with me. We can do this if you work with me."

She thought he was only talking about the spirit cage.
She nodded eagerly, and JC moved as close to the bars
as he dared.

"These bars are made of ectoplasm, drawn out of you
by the Project woman. It's yours; it belongs to you. So
take it back. Concentrate, and take it back inside you,
where it belongs."

Kim looked at him for a long moment, and he held
her gaze steadily, reassuringly. Kim glared at the shimmering bars of her cage, and they quickly unravelled
under the impact of her will, which was so much stronger than anyone had anticipated. She wasn't lost and
dreaming any more. Kim inhaled the ectoplasm, the
blue-grey smoke disappearing into her mouth and nose
in moments; and she was free again.

For a moment, JC and Kim stood face-to-face, the

living and the dead, looking into each other's eyes, smiling at each other, not knowing what to say. They could both feel the powerful attraction burning between them. As though everything they'd ever done had been necessary steps to lead them to this place, this moment. As though the whole world was holding its breath, to see what would happen next.

And then the unseen force seized hold of Kim Sterling and snatched her away again. She receded rapidly before JC, hauled backwards down the long corridor at impossible speed, while she kicked and struggled helplessly and screamed in horror and rage. She held out her arms beseechingly to JC, and he ran after her. He followed her retreating form through corridor after corridor, never looking back once. Because she needed him, and he needed her. Because it was his job.

He knew he was abandoning Happy and Melody to their own devices, but he had faith in them. He hoped they'd understand. Understand that he had no choice in this. Love had come late in life to JC, and he was damned if he'd lose it.

SIX

ALL KINDS OF APPETITES

Melody was fighting well, and Erik was fighting dirty, and it was still as near a draw as could be. Melody spun and pirouetted, her feet cracking out like the wrath of God Himself, and still she couldn't seem to land a blow on the madly dodging and ducking Erik. He was panting hard by then, his face flushed an unhealthy shade of purple, and he was waving his Aboriginal pointing bone around with less and less accuracy; but the little creep wouldn't go down. Melody finally threw caution to the winds, stepped inside his reach, and deftly kicked the pointing bone right out of his hand. Erik watched dumbly as it flew through the air, and Melody moved in to beat the crap out of him. Erik laughed breathlessly, right into her face, and his other hand came up holding his specially modified taser. He jammed the metal horns into her gut and hit the button.

Melody convulsed, her whole body going into spasm after spasm as she was thrown backwards by the massive contractions in her muscles. She crashed to the platform, hitting it hard, and lay there, twitching and shuddering. Her eyes were wide, and drool ran from her slack mouth. Erik strolled unhurriedly forward to lean over her, studied her thoughtfully, and hit her with the taser again. She convulsed once more, arms and legs flailing while her back and the back of her head slammed against the unyielding platform. She made brief grunting sounds of agony, and Erik laughed happily.

He set the taser's metal horns against the trembling skin at Melody's bare throat, then raised his voice.

"Happy! If you don't surrender to Natasha, right now, I'm going to give your little techno-geek girl-friend a full-scale shock, and you can listen to her brains frying."

Distracted, caught between two thoughts and intentions, Happy's concentration was shattered; and Natasha slammed through his mental shields like they weren't even there. Her thoughts overwhelmed his, and, in a moment, she had shouldered her way inside his mind and taken control. Happy didn't even get a chance to cry out. He simply stood there before her, utterly still. A prisoner inside his own head. Natasha relaxed abruptly, like a runner at the end of a race. She breathed heavily and grinned widely, even as sweat ran down her face.

It had been a near thing, much nearer than she'd expected. And it hadn't been the pills, either; Happy was a lot stronger than he allowed himself to believe. It had been a long time since anyone had been able to match Natasha in a fair contest. Mainly because Natasha didn't believe in fair contests; she believed in winning. She moved forward, kicking aside some feebly moving rose petals, so she could laugh right into Happy's unmoving face.

"Think you're so good. Think you're so big-time!

I would have kicked your arse even without Erik's distraction."

Something in Happy's inscrutable face still managed to suggest he rather doubted it. So Natasha took control of his right arm and his right hand, and made Happy punch himself repeatedly in the face. The sound of bone cracking into bone was shockingly loud in the quiet, and Natasha clapped her hands together delightedly as blood gushed from Happy's nose and spilled from his rapidly swelling mouth. Happy hit himself again and again, and Natasha never got tired of it.

"Look over here, Natasha!" said Erik, not wanting to be left out. "Look what I can do!"

And when Natasha looked, he jabbed Melody in the gut with his taser and giggled as she jumped and kicked, her head jerking helplessly back and forth. The agonised sounds coming from her mouth were more animal than human.

Natasha sniffed and looked at Happy. "You can stop that now. Just stand there till I have need of you." She put a hand to her forehead. "You have no idea what it's like inside that man's head, Erik. So many chemicals, so many reactions, so many side effects . . . his thoughts rise and fall like tides, and his emotions surge back and forth like icebergs. It's a wonder to me he still knows who he is. No, Erik; no more taser, no more playtime. Revenge is one thing, giving in to our baser natures is quite another. Control, Erik, control; discipline at all times. We must always be in control of our passions and not the other way round."

Erik raised an eyebrow, considered a very cutting comeback, then quickly decided against saying it. He put the taser away and recovered his pointing bone.

"You're no fun any more," he said accusingly. "How else are we supposed to make them talk?"

"Who cares what these two have to say?" said Natasha. "I doubt very much they know anything we don't. No; we'll use them as bait to get what we want, then kill them. That is what we're here for, after all. Now, did you happen to see where JC went?"

"Last I saw he was running for the exit," said Erik. "Chasing that ghost woman."

Natasha frowned and tapped a single pink-leather-gloved fingertip against her lower lip. "Why would he abandon his fellow team members to go haring off after a ghost? I mean, what's so special about her?"

"Nothing I could see," said Erik. "Maybe he fancies her."

"Oh please!" said Natasha, curling her upper lip magnificently. "One of us and one of them? I don't think so. Necrophilia is so . . . tacky. And JC is, after all, a professional."

"You're jealous!" said Erik delightedly. "You are!"

"You want a slap?"

Erik took a careful step backwards. Natasha turned her back on him cuttingly and considered the motionless Happy and the still-twitching Melody.

"On the whole, I don't think Vivienne MacAbre will be at all pleased with us if we give up now. We were sent down here to kill JC. Having to admit that we let him get away while we concentrated on these two lesser fish . . . would not go down well. So, we use them as bait, to draw him back."

"I could still make use of them," said Erik, hopefully. "I have a full surgical kit in my back-pack. I could do all kinds of interesting things with them. Really. You'd be surprised."

"Quite possibly," said Natasha. "But we don't have the time. There's something really big, and really powerful, down here in the dark with us, something Vivienne never even mentioned. And I want it."

"I don't know," said Erik. "That wasn't the mission. You heard the cat head. *Something very old. Something from the afterworlds.*"

"I know," said Natasha. "I can feel it, like a constant pressure on my mental shields, trying to force its way in . . . It's big, Erik, you have no idea how big. This could be the biggest catch of our career."

"Can you pinpoint its location?" said Erik, cautiously.

"Not without giving the problem my full concentration," said Natasha, glancing at Happy. "He's still fighting me, you know. Like a fox with his paw caught in a trap. The chase is over, but he still won't admit it."

"We need more information on this . . . prize," said Erik.

"Big, powerful, and nasty," said Natasha. "And not in any way human. What more do you need to know?"

"Are you sure you aren't just seeing your own reflection?" said Erik from a safe distance.

Natasha was in such a good mood she smiled at him sweetly. "I shall make you suffer for that, little man, at some future time. For now, make yourself useful and consult your little cat computer. From the mental traces I'm picking up . . . I'd venture that what we have down here is almost certainly other-dimensional in origin."

"Oh crap," said Erik.

"Precisely," said Natasha. "We're going to need a

really sharp hook and a really strong line to haul this one in."

"We need reinforcements!" said Erik. "In fact, we need to get the hell out of here, right now, at speed, and put as much distance as possible between us and London, and let some other poor fool deal with it."

"Where's your spine?" said Natasha. "This is our big chance to prove our worth to the high-and-mighty Vivienne MacAbre. If we deliver not only the heads of JC, Melody, and Happy, but also the tamed and caged remains of an other-dimensional Intruder, on a plate . . . she'll make us an A team, with all their wonderful pay and privileges, on the spot."

"All right, I'm tempted," said Erik. "But I'm not committing myself to anything until I've got some hard data to look at."

"Then unpack your cat thing and get this show on the road," said Natasha.

....

Erik took his time unpacking his cat-head computer and making sure it was all functioning as it should be. Shimmering mechanisms of pure energy whirled and revolved, enforcing their strange designs upon the world; and then the cat head opened its eyes and spat fiercely. Erik tweaked one of its whiskers playfully and snatched his hand back before the teeth could reach him. He knelt before the computer, so he could look right into the cat's slit-pupilled eyes.

"There's something down here with us," he said bluntly. "What is it? What is it doing down here?"

"It's watching you," said the cat head in its harsh, unnatural voice. "It knows all about you. It wants you."

"Who doesn't?" said Erik. "But what is it, precisely? Demon, demiurge, one of the Great Beasts, perhaps?"

The cat head considered the question for a long moment while its glowing mechanisms went quietly mad. "It's not from around here," it said finally. "From over the hill and far away. From out of the past, to put an end to the future. The wolf has come down upon the fold, and it's bigger than anyone ever dreamed of."

"Forget the poetry," snapped Natasha. "What does it want?"

"Everything," said the cat head, turning its eyes to look directly at her. "It's going to eat you up."

Natasha glared at the head. "Technology should know its place. You watch your manners, kitty cat, or I'll pluck out your whiskers."

"Please don't threaten the machinery while it's working," said Erik. "And let us not get distracted, please."

"Well," said Natasha, "the cat started it."

"We should have been told about this before we came down here," said Erik.

"What if . . . nobody knows, but us?" said Natasha, thoughtfully. "We could do anything we wanted, down here, and no-one could do anything to stop us."

"Let's not lose track of what's important," Erik said stubbornly. "I am not going back to Vivienne MacAbre without, at the very least, JC's heart and brains in my little collecting box. As ordered. I have to say, I am far more afraid of displeasing Vivienne than I am of facing some other-dimensional Intruder. I know what your problem is," he said craftily. "All these manifestations down here are giving you an appetite. Why don't you indulge yourself? Maybe you'll think more clearly with a full stomach. So to speak."

"Don't try to get round me, little man," said Natasha. "The ghosts make me stronger. That's all that matters."

"Of course, of course," said Erik. "And you will need to be so very strong, for this."

Natasha turned to Happy, still standing absolutely motionless, where she'd left him. Blood continued to drip from his face. She smiled at him sweetly. "Work with me, little telepath. Lend me your energies. It's time for Daddy's bad little girl to go hunting again."

She reached inside him and drew on his power, despite everything he could do to stop her, sucking it right out of him. Natasha laughed out loud as new strength filled her from head to toe. Faces and figures flickered on and off before and around her, echoes of people and personalities soaked into the surroundings, imprinted on Time itself. They came and went like so many swiftly shuffling cards, until Natasha spotted one that appealed to her and pounced.

A man appeared, standing stiffly on the very edge of the platform, his feet planted well past the yellow safety line. He was only a man, no different from many others, except that perhaps his suit was that little bit too hard worn, too shabby. He looked older than his years, beaten down and hard done by, and his hands were clenched into determined fists at his sides. His face was beaded with sweat and full of a great concentration. There was the sound of a train approaching, and the man's head jerked round to look for it. The sound grew louder and louder, then the man threw himself forwards, into the path of the on-coming train.

His body all but exploded under the force of the impact, blood flying everywhere, and the remains were carried the length of the platform before finally slipping down to be finished off under the grinding wheels. There was nothing defiant or even meaningful about the suicide—only a small broken man, doing something pitiful. It was like looking at a child that had fallen and would never get up again.

There was never any sign of the train itself, only the sound it made and the awful things it did to the fragile human body. The man was the subject of the haunting, nothing else.

And then the man was back, unharmed, standing at the edge of the platform again, waiting for his train. Repeating the last few moments of his life, for all eternity. Trapped in the Hell he'd made for himself. Natasha and Erik watched the ghost kill himself several times until they grew bored with it.

"Could be a stone tape," said Erik, critically. "Nothing there but a recording. Want me to check it out with my little catty box of tricks?"

"No need," said Natasha. She was smiling, and it was not a nice smile. "This was a suicide, so some small part of him remains here still, trapped in the moment. A part of his consciousness, or his soul, whichever you prefer—forever here, eternally suffering. And I want it."

She strode forward, barely controlling her eagerness, and moved in right beside the suicide ghost, concentrating all her attention on him. And when she'd made herself as real to him as the on-coming train, she tapped him lightly on the shoulder, just as he was about to jump. He spun round, startled, and looked right at her. He looked into her eyes and screamed at what he saw there. Natasha enfolded him in her arms and clamped her hungry lips onto his screaming mouth, smothering the sound.

Unlike the homeless man, the suicide ghost fought

her savagely. He had chosen the manner and moment of his death, and he was damned if he'd have it stolen from him. He struggled in her arms and resisted her with all his will; but it didn't stop Natasha, or even slow her down. Because she was a Class Ten telepath, and an experienced eater of souls; and he was nothing more than a sad little ghost. She ate him all up, every last bit of him, until there was nothing left in her arms. Natasha straightened up slowly and wiped her mouth with the back of her hand.

"Oh, you little tease," she said thickly. "I do so love a bit of foreplay . . ."

Erik applauded languidly. You couldn't stay shocked all the time around Natasha; it wore you out. "I do so love to watch a professional doing what she does best. Speaking of which. Perhaps now we can get on with what we're supposed to be doing down here . . ."

"No," said Natasha. "I'm not done yet. He was fine for an appetiser, but I'm still hungry." She jerked suddenly round to glare at Happy. "You! Stop fighting me! Or I'll let Erik play with science girl some more. Now, work with me. Find me something more filling, more satisfying. Because you're starting to look pretty tasty yourself, little man . . ."

And then she broke off, looking round sharply. Something had changed on the platform; she could feel it. Even Erik's head snapped round, looking for something he could sense, if not put a name to. Natasha looked slowly round her, then stopped as she realised something had changed in the poster on the wall beside her. It didn't look like a poster any more. The gaudy colours in the painted advertisement had come alive, taken on depth and meaning and reality, like a window into another world. Natasha moved slowly back to stand with Erik, putting the cat computer between her and the strangely altered poster.

Glorious country-side seemed to stretch away forever under a gorgeous summer sky. A peaceful scene, with wide green fields untroubled by any sign of civilisation. A long, green dream of England. Except for the young man, tall and lithe and almost unbearably handsome, in a stylish white T-shirt and smart new jeans, standing at his ease under the spreading branches of an old oak tree. Almost bursting with glamour and masculinity, handsome as the Devil and twice as smooth, the young man looked out over the country scene as though he owned it. Natasha was pretty sure the original poster had been a somewhat overdone ad for a new deodorant, the last time she looked; but it was alive now, and so was the young man. He turned his head, looked at Natasha, and smiled lazily. The smile of a man who knew he was handsome, and charming, the smile of someone who knew he didn't have to try too hard. Exactly the kind of man Natasha would have enjoyed cutting down to size under normal conditions.

But this was different, and so was he.

"You're not what I was looking for," she said. "You're not a ghost, and you're not a man. What are you, exactly?"

The handsome young man pushed himself away from the tree and stepped casually out of his country-side scene and down onto the station platform. He seemed to bring a little of the other world with him, a breath of fresh country air, rich with the scents of trees and flowers and earth. Natasha gasped, as a sudden erotic frisson rushed through her.

The young man ignored his new surroundings, his dark gaze intent on Natasha. He didn't even glance at Erik. The young man stretched slowly, to show off his fine lithe frame, then walked unhurriedly down the platform, smiling at Natasha with disturbing intensity. She stood her ground, waited until he was almost upon her, then put out a hand to stop him. Her pink-leather-gloved palm actually slammed against his chest before he stopped. She hadn't realised she'd let him get that close. The broad chest under the T-shirt was solid and real. He was undeniably there, smiling right at her, his eyes full of laughter and mischief. Natasha could feel her heart racing.

Behind her, unnoticed by either of them, Erik was kneeling beside his cat-head computer. "What is that?" he said quietly. "Is it a ghost of some sort? Is it real? Really real?"

"No," said the cat head. "Not even close. Real enough to be dangerous, though."

"I know he's not a ghost!" snapped Natasha, not looking round. "I'm a telepath, remember?"

"So what are you picking up from him?" said Erik.

"Mostly . . . appetite," said Natasha. "And I don't mean he's feeling a bit peckish." She fixed the handsome young man with a steady gaze. "Flattery will get you nowhere; and I'm well past the point where I can be swept off my feet by raging hormones. So throw a bucket of water over it and talk to me. You're not a ghost, and you can't be real, so what are you?"

"I'm whatever you want me to be," said the young man. "Your fantasy. Your dream. I am your secret need and your heart's desire. I'm everything you ever dreamed of, including all the things you wouldn't admit to on waking. And you have dreamed of so many things, haven't you, Natasha?"

"How do you know my name?" Natasha wanted to be suspicious and on her guard, but there was something about his voice . . . something in its tone and timbre that made her feel like a teenage girl again, trembling in the grip of her own sexuality. She wanted him, she really did, even while another part of her mind yelled at her to kill him, immediately, while she still had the chance.

"I know everything about you," said the man. "You called to me."

"No," said Natasha. "I'm pretty sure I didn't. You know my name; what's yours?"

He smiled engagingly. "I have many names but one nature. I am the fire on the heath and the shriek in the night. I am the look that challenges and the glance that quickens the heart. I am the cat who is always grey and the cuckoo in the nest. Don't you know me, Natasha?"

"I didn't call you," Natasha said sternly, ignoring her increased breathing, the fluttering in her stomach, and the pleasant ache between her thighs. "I don't want you. You can go now."

"You want me," said the man, so close to her by then she could feel his breath on her mouth. "You need me. You can't live without me."

"Don't put money on it," said Natasha.

Her breath caught in her throat as the man changed subtly before her, becoming even more handsome and glamorous, every detail intense and overwhelming . . . But at the same time, he was too much of a good thing. Like every treat you know is bad for you; like the poison that tastes sweet even as it kills you. Natasha backed away, and the man went after her.

And Erik, forgotten by both of them, stepped in behind the young man and stabbed him in the neck with his
taser turned to full strength. Lightning flared, and the
man stopped dead in his tracks, his mouth stretched in a
wild, inhuman howl. Natasha almost cried out as the
man's face changed abruptly before her, the details blur-
ring and slipping. He lurched forward another step, his
hands reaching imploringly out to Natasha; but they
weren't hands any more. He didn't look like a man any
more. The slumping figure turned abruptly and lashed
out at Erik, one overlong arm scything through the air
with deadly speed. But Erik was no longer there.

He'd put away the taser and taken out his pointing
bone. And as the figure changed still more, sloughing off
its veneer of Humanity to become something so disturbing that human eyes could not bear to look at it, Erik
shielded his eyes and stabbed the pointing bone in its
direction. The figure cried out again, in pain and horror
and thwarted rage, and disappeared.

Erik lowered his trembling hand and moved forward
to make sure the thing was really gone. He waved both
his hands through the air where it had been, and only
then did he go over to join Natasha, who was leaning
against the wall with her eyes shut, breathing hard. Erik
stopped a safe distance away and waited. He knew better
than to touch her, or even say something reassuring. He
looked at the poster on the wall. The countryside was
simply a painted scene again, but interestingly, there was
no trace anywhere of the young man. No-one stood
under the oak tree any more.

Erik glanced down at his cat-head computer. "Don't
suppose you've any idea as to what just happened?"

"It wasn't a ghost, and it wasn't real," said the cold,

inhuman voice. "It was a signal, broadcast by the bad thing that's waiting for you. The taser interrupted the signal, and the pointing bone dispersed it. The bad thing knows you're looking for it. It was testing you. Or perhaps it was playing. Who knows why the gods do anything?"

Erik looked at it sharply. "Gods?"

"Manner of speaking," said the cat head, and it stopped talking.

Natasha pushed herself away from the wall and stood up straight, pulling at her leather outfit here and there to make sure she looked good. She took one last deep breath, let it out slowly, then glared at Erik, herself again.

"Next time, don't take so long."

"You're welcome," said Erik. And then he went for her, his clawed hands reaching for her throat.

Happy had been biding his time. With Natasha weakened and distracted, he eased free of her mental domination without her even noticing. So it was the easiest thing in the world for him to take control of Erik and throw the nasty little man at Natasha. It helped that Erik had often thought of doing it, and for a moment even thought it was his own idea. He grabbed the front of Natasha's pink leather jacket with both hands and slammed her back against the wall. He crowded in close, holding her there with his full weight, pushing his face right into hers, his eyes and his smile full of all the awful things he wanted to do to her. When it came to the domination game, Erik had always been happy to swing both ways. He knew by then that he was acting under Happy's direction, but he didn't care. He savoured the moment, delighting in the chance to do really appalling things and still be able to claim it was nothing to do with him.

And while the two of them were struggling, Happy grabbed Melody, hauled her to her feet, and half led and half carried her to the nearest exit. She was only half-conscious, but once he got her feet under her, she got the idea fast enough.

Natasha kneed Erik in the balls so hard it practically drove his testicles up into his chest cavity. He fell away from her, all but paralysed by the terrible pain between his legs, and Natasha thrust her thoughts inside his head and broke Happy's control in a moment. Erik contracted into a full foetus on the platform, wrapped tightly around his pain, fighting to get his lungs working again. Natasha looked for Happy and Melody, but they were already gone, and she knew better than to go chasing after them. Far too many dark places and ambush points. She tried to follow them with her mind, but Happy had his shields firmly back in place, and Natasha couldn't even detect the shields. She cursed once, briefly and dispassionately. Erik rose slowly to his feet, tears rolling down his face, still bent over the pain coursing through him. Natasha slapped him viciously across the face. Erik rocked on his feet from the blow but took it.

"Talk to your nasty little computer," Natasha said coldly. "Find our two runaways."

Erik was glad of an excuse to kneel again, but the cat head wasn't of much use. Happy's shields really were first-class.

"Interesting," the cat head said finally. "I cannot see Happy or Melody, or JC, or the ghost he's chasing. Something is muddying the aether. But I am picking up another human presence down here in the station with us."

"You're sure it's not JC?" said Natasha.

"I know what he looks like," said the cat head. "This isn't him. No; a very interesting mind, this, very . . . odd. Not one of the Project's people and not one of the Institute's field agents. Very odd . . . I can see him, but I can't lock on to him. He's . . . protected."

Erik and Natasha looked at each other. Erik made himself ask the obvious question. "Who's doing the protecting?"

"Can't you guess?" said the cat head. "The bad thing, of course."

Erik rose painfully to his feet again. "My machine's too limited for this."

"Speak for yourself," said the cat head.

"Shut up," said Erik. "Melody wouldn't have come down here without all the very latest devices the Institute could provide. They might be able to help us more. Can you tell us where they are, cat?"

"Of course. Southbound platform, not ten minutes' walk from here. I can guide you right to it."

"Institute agents always get the best toys," said Erik. "I mostly have to design my own, on a budget significantly less than I was promised. And you have to order parts three months in advance . . . Luckily, I can usually make my own. Providing there's a zoo or a hospital nearby."

"I can feel too much information coming on," said Natasha. "Move it."

||||||||||||||||||||||||||

Melody's precious machines were right where she'd left them, and Erik almost cooed with pleasure as he ran his fat little hands over them. It didn't take him long to get the hang of the sensors and track down the Institute agents. Happy and Melody were still moving steadily through the deepest parts of the system, but JC, surprisingly, wasn't that far away. Still chasing his ghost.

"We'll take him from behind while he's distracted," said Natasha. "No time for anything fun; shoot him down. Aim for the body; I don't want his pretty face damaged. We can use him as bait to attract the other two. And then . . . we can give our full attention to sorting out whatever it is that's going on down here. After all the trouble I've been put through, I think I deserve a really big prize."

"I think we need to think about this some more," said Erik, diffidently. "The cat head said *other-dimensional*, and I'm inclined to believe it. These instruments are picking up some strange readings. Really powerful readings; almost off the scale. We don't want to bite off more than we can chew."

"You speak for yourself," said Natasha.

SEVEN

:::

TO WAR WITH DEMONS

:::::::::::::::::::::::::::::::

If you go to war with demons, you must be pure in your intent.

:::::::::::::::::::::::::

Drawn remorselessly on, like a fish on a line, like bait on a hook, Kim Sterling was dragged struggling backwards through the corridors and tunnels; and JC ran after her. He pursued her up and down stairs and around sharp corners, sometimes drawing close but never, ever, allowed to catch up. Now and then her ghostly form would be pulled suddenly through a solid wall, and JC had to hunt frantically back and forth before he could pick up her trail again. He could always hear her, even when he couldn't see her, calling out to him in fear and anger or richly cursing her unseen abductor, and that kept him going . . . She hadn't given up, and neither would he. He pounded headlong down corridors and passageways, breathing harshly, legs and ribs aching, his arms pistoning at his sides. And somehow Kim was never hauled away so fast that JC couldn't keep up—as long as he pushed himself to his limit. The chase was a challenge, a taunt, goading him on, almost allowing him to catch up, then snatching Kim away again.

JC ran on, back and forth through the maze of corridors, on and off platforms, up and down the stationary elevators, knowing that the chase was meant to break his spirit, to force him to give up and abandon his new-found love. But he wouldn't do that. He had already decided, quite calmly and rationally, that he would drop in his tracks first.

JC was so caught up in the chase that it took him a while to realise that his surroundings were going through subtle, deceptive changes.

Passageways seemed to stretch away before him, their ends growing more and more distant as the walls grew infinitely longer, elongating unnaturally like the passages we run through in nightmares, with no hope of getting anywhere. He ran and ran, and Kim receded endlessly before him. But the floor beneath his feet was still reassuringly hard and solid, so JC lowered his head like a charging bull and ran on. The walls on either side of him seemed to slump and bulge inwards, as though they were melting, then snap back into form again, all their details smudged and meaningless, but it took JC a while to realise that he didn't recognise anything and had no idea as to where he was.

He wished Happy were with him, to tell him whether what he was seeing was real or another illusion broadcast by the unknown enemy. JC scowled and pushed the thought away. He'd had to leave Happy behind, and Melody. Focused as he was on the chase, JC still had it in him to feel bad about leaving them to fight alone. He had faith in them. They were both trained, experienced agents. They'd manage. But that wasn't why he'd left them so readily. He'd abandoned his team-mates because he couldn't abandon Kim to her fate. He hoped they'd understand. He ran on, breathing really hard, a fire in his chest and an almost unbearable pain shooting through his sides.

Endless corridors, endless walls spattered with images out of Hell, howls and screams and hopeless sobbing all around him. Illusion. Had to be. JC kept his head down and concentrated on pursuing the only thing that mattered. His trained will was a match for any illusion. Unless . . . whatever was down in the darkness with him was actually so powerful it could distort Space and Time itself . . . in which case, he was in real trouble.

He rounded a corner and staggered to a halt as he saw Kim hanging in the air at the end of the new corridor. He fought for breath, half–bent over as sweat dripped from his face, glad of the chance for a break but already looking about him for any trace of a new threat. And that was when the walls on either side began to close in, moving remorselessly forward from both sides at once. The suddenly very real and solid walls ground loudly against the hard floor. JC straightened up immediately and looked behind him; but he was too far down the corridor to escape. He couldn't hope to reach either end before the walls slammed together. They were closing in on him steadily, taking their time. They looked heavy and solid enough to crush him to a bloody pulp. And they would do it slowly, inch by inch, while Kim watched. JC risked a glance at her. She was looking at him beseechingly, imploring him to get out of there. Her lips moved, but no sound came to him as she silently begged him to save himself.

JC shot her a reassuring smile. He breathed deeply, dragging air far into his lungs, gathering his strength and calming his mind. Sweat was still running down his face and stinging his eyes, and he took a moment to pull out a handkerchief and mop his face clean. Kim stared at him wildly, hardly believing he would waste time while the walls were closing in to crush him. JC put his hand-kerchief away with a flourish and looked left and right to check how close the walls were. The harsh grinding sound of their progress across the floor was very loud, and very near. At the speed they were moving, his death would be a slow and horrible thing, with the cracking and breaking of bones first, then the slow crushing of inner organs, as he literally died by inches. He'd proba-bly be alive right till the end, so Kim could suffer as much as he did.

JC was really looking forward to meeting his unseen enemy and teaching it the error of its ways.

He stretched out both arms, hands splayed, as though he intended to stop the incoming walls with sheer brute strength. But JC had been trained better than that. The Institute prepared its agents to be strong in all kinds of ways. JC calmed his mind with familiar and well-rehearsed routines, drew on his inner resources, and quite simply refused to accept what was happening. The walls couldn't be moving because the unseen enemy wasn't strong enough to rewrite physical reality. It couldn't be. JC defied the evidence of his senses and denied the movement of the walls through sheer strength of will. He closed his eyes and stood there with arms outstretched . . . and nothing came forward to touch his waiting hands. He slowly opened his eyes, and the corridor walls were back where they belonged as though they had never moved. Because, of course, they hadn't. JC slowly lowered his arms. He smiled at Kim, still hanging unsupported at the end of the corridor, and she smiled back.

Inside, JC was laughing his head off. He'd bet his shirt the enemy had been bluffing, and he'd won. It wasn't that powerful, after all. And that . . . was good to know.

He walked forward, and Kim hung there before him, dangled before him like a toy, or a lure. JC kept his approach slow and careful, not allowing himself to run to her, and his heart leapt a little when Kim didn't move. He made himself stop a careful distance away, somehow knowing that if he tried to free her from whatever held her, she would immediately be snatched away again. So he stood before her and smiled at her, and she smiled back, and they talked in quiet, calm, rational voices.

"You have to give this up," said Kim. "You can't keep chasing me. It's killing you. I don't want that."

"I have to run," said JC. "I have to try. I can't give up on you. Not so soon after finding you."

She smiled again, but there was sadness in her eyes. "I'm afraid we found each other a little too late, my sweet. I'm dead, aren't I? Only a ghost now, a memory of the person I once was."

"Yes," said JC.

"Then go back," said Kim, kindly but firmly. "There's no sense in both of us being dead. So far, I haven't seen anything to recommend it. You have your whole life ahead of you. All the years that were stolen from me. So go back, find someone else, someone with a future, and love her. Forget me, and be happy."

"I could no more forget you than I could forget me," said JC. "It wouldn't be living, and it wouldn't be love if it wasn't you."

"Now that is crap, and you know it," said Kim. "You hardly know me. And no-one ever really dies of a broken heart. You will forget me, and you will move on, because that's what people do."

"It's not what I do," said JC. "Don't give up, Kim. Because I won't. I will follow you wherever this force takes you. I will find you wherever he hides you, and I will break you free and take you up out of this place and into the light again. Because that is what I do."

"And then what?" said Kim. "I'll still be a ghost. What kind of life could we have together?"

JC grinned at her. "I'll think of something. Don't push me; I'm still working this out as I go along. Never give up hope, Kim."

"Never," she said.

Kim started to drift backwards again. JC went after her at his own pace, refusing to be hurried. Kim's speed remained the same, and JC smiled inwardly. It seemed he'd achieved some measure of control over the situation.

And then she and he rounded the corner into the next passageway, and JC stopped abruptly. Kim kept going, floating slowly but steadily backwards down the corridor, her feet dangling a good few inches above the thousands of razor blades covering the floor. Jammed in sideways, their glistening sharp edges pointing upwards. Thousands of them, covering the floor from one end of the corridor to the other, blue steel gleaming brightly in the fierce electric light. Kim kept going until she reached the far end, then stopped. JC's heart sank as he realised there was no way past the razor blades and no way round them.

His shoes wouldn't protect him for long. The blades would slice through the soles in half a dozen steps, then there would be nothing between his feet and the razor-sharp blades. And once he fell . . . it would be a bad way to die, crawling across the razor blades, bleeding out slowly.

He looked at Kim, held motionless at the end of the corridor, and she seemed miles away. Once again the chase had been stopped, so she could watch him suffer and die because of her. This unseen enemy really did love his mind games. It was saying to Kim, *How much is this man prepared to do, how far is he prepared to go, how much will he risk to come after you?* And JC had to wonder: *Why does the enemy care? Why doesn't it just kill me?*

JC knelt before the first row of razor blades, hardened his mind against all illusion, and stretched out a single finger. The nearest steel blade sliced into his fingertip so gently he didn't even feel it until he saw the blood welling up. Then he felt the pain and snatched his hand back to suck thoughtfully at the wounded finger. So, real blood and real pain. If this was an illusion, it was such a powerful one his body believed in it. JC frowned, concentrating, remembering how the Institute had taught him to walk barefoot across live coals. He'd protested about that very loudly at the time, demanding to know when such a thing would ever come in handy. But the Institute had insisted, and he'd learned. It was all about faith, and balance. JC smiled briefly, took a slow, calming breath, and stepped lightly up onto the first row of razor blades. He stood there, for a moment, centring himself, then walked slowly and deliberately forward across the sea of razor blades.

He took his time about it, letting each foot come down calmly and naturally, never once looking down but always straight ahead, at Kim. She was smiling widely, hardly daring to believe what she was seeing. He walked on, and it felt like walking on solid ground. He took no damage, and he felt no pain. Knowing all the time that if he flinched, or lost concentration, even for a moment, he would stumble and fall, all his weight crashing down onto the tightly packed steel blades.

And he would not rise again from a fall like that.

Thunder exploded in the narrow corridor, close and huge and deafeningly loud. The sheer sound of it vibrated in his bones and shuddered through his flesh. Lightning stabbed down out of nowhere, melting patches of razor blades into puddles of molten steel. The lightning was close enough to JC that he could feel the tingling on his skin, but it never hit him. The storm roared all around him, but he walked steadily right through the raging heart of it. The air was blisteringly hot, then bitingly cold, and Kim convulsed in the air before him, crying out as though tormented. But JC would not allow himself to be disturbed. Inside his head he was calm and serene, untouched by the untrustworthy world, his concentration fierce and unyielding. The enemy was playing games with him, and that thought made JC calmly, coldly, implacably determined to press on, rescue Kim, and take his revenges.

He came at last to the end of the corridor and stepped down from the last of the razor blades. Kim was yanked suddenly backwards, hauled out of sight around the corner into the next corridor. JC went after her. There were no more razor blades before him, and he didn't look back. The air was still and quiet and normal. But when

JC rounded the corner, the corridor ahead was packed full of spider-webs.

"Aren't you repeating yourself?" JC said loudly, but there was no reply.

Kim hung in the air at the far end of the passage, and between her and JC, huge masses of dirty grey spider-webs filled up all the space. They hung down from the ceiling and clung to both walls: thick sticky strands, trembling slightly, and thick grey veils that pulsed slowly. And before JC, hanging in mid air, strung up in thick and nasty cocoons, were Happy and Melody. Or at least, what was left of them.

JC's breath caught in his throat, and his heart hammered painfully in his chest, but he wouldn't let any of it show in his face. He wouldn't give his unseen enemy even that small satisfaction. JC moved slowly forward. Happy and Melody were both dead. They had to be dead. They were . . . shrunken, desiccated, what was left of their faces little more than skin and bone. As though all the living juices had been sucked out of them. Deep dark holes had been burrowed into their guts, great areas of flesh eaten away. As JC watched, a single dark spider pulled itself out of Happy's empty left eye socket and scurried quickly across Happy's unmoving features. JC stood before what was left of his good friends and colleagues, and could hardly breathe at all.

You shouldn't have left us behind. You shouldn't have left us alone. We didn't stand a chance, without you. If you had stayed, we'd still be alive. This is all your fault.

"Shut up! You aren't dead!" JC said loudly. "You can't be dead. I would have known. I would have felt it."

He lurched forward, tearing the grey veils apart with

his bare hands. They clung to his fingers and stuck to his face, but he brushed them roughly away and kept going. He plunged through the webbing, refusing to be slowed by it, but when he came to the two cocoons holding what was left of his friends, they remained stubbornly firm and solid, and he had to push and force his way between them. The webbing seized him from all sides, resisting his progress and tearing only slowly and reluctantly. JC pressed on, refusing to be stopped, but in that moment when he was caught between the two cocoons, shouldering them aside to get past, Happy and Melody opened their eyes and looked at him. Three dead eyes, bereft of feeling or Humanity, but full of awful, hard-won knowledge. JC paused despite himself, and Happy and Melody spoke to him in the soft whispering voices of the dead.

"I hate being dead," said Melody. "I can't stand it. Everyone cries here."

"They should have told us what it was like," said Happy. "They should have warned us. They should have told us about the Houses of Pain."

"You'll be with us soon," said Melody. "You won't like it."

"They keep a special place here, for people like you," said Happy. "For those who betray their friends."

"You're not Happy and you're not Melody and you're not real!" yelled JC. He tore at the webbing with desperate hands, forcing a way through, leaving the figures and their cocoons behind. They stopped talking, but JC could still hear them crying. He fought his way through the webs to the end of the corridor, then it all went suddenly quiet. JC didn't look back to see if the webbing and the cocoons had disappeared.

Kim moved on, and JC went after her.

....

Maybe it ran out of corridors, or maybe it ran out of tricks, but eventually JC followed Kim through a particularly low-arched entranceway and found himself on an unfamiliar platform. He stopped to get his breath and looked around, wondering why he felt so strongly and obscurely disturbed. He didn't recognise anything. Not only had he never been on this platform, he wasn't sure anyone had. Everything looked different, felt different . . . subtly *alien*, as though he'd stepped out of the world he knew and into some new and very dangerous place. It was a Tube station platform, but more like Oxford Circus seen through a distorting mirror. The overhead lights flickered, plunging this part of the platform and that into patches of impenetrable gloom. The station's name wasn't Oxford Circus. Instead, daubed on the far wall in old dried blood, was a single phrase.

ET IN INFERNO EGO.

There was no destination map, and the posters on the wall beside him made no sense at all. The landscapes and views were alien and unsettling and utterly inhuman. Houses made out of porcelain, horribly fragile and sickeningly gaudy. Hanging gardens tumbled down the sides of ruined office buildings, with long grey fronds twitching hungrily. Seas and skies of unknown colours, and the shadows of things passing by. The scenes seemed to shift and stir, sluggishly, as though the posters were dreaming.

Kim floated in mid air at the very end of the platform, rising and falling slowly, her feet dangling helplessly above the platform, her great mane of red hair streaming away from her as though she were underwater. Her eyes were fixed only on JC, and she was still trying to smile for him. He started slowly, cautiously, down the platform, and she stayed where she was, waiting for him. He stopped before her, still careful to maintain a respectful distance, and again they talked. In quiet, low, confidential voices.

"I'm remembering more," said Kim. "About how I died. I was murdered, wasn't I?"

"Yes," said JC. "I'm so sorry."

"Why would anyone want to kill me?" said Kim, plaintively. "I'm not anyone important, or special. Or at least I wasn't. Damn. I can see I'm going to have to work on my tenses."

"Everyone's important," said JC. "First thing they teach you, in this job."

"You're sweet," said Kim. "JC . . . If all else fails, promise me you'll find whoever it was that killed me. And make him pay. I never thought of myself as the kind of person who believes in vengeance, never thought of myself as vindictive . . . but I suppose death changes you."

"I will find him," said JC. "And I will make him pay for what he did to you. Whatever it takes."

"I wish I'd met you before. There was never anyone special while I was alive. Never anyone who mattered. I was young, I was enjoying myself, and I thought I had all the time in the world . . . Was there ever anyone, for you?"

"No," said JC. "No-one special. I guess I was waiting for you."

"I think you've left it a bit late," said Kim.

They laughed quietly together.

"I love you, Kim," said JC. "A bit sudden, I know, but . . ."

"I know," said Kim. "We have to say what we need to say, and say it now, because who knows how much time we'll have together. I love you, JC. However this all works out. If nothing else . . . I'll have one good memory to take into the dark with me. Do you know where we go, when we . . . go?"

"Not for sure," said JC.

"Terrific," said Kim.

"It's all a mess, isn't it?" said JC. "We shouldn't be doing this. Our feelings make us vulnerable. The enemy will hurt you to get at me."

"How can he hurt me?" said Kim. "I'm dead. The worst thing that can ever happen to me has already happened. Who is this enemy, anyway? What does he want with you, and me? What's going on here, JC?"

"Damned if I know," said JC. "But I'm beginning to think it may be more of a What than a Who. Can you see, or feel, anything? The dead can see many things that are hidden from the living."

"At some point you're going to have to tell me how you know things like that," said Kim. "Hmmm . . . I seem to see, or sense, a whole new direction I never knew was there, before. There's something there . . . but I'm afraid to look too closely. It would be like taking a final, irrevocable step, admitting I was no longer alive and limited to the things that only living people can do. I don't feel dead. I don't! I still feel human things, living things; and I'm afraid to give up on them because that would mean giving up on you, JC, and how I feel about you."

"Then don't do it," JC said immediately. "Look away. Dealing with things like this is my business. I'll find out Who or What is behind all this and make them pay. That's what I do."

"I love it when you sound all cocky and confident," said Kim. "It gives me hope. Tell me . . . what does JC stand for?"

"Josiah Charles," said JC, after a moment.

"Ah." Kim considered this, for a moment, then smiled broadly. "JC is fine."

"I thought so," said JC.

"Why is life so unfair? Why did I have to die to find true love?"

"Life's like that," said JC. "And death, too, sometimes."

From out of the darkness, at the end of the platform, there came the sudden thunder of an approaching train. It beat on the air like the roar of some great, hungry, beast. JC moved forward automatically, to put his body between Kim and the approaching train, to protect her. Kim giggled, despite herself.

"JC, sweetie, I'm a ghost, remember? I don't need protecting."

"Being dead doesn't necessarily mean you're beyond all harm," said JC.

"What?" said Kim. "I'm not safe even now I'm dead? How unfair is that? And exactly when were you planning to tell me that?"

"I just did. Can we concentrate on the on-coming threat, please?"

"We will have words about this later," said Kim.

"Oh joy," said JC.

The growing roar of sound became too loud for further conversation, then the train slammed into the station. The compressed air blasted ahead of the engine stank so badly that JC actually recoiled from it. The train roared past him, dripping blood, as though it had been doused in gallons of the stuff, and behind it came cars covered in graffiti, daubed in fresh blood. Some of it was still running down the steel sides. As the cars slowed to a halt in the station, JC recognised some of the graffitied words, and he winced despite himself.

"What?" Kim said immediately. "What is it, JC? Do you know that weird writing?"

"Yes," JC said reluctantly. "It's Enochian. An artificial language created in Elizabethan times, so men could talk with angels and demons and spirits of the air."

"Enochian? I never heard of it."

"Not many have, and it's better that way. It's not a language for everyday conversation. The name comes from Enoch, the first city of men, according to the Old Testament."

"Never mind the history lesson, sweetie. Can you read it?"

"No. I really should have studied more. Though I doubt very much it's saying anything we'd want to know."

Steam curled up around the long line of cars, thick and rancid, smelling of brimstone and bitter honey, blood and shit and sour milk. Kim pulled a face.

"What is that awful stench?"

"Trust me," said JC. "You really don't want to know. Wait a minute . . . you can smell that?"

"I can see and hear," said Kim, defensively. "Why shouldn't my other senses work as well?"

"I'm going to have to get back to you on that one," said JC.

The doors slammed open, one after another, all down the long row of cars, sounding like firecrackers in Hell. Suddenly every car was illuminated from within by a fierce blood-red glow; and in that hellish light, demons glared out the windows and through the open doors, all their glowing eyes locked onto the living man and the dead woman. And then the demons laughed, a harsh, awful sound that hurt the ears of the living and the dead. They laughed and howled and stamped their misshapen feet, seething together in their packed cars like maggots in an open wound.

JC's blood ran cold at the sight of them. His heart lurched in his chest, and he could barely get his breath. These were no traditional, medieval demons, with scarlet skin and barbed tails, claws and fangs and batwings. No simple distortions of Humanity, like those old familiar monsters carved into stone on churches and cathedrals all over Europe. These were the real thing, low-level demons made flesh and bone so they could operate in the material plane. The dregs of the damned, the gutter sweepings of Hell.

They wore forms calculated to horrify, intended to disgust. Shapes that held only a little Humanity, the better for Humanity to be mocked and insulted. Sin made plain in flesh and bone, stamped with the imprint of all the evil they had ever done. Monsters, in the flesh and in the soul, they all bore the mark of the Beast upon them. There were claws and fangs, cloven hooves and membranous batwings, distorted forms and exaggerated sexual characteristics, barbed tentacles and needle teeth crammed into round lamprey mouths . . . but that was incidental. All you had to do was look into their eyes to know all you needed to know. That they were evil, and they gloried in it. Some stamped impatiently on the floor, some scuttled along the windows, some hung down from the ceilings. And some crawled back and forth over and across the others like oversized insects.

Hell had come to town, looking to play.

They laughed and howled and leered at JC and Kim, held back only by some unheard command, some unseen authority. JC glared right back at them.

"Am I supposed to be impressed by this?" he said loudly. "Am I supposed to be intimidated by this half-arsed fun-house ghost train? I've fucked scarier-looking things than you!"

"Really?" said Kim.

"Never let the truth get in the way of a good insult," said JC.

"I see," said Kim. "Something else for us to discuss later."

"Look, I really am rather busy at the moment . . ."

And then Kim cried out, as the unseen force took hold of her again and hauled her backwards all the way down the length of the platform. JC ran after her, goaded by the awful laughter of the demons, but he couldn't catch up. He was helpless to do anything but watch as Kim was thrown through the open doors of the front car, right into the midst of the waiting demons. They fell upon her, and she disappeared in a moment, swarmed over by vile and vicious things.

JC ran to the front car, and the doors slammed together in his face at the very last moment. He hammered on them with his fists, then hit them with his shoulder, but the doors wouldn't budge. He pounded on the windows, but his fists made no impression. He pressed his face against one window and screamed Kim's name, but if she made any sound, it was lost in the triumphant howling of the demons.

The train pulled slowly out of the station, not hurrying, taking its time, and JC ran alongside it, half out of his mind. He shouted threats and pleas and promises as he beat at the moving windows with his bare hands and tried to force open the closed doors as one by one they passed him by. The train sped up, leaving him behind. JC's fear and rage turned cold, and a fierce, implacable purpose took over. He waited for the last car, then threw himself onto the end of the train, hanging on to the end door with both hands. The train speeded up and roared away, plunging into the darkness of the tunnel; and JC went with it.

꜒꜒꜒꜒꜒꜒꜒꜒꜒꜒꜒꜒꜒꜒꜒꜒꜒꜒꜒꜒꜒꜒

The only light was the hellish crimson glow spilling out of the car windows and end door. The train rattled and swerved, as though trying to throw JC off, but he held on grimly with one hand while searching through his jacket pockets with the other. He finally pulled out a withered monkey's paw that had been crudely made into a Hand of Glory, in defiance of all international laws and conventions. Just one of the many things JC wasn't supposed to know about, let alone possess. Not actually black magic, as such, but close enough that you could damn your soul using it in the wrong way. JC was a great believer in all the modern technology the Institute provided; but sometimes you had to go Old School on your enemies, and to hell with the consequences.

The slender wrinkled fingers on the monkey's paw had been made into crude candles, complete with wicks, and when JC forced out the exact Word of Power, they all burst into flames at once, activating the Hand. A properly operated Hand of Glory can undo any lock, open any door, and reveal any secret. The end door of the hell train was no match for it and sprang open so suddenly it nearly threw JC off. He hung on to the door precariously with one hand, the rails shooting by beneath his dangling feet. The turbulence of the racing train buffeted him viciously back and forth, but his grip held, even as his fingers screamed at him; because he knew that letting go of the door would mean letting go of Kim. And he would die before he did that.

He waved the Hand of Glory sharply to put out the flames and stuffed it back into his jacket pocket. Only then did he use both hands to grab the open door and haul himself forward into the car. The door slammed shut behind him, and JC took a moment to crouch on the rocking steel floor and get his breath back. His head was spinning, he was shaking all over, and his heart felt like it was trying to leap out of his chest. It was at times like this that JC really wished he went to the gym more often. Or at all.

He forced himself back onto his feet, and looked around. The car was empty, its light surprisingly normal. And then a bitterly cold wind blew up out of nowhere and slapped him bluntly in the face. The cold soaked into him, biting at his bare hands and face, stealing away all sensation even as it numbed his brain and slowed his thoughts. This was the cold of the space between worlds, untouched by the warmth of suns, cold enough to blast the soul. One of the many faces of Hell; a taste of what was to come. A slow certain knowledge came to JC then—that if he insisted on going on, if he persisted in his attempt to rescue Kim . . . he would die. And his soul

would be trapped on the hell train forever, or at least
until such time as the Institute sent a team to exorcise it
and him. JC knew that, as surely and certainly as he
knew anything, and didn't give a damn. It might be true,
or it might not; you couldn't trust anything on a hell
train. But even if someone he trusted had told him he
was doomed, and damned, he would have gone on anyway. Because Kim needed him. So he thrust his face into
the bitter cold wind, stamped his frozen feet, and forced
himself down the length of the car, one hard step at a
time. Forcing himself on, against everything the train
could throw at him.

　　Because in the end that's what love is. To go on, despite everything, driven by hope and faith alone.

　　　　　　　　　,,,,,,,,,,,,,,,,,,,,,,,,,,

The door at the end of the car opened abruptly before
him, then the door into the next, and he stepped through
into the crimson hell glare of demon territory and the
company of Hell. Dozens of the creatures filled the car
from end to end, packed in tight, facing him with antici-
patory smiles, with teeth and claws and long, barbed
arms with too many joints. Foul, horrid things with inhuman needs and appetites made clear in their misshapen
flesh, all the better to inflict suffering upon the living.
They laughed in JC's face and stamped their cloven
hooves upon the steel floor.

　　JC laughed right back in their awful faces, and the
demons actually paused a moment, taken aback. They
weren't used to being so openly defied and mocked, in
the face of certain torment and slow death. The sight of
them was usually enough to drive mortals out of their

minds. JC struck a studiedly casual pose and addressed the waiting host of Hell with contemptuous disdain.

"I don't know if you really are demons called up out of Hell or only living extensions of my unseen enemy; and I don't give a damn. It doesn't matter what you are. You stand between me and my Kim; and I am here to rescue her. Get in my way, and I swear I will strike you down like the hammer of God."

The cold, certain implacability in his voice held the demons motionless. And in that long, extended moment, JC took out a heavy brass knuckle-duster and slipped it onto his left hand. He reached down with his other hand and drew from a concealed ankle sheath a long, rune-etched silver dagger. He showed both weapons to the demons and laughed as they seethed uncertainly. JC took a glass phial from his inside coat pocket, pulled out the rubber stopper with his teeth, and spat it away. And then he poured some of the holy water over his silver blade and some over the knuckle-duster. He drank the rest, tossed the empty phial aside, and smiled a really nasty death's-head smile at the demons assembled before him.

"All right, you ugly pieces of shit. Let's do it."

He strode forward, weapons at the ready. Not to punish the demons, or to take vengeance for all the missing commuters, or even to strike them down for what they were. He was doing what was needed to reach and rescue Kim because that mattered more to him than life itself.

To fight with demons, your intent must be pure. And even then, there's no guarantee you'll win.

The demon host rose up before him, and he hit them

hard, lashing out with his silver blade and punching in misshapen faces with his brass knuckles. The silver blade sliced cleanly through demon flesh, opening them up like garbage bags. They fell screaming and howling to the floor, their steaming insides spilling out even as they tried to stuff them back in. The brass knuckles shattered bones and stove in fanged mouths, and the touch of the blessed metal was enough to burn demon flesh. JC worked his way forward, one step at a time, striking down the demons with a cold, implacable fury and trampling them underfoot. They fell before him, shocked and dismayed, unable to believe any mere mortal could do this to them.

JC fought his way into the midst of them, never dodging or ducking, always pressing forward, right into the teeth of anything they could do to him. He struck the demons down and stamped on their heads and sides, forcing his way through the whole pack of them. All the way down the car, to the next door, then through the door and into the next car, where a whole new host waited for him. JC fought on, opening up a path through the demon horde using sheer brute courage and tenacity, and a simple dogged refusal to be stopped or turned aside while Kim still needed him.

They hurt him horribly, but he kept going. Jagged claws sliced and tore through his flesh and grated on the bones beneath. Heavy blows knocked him this way and that, but he wouldn't fall. Sharp-toothed jaws buried themselves in his flesh, and even found his face more than once. Blood-stained and terribly injured, he kept going, ignoring the pains that threatened to drain his strength and resolve, ignoring the blood that poured from him and dripped down to steam on the hot floor. JC threw himself at the leering demon faces before him, giving blow for blow and hurt for hurt, and never once allowed himself to be stopped, or slowed. Claws came at him from every side, teeth buried themselves in arms and legs and had to be jerked or shaken free. Overlong arms tried to wrap themselves around him and drag him down. But still, he went on. Sometimes he cried out, and sometimes he sobbed, and sometimes he roared and cursed and spat at the snarling faces before him; but none of it meant anything. He had a thing to do, and he was going to do it.

Despite everything he did, and everything that was done to him, he thought only of Kim. And what the demons might be doing to her. Being dead was no defence against the torments of Hell. He went on, and not all the demons on the hell train could deny him.

Until finally JC fought his way through to the last car but one; and there, at last, they stopped him. Because in the end, he was only a man, with a man's limits. The demons blocked the way to the next car through sheer strength of numbers, their horrid shapes packing the car from wall to wall and floor to ceiling. They surrounded JC, coming at him from every direction at once. And so, finally, he was forced to a halt and stood swaying in the middle of the car: a ragged, tattered, and bloody mess of a man. His wonderful cream suit was ruined, soaked and stained with his blood and that of the demons. He had been cut and gouged and torn open, and a long trail of blood lay behind him. He had to keep spitting out blood because it kept filling his mouth. He could feel broken and splintered ribs grinding against each other with every breath, tearing into his lungs; and he was tired, so terribly tired. Every movement hurt him, and lifting his savaged arms was an effort that would have made him cry out if he'd had any voice left. But he'd worn it out screaming, several cars back.

The demons blocked his way, but still he lurched forward and struck out at them with stubborn fury. Because they stood between him and Kim. He was close by then; he could feel her presence. He was damned if he'd be stopped. Not after he'd come so far. He called out Kim's name, a single breathy rasp of sound; but the demons howled and shouted him down, mocking him by yelling out her name in their sick and rotten voices.

JC swung his silver blade, and missed, and a demon surged forward. Its vicious jaws snapped together and bit off three of JC's fingers. He hardly noticed the pain; it was one more, among so many others. He looked down stupidly as the silver blade fell from his mutilated hand, and blood jetted from the stumps of his missing fingers. And while he hesitated, thrown off-balance for a moment, a clawed hand came sweeping round and sliced clean through both his eyes.

Blood filled his view, then darkness, and a sudden agony roared inside his head. He howled in rage and loss, and lashed out blindly with his knuckle-duster and his maimed hand. It didn't feel like he hit anything. He could feel viscous tears running down his face, blood and vitreous fluids from his ruined eyes. He could hear mocking demon laughter all around him. Claws cut at him from every side at once, darting in and out again, taunting and mocking him. A set of heavy jaws fastened on to his right hip, worrying right through to the bone, and he couldn't shake them off. He staggered and almost fell, blind and alone, flailing helplessly around himself, shouting incoherent defiance; his only regret was that in dying he had failed Kim.

I'm sorry, Kim, he said, or thought he said. *I'm so sorry.*

And then, incredibly, he could see again. A great Light blazed up within him, filling him from top to bottom, and burst from his eyes. The demons screamed in rage and horror to see it, and fell back, unable to face the terrible Light that blazed from JC's miraculously restored eyes. And still the Light blazed through JC, growing stronger and more terrible, building and building until it seemed impossible one small mortal frame could hold it all. The Light healed and restored JC, repairing all his wounds in a moment and filling him with incredible new energy. JC stood tall and strong in the middle of the car, surrounded by weeping, terrified demons, crouching and shrinking away from him; and he laughed in their terrified faces.

He hadn't called for the Light, or expected it; but he had heard of such things. That sometimes, on very rare occasions, there was a Light that would come as a gift from Outside, from some great Force in the afterworlds . . . but it was rare, so very rare. Certainly he had never thought of himself as worthy. But the Light was there, and it was his to use, and he was strong and whole again. He looked about him, and thought he'd never seen so clearly before. He raised his hands, and they were both whole again. He dropped the pitted and scorched knuckle-duster. He didn't need it any more. He strode forward, towards the end car, and Kim.

Some of the demons tried to fight him, only to quickly learn they couldn't. They couldn't face the Light that

shone from his restored eyes or match the new strength
that filled his arms. He beat them down, shattering their
bones and tearing their foul bodies apart with his bare
hands. His touch was enough to blister and burn demon
flesh; and even their strongest blows couldn't hurt him
any more. The Light blazed ever more fiercely within
him until all he had to do was touch the demons, and
they burned up in a moment, leaving nothing behind but
ashes.

Most of the remaining demons disappeared. They ran
away, falling back into Hell rather than face what he had
become. By the time JC reached the end of the car, the
light from his eyes was enough to make the last few
demons fade away into nothing, like the final remnants
of a bad dream.

JC looked at the closed door before him, and it melted
and ran away in streams of molten metal. The door beyond, into the next car, exploded inwards under the pressure of his gaze. And so he came at last to the end car, and
there, waiting for him, was Kim Sterling. No more demons, no hell light. Only Kim; crucified against the end
door. Glowing ectoplasmic nails hammered through her
ghostly hands and ankles. Her head hung down, her long
red hair covering her face. She didn't move. But when JC
said her name, her head came up and she saw him, and
she smiled. Their eyes met, and the Light in JC's eyes
blazed so very brightly.

The glowing nails disappeared under JC's gaze, and
Kim's ghostly flesh repaired itself at once. She flew
down the car towards him, her long white dress billow-
ing in some unfelt breeze, and JC walked in glory down
the car to meet her. They came together in the middle,

and the whole of the car was full of their love, a force so powerful it seemed to beat on the air like great wings.

JC reached out to her, and she put out her hands to take his; and his fingers passed right through hers. Because he was alive, and she was dead, he was flesh and blood and she was just a ghost; and because there were some things even the Light could not change.

They stood together, as close as they could get, looking into each other's eyes. The Light didn't bother Kim at all.

"We can never touch," said JC. "But we have each other."

"You say the sweetest things," said Kim. "You sentimental old softy. I knew you'd come for me. I knew they could never stop you."

"Well," said JC, "I'm glad one of us was sure."

They laughed quietly together. The train roared into a station and skidded to a halt. The doors opened, and JC and Kim stepped out onto what appeared to be a perfectly ordinary platform. No demons, no webbing, no illusions . . . and no-one tried to haul Kim away again. JC had broken that hold. When they looked behind them, they found the train had gone. Not departed; disappeared.

The Light within JC suddenly died down and was gone. He wasn't surprised. Such gifts were never granted for long. JC didn't think he'd miss it. He preferred being human, with its small but real comforts and rewards. He smiled at Kim, and she smiled back.

EIGHT

,,

BLOODBATH

There are some advantages to being a ghost. Kim discovered that by concentrating in a certain way, she could change the colour of her dress; and after that, there was no stopping her. Her long white dress went through a dozen different colours and styles, and then as many completely different outfits, as Kim imagined herself wearing all the expensive and stylish clothes she'd never been able to afford. She finally settled on a marvellous off-the-shoulder emerald-green creation she'd once seen in a shop window that went well with her eyes and contrasted nicely with her mane of red hair. JC had to insist she stop there, as he was getting dizzy. They were still laughing quietly together when Happy and Melody burst through the entrance beside them.

JC grinned widely to see them both safe and well but was somewhat taken aback when Happy and Melody stopped abruptly in their tracks and stared at him with something very like shock. His first thought was that they were surprised at Kim's presence; but no, they only had eyes for him. Melody in particular was looking at him as though he'd just risen from the grave.

"JC, what happened to you?" she said, open horror in her face and in her voice. "Your clothes are . . . All that blood . . . Who did this to you?"

"Hell with the suit," said Happy. "JC, what happened to your eyes?"

JC glanced at Kim, then back at his colleagues. "What's the matter with my eyes?"

"They're glowing," said Happy. "And not with any kind of light I've ever seen. It's so intense, it's like looking into a spotlight. Or possibly the headlights of an oncoming car. Those are spooky eyes, JC."

"Are you dead?" Melody said abruptly. "Is that why you're hanging out with a ghost?"

"Of course he's not dead!" said Happy. "I'd know if he were dead. This . . . is altogether more disturbing."

"But look at how much blood he's lost!" said Melody. "Look at the state of his marvellous ice-cream suit! It looks like a pack of wild dogs tried to bite it off him."

"I have wrestled with demons and defied a god," said JC. "That kind of thing does take it out of you."

"He has," said Kim. "He really has. And all for me. Isn't he wonderful?"

"Hold everything," said Happy. "You can see us? You're aware of the world around you? When did that happen?"

"A lot has happened since we . . . became separated," said JC. "Kim, allow me to present my friends and colleagues from the Carnacki Institute: Happy Jack Palmer and Melody Chambers. My friends, this is Kim Sterling.

Happy . . . what happened to your face? Did someone take a swing at you?"

"Yes," said Happy. "I did. But don't change the subject. What happened to you?"

"I rescued Kim from the grip of our unseen enemy," said JC. "And . . . we're an item now. Don't ask me how that happened. I think we're both equally baffled."

"And delighted," said Kim, reproachfully.

"Oh yes, delighted, absolutely," said JC. "I was making the point that it rather sneaked up on us when we weren't looking."

"Isn't it always like that?" said Kim. She smiled sweetly at Happy and Melody. "I'm glad JC has friends. He's going to need a lot of help and support, now that he has a ghost for a girl-friend."

"That's the spirit," said JC.

"Oh you," said Kim. She elbowed him playfully in the ribs, but her arm passed swiftly through him.

"I hate new couples," said Happy. "They're always so pleased with themselves . . . Look, you're doing the distraction thing again! What the hell have you been up to, JC? You've been blazing inside my head like a sun going supernova! That's how I was able to find you so quickly. For a while there, you were the most powerful thing in this station."

"I fought an army of demons," said JC. "And I lost. But at the very last moment . . . a Light came out of no where and made me strong enough to fight any number of them. It's gone now, but . . ."

"It's still there, in your eyes," said Melody. "The Light has put its mark on you, JC."

"And that is rare, so rare," said Happy, sounding impressed despite himself.

"I know!" said JC. "I think it's another sign of how important all this is. Whatever it is that's going on down here. Now, what have you been doing while I was away? What happened to the Project agents I left you fighting?"

"We got away," said Melody. Her voice was suddenly quiet, and she folded her arms tightly across her chest.

"They hurt us," said Happy, staring steadily at JC. "They hurt us bad. We could have used your help."

"You left us!" said Melody. "To chase after her." She couldn't even bring herself to look at Kim. "You have no idea what they did to us, JC."

"I'm sorry," said JC.

"I'm sorry," said Happy, "but you and ghost girl can't be a couple. You just can't. You know that, JC."

"You said it yourself," said Melody. "The living must never get emotionally involved with the dead. It's not fair to either of you. Love is for the living, for people with a stake in the future."

"Love conquers all," murmured Kim. "I heard it in a song, so it must be true."

"Not this time," said Melody. "You may not even have an immediate future. It's looking more and more as though you're the focal point of this haunting. The central event that supports everything else."

"Which means," Happy said slowly, "that the only way to be sure of stopping all this . . . may involve putting you to rest, Kim. Our other-dimensional Intruder is using you to maintain its hold on the material plane. Unless we remove you, and break his hold, he'll grow stronger and stronger, spreading his horror show across the whole of London. Maybe even further . . ."

"We'll exorcise that bridge when we come to it," JC

said cheerfully. "I have a plan, a scheme, and a whole bunch of really nasty dirty tricks to try out on our unseen enemy. But first things first. Kim, you're the only one to have had direct contact with the Intruder. And your dead eyes can see the greater world far more clearly than ours. What can you tell us?"

"Not much," said Kim. "I'm still getting used to being a ghost. The more I talk with you and your friends, the more awake I feel, the more me . . . But the more human I feel, the harder it is to interpret what I'm seeing and feeling. As though being human . . . limits me. I've never seen your Intruder, never heard its voice. But I seem to have this sense of . . . something wild. Something horribly powerful, beyond the laws and limitations of this small world."

"Not really what I wanted to hear," said Happy. Melody ignored him, intent on Kim.

"What's the last thing you remember?" she said bluntly. "From when you were alive?"

Kim frowned, as though trying to remember something that had happened long ago. "There was a phone call, early in the morning. From my agent, telling me I had to come in for a special audition. A really big part, he said, that could make my career. I started to ask for details, but he gave me the address and the time, and told me to hurry. I was so excited . . . I came down into the Underground, waited for my train to come, then someone stabbed me in the back. I never even saw his face. I didn't understand what had happened, at first. The pain, and falling, and the platform rising to hit me in the face. There were people all around me, but I couldn't hear what they were saying. And then . . . I was back standing on the platform, completely alone, waiting for a train that never came. I'd still be standing there if JC hadn't come and found me . . ."

"This is why I never get anywhere with women," said Happy. "I can't stand this soppy sentimental stuff."

"Trust me," said JC. "That's not the only reason."

"But . . . how does her death tie in with everything that's happened here?" said Melody. "And why has the Intruder made such a point of using her?"

"Because she's important to me?" said JC.

Melody sniffed. "Not everything is about you, JC."

"Look me in the eye and say that," said JC.

"Sounds like necromancy to me," Happy said quickly. "Murder magic. Energy generated by the destruction of a life and the loss of all the things that person might have done. Lot of energy in murder. You were lured down here just to be killed, Kim."

"I want my machines!" said Melody. "Theories are all very well, but I need hard, solid facts to work with! I have got to run some tests on you, Kim. I've never encountered such a conscious, interactive, alive-seeming post-mortem presence."

She walked quickly around Kim, several times, examining the ghost girl from all angles, much to Kim's quiet amusement.

"Most ghosts run in circles," said Melody, at least partly to herself. "Endlessly repeating old actions, old emotions, significant events. They don't react to, or interact with, the real world because they can't see it. Quite literally lost in their own worlds. The future isn't important to them because they're locked in the past." She turned abruptly to study JC. "And I'm dying to put you under the microscope and see what makes you tick.

You've changed . . . and I don't mean only those highly unsettling eyes of yours. I want to know what hosting the Light has done to you. There's a whole series of serious scientific papers in you, JC, and I want my name on them."

"You've got to do something about those eyes, JC," said Happy. "They're too disturbing for mere mortals like us. How about a nice set of designer shades?"

He produced a pair of sunglasses that might have been borderline fashionable, several years previously, and handed them to JC. He slipped them on with a certain amount of self-consciousness.

"Okay, that's weird," said Melody. "The glow is actually shining through the sunglasses."

"Well, yes," said Happy. "But it is more bearable."

"Oh yes," said Melody. "Definitely more bearable."

JC looked at Kim. "How do I look? Seriously?"

"Well, the shades do help detract from the somewhat shredded suit," said Kim. "But to be brutally honest . . . you look like a second-rate spy who's been dragged through a car wash, backwards."

"I can live with that," said JC. "Now, let us concentrate on more important problems. We need more information on our unseen Intruder. Happy, crank up your amazing mind and scan Kim. See if you can pick up any traces left behind from contact with our enemy."

"I can try." Happy smiled diffidently at Kim. "Don't worry; you won't feel a thing. I'm going to take a quick poke around through your recent past."

"Go ahead," said Kim. "I've always been pretty transparent. Little ghost humour there. Don't let me spook you."

Happy scowled, concentrating, all his attention fixed

on Kim, then he blushed suddenly and backed away. "Ah. Yes. I see. Sorry!"

"What's the matter?" said Kim. "I didn't feel anything."

"I did," said Happy. "In fact, I feel in definite need of a cold shower, and a lie-down with an instructional book. Sorry, JC . . . All I'm picking up from her is, well, love. Her love for you. Her feelings are really quite . . . overwhelming. Can't see anything else through it. I haven't felt so embarrassed since I walked in on Great-uncle Sebastian and the two parlour-maids. Haven't felt the same about feather-dusters ever since. I'm babbling, aren't I? Don't mind me. I'll go stand over there by myself and think pure thoughts for a while if that's all right with everyone."

"Stand firm, man," said JC. "You still have work to do. Scan me. See if you can identify the source of the Light that saved me."

"You don't want much," grumbled Happy. He considered JC thoughtfully for a long moment. "Hmmm . . ."

"What does that mean?" said JC. "Hmmm . . . what?"

"It would appear," Happy said carefully, "that in the hour of your greatest need, something very high up in the pecking order of the Good reached down from the afterworlds and touched you, briefly, with its power."

"Then why are you looking so concerned?" said Kim, drifting forward to stand beside JC. "Isn't that a good thing?"

"It's never a good thing when the Outer Forces start taking a direct interest in you," Happy said grimly. "Unless you want to end up as a conscript foot-soldier in their never-ending war between Light and Dark, Law and Chaos, Good and Evil."

"Well," said JC, after a moment, "who knows? Maybe I'm officer material."

And that was when Natasha Chang and Erik Grossman burst onto the platform, guns blazing. Once again, it was only Happy's last-moment apprehension of danger that allowed the Institute agents to survive. Natasha's mental shields were powerful enough to hide both her and Erik's approach, but the presence of such a strong mental shield was enough to alert Happy's well-nourished sense of paranoia. He yelled a warning and was actually diving for cover even as Natasha and Erik made their entrance through the archway. JC and Melody were off and moving even as the first bullets were fired.

Kim stayed where she was, lacking both Institute training and self-preservation instincts. She looked confusedly about as bullets punched harmlessly through her ghostly form. Melody threw herself behind a vending machine, produced her machine-pistol from somewhere about her person, and returned fire. Natasha ducked back into the archway and kept up a steady barrage on the vending machine, which jumped and shuddered as bullets slammed into its steel side.

Happy peered out from behind a row of metal seats and hit Erik with a powerful mental probe, freezing him in place. Natasha spotted her partner's plight immediately but ignored it, concentrating all her mental powers on Melody, to make her miss. Puffs of plaster flew through the air as Melody's bullets pock-marked the archway, but not one of them came anywhere near Natasha. Emboldened, she stepped forward and drew a bead on Melody. And that was when JC stepped out of the shadows, whipped off his sunglasses, and fixed the startled Natasha with his gaze. She froze in place, the gun slipping from her nerveless fingers. And then she sank abruptly to her knees, crying out and covering her eyes with both hands. Unable to face what she'd seen in JC's new eyes.

"What have you done to yourself?" Natasha said sickly. *"You're not human any more!"*

"I don't think you're in any position to judge," said JC.

....

Natasha and Erik were made to sit with their backs to the wall, hands clasped together on top of their heads. Neither of them gave any trouble. Between Happy's telepathy and JC's eyes, they felt seriously outgunned. They both looked dazed, and a little disturbed, at how easily they'd been taken down. Natasha wouldn't so much as look in JC's direction even after he put his sunglasses back on. He stood over the Project agents, frowning thoughtfully. Happy and Melody stood on either side of him, doing their best to look dangerous. Melody was the most successful at that because she still held her machine-pistol at the ready.

"Talk to me," JC said coldly. "No use playing dumb. I know who you are; I've read your files at the Institute. Natasha Chang and Erik Grossman, field agents for the Crowley Project. So what are you doing here?"

"Wouldn't you like to know," said Erik, but his heart wasn't in it.

"Happy," said JC, "see what you can dig out of them. No need to be gentle about it."

"Way ahead of you," said Happy. "I can't see much; the Project's installed really good shields. Still, this pair isn't exactly A team material; they operate on our level, more or less." He smiled nastily at Natasha. "Don't think you can keep me out forever, though. I already know things about you. You're a soul eater, you nasty little cow. And your fat friend tortures animals. For fun."

"For science!" said Erik. But he still wouldn't look up.

"What are you doing down here?" said JC. "What's your mission? Talk to me; or I'll take my shades off again."

"This is all the Project's fault, isn't it?" snapped Happy. "One of your Workings gone wrong! Your higher-ups let something nasty into our world, and you were sent down here to clean up the mess and wipe off the finger-prints."

"No!" said Natasha. She looked up at Happy, avoiding JC. "We're not here for the haunting; we're here for you. Vivienne MacAbre put a death mark on all three of you for being too good at your job. We don't like competition. Your deaths were supposed to send a message to the Institute. No-one told us what was really going on down here, or we wouldn't have come. We're no more fit to deal with a mess of this magnitude than you are."

"If you didn't know what was going on down here," Happy said craftily, "then you can't be sure the Project isn't behind it, can you? Hah! Got you there!"

"If the Project is in any way involved, it would have been decided at a much higher level than we have access to," Erik said tiredly. "All field agents are mushrooms, you know that, kept in the dark and fed shit on a regular basis. How do you know this isn't the result of some major cock-up by your higher-ups?"

"Because we don't do things like that," said Melody.

"Yeah, right," said Erik.

Happy looked at JC. "Sounds like they were dropped in the deep end, unarmed and unprepared, just like us. If you believe them, which I prefer not to, on general principles." He glared at Natasha. "And don't you think I've forgotten what you did to me, bitch. What you made me do. I can still taste blood in my mouth and feel loose teeth with my tongue. I should smack you a good one right in the mouth, so you can see what it feels like. Except that I'm a better man than that. I am. I really am. Oh the hell I am . . ."

He punched her in the mouth. Her head swung round under the impact. Happy stood over her, breathing hard. And then Natasha turned her face back and sneered at him.

"Is that it? You punch like a junkie."

Happy went to hit her again. JC grabbed his arm, stopping him. Happy glared at JC, meeting his gaze un-flinchingly.

"Why not, JC? Give me one good reason."

"Because we're supposed to be better than that."

Happy pulled his arm free. JC didn't try to hold on to him. Happy sniffed. "You might be, JC. I'm still work-ing on it."

"You don't know what they did to him, JC," said Melody. "What they did to us when you weren't there to protect us. That little toad used a taser on me. Over and over again. And laughed while he did it." Melody's machine-pistol moved closer to Erik's head, as though pulling Melody's hand behind it. "You have no idea how much it hurt, JC. My gut muscles still ache. You don't know how helpless and violated he made me feel while he hurt me. Do we really need both of them alive, JC?"

"Yes," he said. "If you feel the need to do something,

you can search them both for weapons. Feel free to be exceedingly thorough."

"Sounds good to me," said Melody.

She stuck the barrel of her pistol under Natasha's chin and made her stand up. Then she made Natasha turn around and lean forward against the wall, with all her weight on her hands. Melody searched Natasha from head to toe, with a carefully impersonal roughness. She found a whole bunch of hidden pockets and concealed pouches, and soon a small pile of assorted weapons and devices had formed at Natasha's feet. Melody checked her over twice, to be sure, then stood back and allowed Natasha to turn around. The Project agent looked at the pile on the ground and smiled disarmingly.

"A girl should always be prepared."

"Shut up," said Melody.

She was even more thorough, and rougher, with Erik. His pile of weapons and assorted weird shit turned out to be even bigger than Natasha's. Including several guns, three knives, a full surgeon's kit, a whole bunch of arcane items that Melody was careful to handle only with her fingertips and at arm's length, and an Aboriginal pointing bone.

"Oh goody," said Happy. "I've always wanted one of those."

"Hands off, man," JC said sternly. "You know very well you're not allowed killing tools." He nodded to Melody, and she tucked the bone away in one of her inside pockets. She then searched Erik again, and when she finally gave up and stood back, he turned around and smiled at her.

"Thank you. A little rougher next time, perhaps. Still, was it good for you, too?"

Melody kneed him briskly in the groin and walked away. Erik bent painfully forward.

"I do wish people would stop doing that."

"You're weird," said Happy. "And I know weird." He looked at the pack on Erik's back. "Melody . . ."

"He can keep his cat computer," said Melody. "I don't want anything to do with the nasty thing."

"Maybe you should take a few pills, Happy," Natasha said sweetly. "Oh yes, we know all about your little adventures in chemistry. You should really be working for us. We don't have to hide our vices, at the Crowley Project; we glory in them. They make us stronger." And then she looked at JC, and Kim. "Although there are limits. What is *that* doing here, JC?"

"She's with me," said JC.

"With you?" Natasha looked like she wanted to spit. "And you have the brass balls to look down on us? Such relationships have always been strictly forbidden! You know that! The living and the dead cannot join together! It's . . . unnatural!"

"So it's all right to eat ghosts," said JC. "But not love them?"

"Yes! Exactly!" said Natasha. "Pervert!"

"Ectophile!" said Erik. "I may puke."

"That's enough," said JC, and immediately Natasha and Erik looked away, unable to meet his gaze, even muffled behind sunglasses.

And then everyone on the platform looked round sharply, as the sound of something large and heavy approaching blasted out of the far tunnel-mouth. The deafening roar drew steadily nearer, building and building until the platform itself began to shake and tremble beneath their feet.

"What the hell . . . ?" said Melody.

"It's not a train," said Happy. "Doesn't sound even a bit like a train."

"Could be another hell train," said JC, again moving automatically to put his body between Kim and danger.

"I don't think so," she said.

And then a great dark tidal wave of crimson blood slammed out of the tunnel-mouth, pouring into the station and swamping the rails. More blood gushed out of the other tunnel-mouth, and when the two crimson waves met in the middle of the station, they pounded together so hard the blood flew up to slap the ceiling. More blood came pouring in, blasting out of both tunnel-mouths at once as though it was under tremendous pressure, forced on by more behind. Gallons and gallons of the dark red blood poured in, as though an ocean of blood had found an opening into the everyday world. The stench was appalling, filling the air. The level of the blood rose quickly, lapping against the side of the platform. By the time they had all gathered their senses enough to start backing away, the blood had already overrun the edge of the platform and spilled across the yellow safety line. And still more blood came rushing in, from both sides at once. JC turned to the exit, only to step quickly aside as a great rush of blood surged through the archway, spilling across the platform. Everyone backed quickly away.

Kim hovered in mid air, keeping her feet well above the rising level of blood; but the others had no such escape. The blood was already up to their ankles and rising fast. The spoiled-carrion stench of the stuff was overpowering. Melody glared at Happy.

"Is this real? Or another illusion?"

"Of course it's real, it's already past my ankles! Can't you smell it? This is extremely real blood; though I hate to think where it's all coming from."

"Not just blood," said Erik. He dipped a fingertip into the rising blood and sucked it thoughtfully. "This is human blood."

"How can you be so sure?" said Melody.

"Trust me," said Natasha. "You really don't want to know."

"I think you can forget about rescuing any of those poor lost commuters," said Erik. "I wonder what it's done with the bones . . ."

"Look, this blood really is rising very quickly," said Happy. "If we don't find a way out of here soon, we're going to be swimming in the stuff. Until it reaches the ceiling . . ."

JC looked at him, then at Natasha. "You're telepaths. Our enemy has to be behind this, controlling the blood. So, working together, could you disrupt his control?"

"Not a hope in hell," said Happy. "We have to find a way out of here!"

"Keep calm, man," said JC. "Panic never solved anything."

"It's always worked for me!" said Happy.

JC produced his monkey's paw and activated the Hand of Glory. The others stared at the thing, fascinated.

"Where the hell did you get that?" said Melody, genuinely shocked.

"Yes, JC," said Natasha. "Where did a Goody Two-shoes like you get hold of a forbidden artefact like that?"

"Could you get me one, too?" said Erik.

"A Hand of Glory can reveal hidden doors and exits," said JC, waving the Hand this way and that. "But unfortunately . . . it seems there aren't any. What you see is what you get; and they're all full of blood."

"I need some of my pills," said Happy.

"Could I have some, too?" said Erik.

Melody lost her footing and fell, slipping under the rising blood. Happy surged forward, blood splashing up against his chest. He thrust an unerring hand beneath the surface, grabbed Melody, and hauled her back up onto her feet again. She clung to him, hacking and coughing, soaked in blood. Happy held her until she got her second wind, then she pushed herself away from him, and he let her go.

"Thanks," she said roughly.

"Try not to be so sentimental" said Happy. "Oh God, I'm going to smell of this blood for months, I know it."

"Hold it!" Natasha said abruptly. "Listen . . ."

They all stood very still, listening. The roar of the inrushing blood seemed to swamp everything else.

"What is it?" said JC.

"There's something in here with us," said Natasha, looking quickly around her. "Can you feel it, Happy?"

"Yes," he said slowly. "There's something . . . in the blood. Something hungry."

They all turned this way and that, but the dark red surface of the blood was all but impenetrable. JC bent forward and stuck his face right next to the surface. And perhaps it was his new eyes, but he thought he saw large dark shapes, moving in the blood . . .

"Get back-to-back!" Erik yelled suddenly. "Don't let them sneak up on us!"

"What is it?" said Melody. "You think we're under attack by sharks?"

"No! Vampires! There are vampires swimming in the blood!"

As though in answer to his naming them, several of the creatures leapt out of the blood, showing themselves to their new prey. The vampires of the blood ocean had shape-shifted into a new hunting form, long sleek shapes with all of a shark's brute power. They had great lashing tails, pale grey scales, and two long arms with clawed hands, to stuff food into the wide mouths that took up most of their blunt heads. They had flat black eyes, without a single human emotion in them, and their mouths held row upon row of cruel, jagged teeth.

One went for JC, and he hit it in the head. It immediately sank back into the blood and disappeared. Melody opened fire with her machine-pistol, and the heavy bullets blew great chunks out of the vampire nearest her; but the wounds healed almost immediately. The vampire sharks drew back a little, considering, as they circled the small knot of people. They swam easily through the blood, as though they'd been born to it, and JC wondered briefly where the Intruder had found such foul creatures. In what bloody alien sea were such things spawned . . . ?

"Before anybody asks, yes, they are quite definitely real!" said Happy. He seemed to be on the edge of hysteria. "I can feel their bloodlust in my head. I'm getting brief flashes of their thoughts, and I do wish I weren't. They were brought here from Somewhere Else by the Intruder. It's another sign of how powerful it's becoming."

"It's planning something," said JC. "And it must see us as a real threat to its purposes if it's trying this hard to stop us."

"Really," said Happy. "How about that? Colour me surprised. Bloody do something!"

A vampire shark reared up out of the blood, its mouth

stretched wide, its clawed hands reaching for Melody. It was almost upon her before she brought her pistol to bear and opened fire. Once again, the bullets slammed into its flesh, blowing whole chunks away. But this time the wounds didn't heal, and the creature fell helplessly back into the blood, thrashing wildly as more bullets tore into it. Others of its kind surged forward to attack the wounded creature and feast on its flesh. The bloody sea churned and frothed. It was past everyone's waist now, and still rising.

"Wooden bullets," said Melody, breathlessly. "I changed magazines. I've always believed in being prepared, too."

"How many wooden bullets have you got?" said JC.

"That was most of them," Melody admitted.

Another vampire shark reared up, exploding into the air and splashing blood right into Natasha's face. The creature's clawed hands slammed down onto her shoulders, the mouth opening wide enough to bite off her whole head. JC spun round and punched the thing in the side. Ribs cracked and broke under the blow, and the creature fell back from Natasha. JC hit it again, in the head, and felt as much as heard the vampire's thick skull collapse under the blow. The vampire fell back, mouth stretched wide in agony, and Happy deftly tossed a handful of pills into its mouth. The vampire's jaws snapped closed automatically, then the whole long body convulsed, and it thrashed helplessly in the blood, as the other vampires turned on it. Natasha shot JC a grateful smile.

"You saved my life . . ."

"I helped," said Happy.

"You saved me, JC. I won't forget that."

Kim sensed a moment coming on and quickly intervened. "Hello? Still lots of vampires all around you, and the blood is rising! Get away, you. Shoo."

A vampire snapped at her foot, dangling directly above the blood, and its jaws slammed harmlessly together.

JC glared about him, thinking hard. The vampire sharks were still circling, though at a slightly wider radius, made wary by their failures. Why were they so determined to attack?

"Happy, these vampires are swimming in blood. Any idea why they're so keen to taste ours?"

"Apparently there's nothing like the real thing," said Happy. "The need to hunt and feed from the source is built into them at the genetic level. I really think we need to get out of here, JC."

"I'm working on it!"

JC's gaze fell upon the far tunnel-mouth, three-quarters full of blood. No way out that way . . . but it did give him a sudden inspiration.

"Listen," he said urgently. "I fought and banished a whole army of demons on a hell train, and once it was empty, the train let Kim and me off at this station. The train then disappeared. Vanished. It could still be out there, somewhere in the Underground system . . . If we could summon it back here, maybe we could use it to escape!"

There was a pause, as everyone considered that.

"Have you got any other ideas?" said Happy.

"It could work!" said JC.

"Yeah, and monkeys could fly out of my butt writing Shakespeare's plays as they went!" said Natasha.

"It's our only chance to get out of here," said JC.

"It's a great idea!" said Erik. "I love this idea! I want

to marry this idea and have its babies! But could we please get a move on because the blood really is getting very close to my chin now!"

"Serves you right for being such a short-arse," said Melody. "JC, how the hell are we supposed to control a hell train? One that presumably works for, and takes its instructions from, the same Intruder that's trying to drown us all in blood?"

"I'd bet Happy's and Natasha's minds against a hell train any day," said JC.

The two telepaths looked at each other.

"Might work," said Happy.

"Agents of the Institute and the Project, working together in common cause, against a common enemy?" said Natasha. "If word of this ever gets out, I'll never hear the end of it. Still, needs must when the Devil vomits in your shoes. Let's do it. But I want a piece of the Intruder just as badly as you do. If we get out of this alive, we go after it together. Fair shares for all. Yes?"

"Works for me," said JC.

Happy and Natasha forced their way through the blood, to stand facing each other. The vampire sharks were still circling, drawing steadily closer as hunger drove them on. Erik stabbed at one of them with his pointing bone, and the creature immediately rolled over onto its back and sank beneath the waves. Blood churned and frothed around it as the others moved in. Melody gaped at Erik.

"How did you get that bone out of my pocket?"

"Heh-heh," said Erik.

"We can call the hell train," Happy said to Natasha. "But will it come? I don't think we have the power to compel it, even working together."

"You want power, I got power," said Erik. "Or rather, my marvellous machine does. Excuse me . . ."

Another vampire shark blasted up out of the blood, rising high into the air to crash down on the group from above. Erik shot it down with his pointing bone, and it was already dead in mid air when JC backhanded the body away. It landed some distance away, and several of the creatures went after it.

"How can they still be hungry?" said Melody.

"Flesh is good, but it doesn't satisfy," Happy said absently. "They want blood. Our blood. Hot and spurting, right from the source."

"We've killed enough of them! Why don't they take the hint and go away?"

"Feel free to ask them," said JC. "Erik, get your damned machine out."

"Way ahead of you," Erik said smugly.

He eased the cat-head computer out of his back-pack. The pack was soaked in blood, but the machine was untouched. Erik held it carefully out before him, above the surface of the rising blood, and turned it on. The three Institute agents watched with varying degrees of horror and disgust as the cat head opened its eyes wide and howled miserably.

"It's crying," said Happy. "The whole thing, not only the cat head. It's alive and crying all the time."

Erik smiled modestly, as though he'd been paid a compliment.

"I do good work. Now, pay attention. Happy, Natasha, reach out with your thoughts and locate our elusive hell train, and the computer will boost your strength, for a time. Make you powerful enough to compel the train to come here and pick us up. But don't take too long, or you'll burn out the box. Or yourselves. We're working in unknown territory here. Come on, come on, shake something useful. You don't want the nice cat head to explode, do you?"

"Ignore him," said Natasha. "I do, as much as possible."

The two telepaths leaned forward until their foreheads were almost touching, and their thoughts jumped out and meshed together, joining with the cold machine thoughts to form a single gestalt consciousness, far greater than the sum of its parts. The wildly moving parts of the machine blazed up, blindingly bright, and Happy and Natasha and the cat head howled together like a crazed animal. Erik looked thoughtfully at his machine and wondered if he truly understood what he'd created.

Three minds in one reached out through the miles of underground tunnels and quickly found the hell train, hiding in a side tunnel that didn't properly exist. It screamed briefly as they took hold of it, and *pulled*, and the hell train erupted out of the far tunnel-mouth, pushing a great bow wave of blood ahead of it. Vampire sharks made harsh grunting sounds as the train ran them over and crushed them under its great weight. The hell train ploughed more of them under as it slammed though the blood, finally slowing to a halt beside the platform. The blood rose half-way up the cars, steaming and boiling where it touched the steel sides.

The car doors nearest the telepaths jerked open. Blood immediately gushed into the empty space. JC led the way forward, broaching the still-rising blood with his chest, forcing his way through the sheer weight of it. The others pressed in close behind him. Kim drifted above the surface, murmuring encouraging words and keeping an eye out for attacking vampires. By the time all of them had struggled through the doors, Erik carrying his computer on top of his head, the car was half-full of blood. The doors moved jerkily forward, tried to close, then stopped abruptly. JC and Melody grabbed a door each and forced them together. One last vampire shark threw itself against the closed doors, and they shuddered under the impact. The vampire fell away, still snapping its great jaws. The blood surged up, rising above the door, as though angry at being cheated of its prey.

JC turned to Happy and Natasha. "Right, we're all in. Get us the hell out of here!"

The train surged forward, throwing them all off-balance. The blood in the car rolled heavily back and forth. And then the train picked up speed, driven on by the three joined minds. The blood finally filled the station, but the train was off and moving, plunging into the tunnel, through the blood and out into the darkness beyond.

....

The train roared on through the dark, the car lurching heavily from side to side as the blood slowly drained away. The five agents waited until the seats reappeared, then collapsed onto them and relaxed as best they could. Happy and Natasha sat shoulder to shoulder, the same radiant expression on their faces. Melody watched them warily, her machine-pistol on her lap. Erik cuddled his computer on his lap and spoke comforting nonsense to the cat head, which ignored him. Kim couldn't actually sit down, as such, but she did her best, floating a few inches above the seat next to JC. He smiled, to show he appreciated the effort. They were all soaked in blood, to varying degrees, and the smell was appalling. Melody frowned suddenly.

"Excuse me. This may be a silly question, but who's driving this train? And do they have any particular destination in mind?"

"We are driving," said Natasha, not looking round, her voice disturbingly far away. "We are in control. And a little less distraction would be fine by us. This isn't easy, you know."

"The train is fighting us," said Happy. His voice sounded eerily like Natasha's. "It isn't really a train, you know. It's something the Intruder brought with it and made over into a train. So it could abduct commuters without being suspected. The Intruder has a use for commuters."

JC leaned forward. "What use?"

"The train doesn't know," said Natasha. "It doesn't ask questions. I don't know if I'd go so far as to say it's sentient, but it's as close as dammit. A living construct, something the Intruder made to love and serve it."

"So the enemy can make real things," said JC. "Not only illusions."

"It's growing stronger all the time," said Happy. "The longer it stays in our world, the stronger it gets. Our world . . . is just something for it to play with. To change and manipulate as it chooses."

"What is it?" JC said urgently. "Can you see what it is?"

"Old," said Natasha. "So very old, and wild, and horribly powerful. It's come here to kill us all. Isn't it all simply too exciting for words?"

"Ignore her," said Erik. "I do, as much as possible."

"Take us back to our original base, on the southbound platform," said JC. "You said you needed your equipment, Melody."

"Damn right." She looked at Happy and leaned forward to stare into his face. "Are you all right? Your face is flushed, and the sweat is pouring off you. Have you been . . ."

"Don't need them," said Happy. "For the moment. I've never experienced power like this. It's like running in a top gear you didn't even know existed."

Melody checked the pulse in his neck, then laid her hand briefly across his sweltering forehead. "Happy, you're burning up! Your body isn't designed to operate under such pressure!"

"Nothing we can do," said Natasha. Her face was flushed and perspiring heavily, too. "If we lose control of this train, even for a moment, it'll turn on us. But don't worry. This really is quite exhilarating."

"Yes," said Happy. "Lovely."

Melody moved to sit at JC's other side, so she could lean in close and whisper. "They're spending too long locked together. They're already acquiring each other's speech patterns. God knows what information she's picking out of his brain, or what nasty habits he's picking up from her. We need to separate them while we still can."

"We can't do anything until the train gets us where we're going," said JC. "You have to work your instruments, find us a way to fight back."

"Oh right; load everything on me."

"We all do what we have to," said JC. "Now concentrate. The first thing we need is some idea of who or what our unseen enemy is. We need a name, an identity, some indication of its powers and limitations. And, hopefully, its weak spots. Next, we need to nail down its exact physical location in the Underground. It used the energies created by Kim's murder to open a portal onto this plane, and now it's using her continued ghostly existence to maintain its presence in our world. That makes it vulnerable. So we have to find and face the Intruder, hurt it enough to weaken it, then break the bonds that connect it to Kim so we can drive it out of our world and slam the door shut behind it."

"Oh," said Melody. "Is that all?"

"Isn't he wonderful?" said Kim, beaming. "He's got a plan for everything!"

"Not necessarily," said Melody. "It could be that the only way to banish the Intruder from our world . . . is to remove the focal point that holds this haunting together. Which is you, Kim. Your existence makes the Intruder's presence possible. To get rid of him . . ."

"We don't know that for sure," said JC. "There's a lot of things we don't know for sure yet."

"But could you sacrifice her?" said Melody relentlessly. "If that's what it takes?"

"He won't have to," said Kim. "I'll do whatever's necessary to save my world."

"Isn't she wonderful?" said JC.

"You poor damned fools," said Melody. "There's no way this can have a happy ending."

She turned her back on JC and Kim and wouldn't look at them for the rest of the journey.

||||||||||||||||||||||||

The train brought them back to the southbound platform without incident. The car doors opened, a little blood leaked out, and everyone disembarked. Melody ran straight to her waiting equipment and did her best to embrace them all at once.

"Babies!" she said, not caring who heard her. "Mommy's back, and everything's going to be fine again." She straightened up suddenly. "All right, who's been messing with my equipment? These aren't the settings I established. Somebody had better speak up right now if they like having their testicles where they are."

"It was me, I admit it!" said Eric. "I was very careful, and very respectful." He looked at Natasha. "And I think I'm going to hide behind you for a while if that's all right with you."

Natasha's head snapped round suddenly, looking behind her. Happy's head turned, too, at the exact same moment. Everyone else turned to look and found that the hell train had vanished, without a sound. Natasha let out her breath in a long sigh and shook her head slowly. Happy mopped sweat from his face with a handkerchief and smiled sickly.

"Wow, what a rush . . . Can't say I'm sorry it's over, though." He glared at Natasha. "That woman has a mind like a bucketful of boiling cats. Sharp and vicious and downright nasty."

"You loved it," Natasha said calmly. "Your mind isn't exactly a luxury hotel. I've never lived in such a small place. Though there were many interesting new chemical flavours . . . It's a wonder to me your synapses still function."

Happy looked at JC. "Don't ever ask me to do that again. There aren't enough pills in the world to flush that woman's thoughts out of my head. I may put in for compensation for post-traumatic stress disorder."

"You were born with that," said JC.

"True."

And then they all stopped talking to look at Kim as she advanced slowly but remorselessly on Erik. He backed away, clutching his cat-head computer to his chest. There was something new about Kim, something different, and disturbing. As though she wore the cold presence of death like a cloak. Erik swallowed hard as Kim drifted down the platform after him.

"What . . . what do you want?" he said, his voice catching in his throat. "I've been good. I've done everything that's been asked of me."

"Put down the computer," said Kim.

Erik clutched the machine tightly. "No. It's mine. I made it. I dreamed it up. I made it real."

"Put down the computer," said Kim. "While you still can."

Erik looked into her eyes, and whimpered. He put the box down on the platform and scuttled quickly backwards. Kim knelt and peered into the cat head's unblinking eyes. It tried to purr for her.

"Poor little kitty," said Kim. "No more screaming, no more crying. Sleep." She extended her ghostly hand down through the cat head and into the glowing workings of the box beneath; and the whole computer shuddered. It turned and twisted unnaturally, imploded, and was gone in a puff of displaced air. The cat's head was left behind on the platform, quite dead. Kim smiled and turned back to face the others.

"It's at peace now," she said.

Melody looked at JC, but he stopped her with an upraised hand.

"Work your equipment," he said. "Find me the answers

I need to take the fight to the enemy. I want this over with."

He walked off down the platform, and Kim drifted after him. They tried to walk arm in arm, but their arms kept passing in and out of each other.

NINE

....

LITTLE BILLY HARTMAN GETS HIS REWARD

Unknown to all the agents in the Underground, there was someone else down in the station with them. Lost and alone, little Billy Hartman went scurrying through the empty corridors like a rat in a sewer. Not very big, never very big, Billy stuck to the shadows, hiding behind corners and peering warily through entranceways. No coat, only a grubby sweater and stained jeans, and a pair of knock-off trainers that had never been fashionable. Half out of his mind with fear and panic, driven on by rage and resentment, tormented by horror and loathing for the awful thing he'd done, little Billy spied on all the other people from a safe distance. None of them noticed him, but then, no-one ever did. He was far too small to be noticed by such powerful people.

And besides, Billy was protected.

He heard them speak, heard them argue, heard of the Carnacki Institute and the Crowley Project; but these names meant nothing to him. He listened to the great people, as they spoke of theories and fears and intentions, and didn't care about any of that, either. He only had thoughts for himself and what might become of him. He'd done something, something big and important that no-one could ever put right again. If they knew, if they only knew . . .

The day before, Billy Hartman had murdered Kim Sterling. Even though he had no real reason, no motive, no idea who she was. He'd never killed anyone before, never really wanted to. He wasn't a murderer, wasn't a beast or a monster. He was a little man with a little life and less ambition. A small cog in a small wheel in a small company that no-one else gave a damn about. But he woke up that morning with murder on his mind, and he couldn't seem to shift it. He wanted to kill a beautiful woman . . . like all the ones who'd laughed at him, or spurned him, or worse still, ignored him. He wanted to hurt one of them the way they had hurt him. To strike back, just once, and let them feel the pain.

So he took a big knife from his tiny kitchen in his shabby little flat and went out into the great big world, humming cheerfully. He descended into the Underground, and travelled up and down the lines, switching from platform to platform until finally . . . he saw her. And knew immediately that she was the one. He'd thought it would be a hard thing, a difficult thing, to actually kill another human being; but when the time came, he walked up behind her, stabbed her once in the back, and walked away. No-one saw or suspected him. Why should they? He was far too small and unimportant to be noticed. He went back to his flat, still humming cheerfully, made himself a meal-for-one in his little microwave, watched television, and went to bed.

To dream of how it felt when the blade went in, and he twisted it, before withdrawing. He didn't enjoy it. It felt like someone else's dream.

But this morning, a new feeling had driven him from his bed. The feeling that something had gone wrong. The morning news said that Oxford Circus Tube Station had been shut down, and serious news presenters said the word *murder* in their serious voices. And suddenly Billy knew he had to go back, that he had to go back down into the Underground and make sure there was no evidence left to link him to the crime. He couldn't have anyone finding out what he'd done. That would be awful.

Sneaking back in had proved surprisingly easy. On any other day the massed forces of uniformed police and security guards would have intimidated him into a frozen panic; but not that day. He walked right past them, and they never saw him. Partly because he was, after all, a small and insignificant person, but also because Someone was looking out for him. He could feel it. Someone big and powerful was protecting him.

He walked right past them, right under their noses, and they couldn't see him.

But once he was down in the tunnels, moving in scurrying little runs through the fiercely bright light, from shadow to shadow and hiding-place to hiding-place, things happened that destroyed what little confidence he had. Bad things. Billy saw bad things. He saw ghosts and monsters and horrible, impossible things, nightmares broken loose and running wild in the world; and he ran and ran until finally he saw the worst thing of all. The ghost of the beautiful woman he'd killed the day before. She looked just as beautiful, dressed in white like an angel, her hair the same colour as the blood that had spilled down her back when he pulled out the knife.

He crouched, in the deepest and darkest of the shadows, watching her with wide, confused eyes, scared out of his mind. He didn't feel guilty, and he didn't feel sorry; he knew now he'd only done what he'd done in the service of his Protector. But he was terrified that these big and important people, with their big and important voices, would tell the authorities what he'd done, then everyone would know. He'd be caught and punished and locked up in a cage, forever and ever. Billy had gone through most of his life afraid of being punished.

First, he spied on JC and his team, then he spied on Natasha and Erik, trying to figure out who they all were and what they were doing. Trying to figure out what he should do. He saw them do amazing and awful things, then he saw them fight each other, and he saw them working together. None of it made any sense to Billy. The ghost was there, too, acting like she was still alive; and once she turned her head and looked right at Billy. He shot off immediately, running and running and not looking back, and when he finally stopped to glance fearfully around him, he was on a platform he didn't recognise.

He moved slowly, diffidently, down the platform. He was meant to be there. He could feel it. His unseen Protector had brought him there, for some important purpose. A train pulled into the station, moving smoothly and silently—a dream of train, come just for him. Billy made *ooh* and *aah* noises. The train was painted in bright colours, from end to end, all the fresh and vivid shades of childhood. A great big toy train, just for him. Bright and cheerful and not threatening at all. (So why were all the hairs standing up on his arms and the back of his neck?) The Protector had sent this train, the Protector who had hidden him from the authorities, who loved him and cared for him and looked after him. Who now called to Billy in the sweetest of voices, calling him . . . to come and meet his Protector, and get his reward for killing the beautiful woman.

(Except . . . Billy hadn't wanted to hurt her. Not really. He never wanted to hurt anyone. At the last moment he had hesitated; and some other force had moved his hand. Hadn't it?)

Billy stared in wonder at the candy-coloured train and was sure it was there to take him to a wonderful place, where he would find all the answers to all the questions that had ever troubled him. And in that place he would be made safe and happy and know pleasures he had only ever dreamed of before. Wriggling with excitement, little Billy Hartman walked confidently forward, and the brightly coloured car doors opened before him. He stepped on board and sat down, the doors closed silently, and the train took him away.

....

He passed through station after station, and many strange and wondrous sights revealed themselves to him through the car windows. Platforms made out of interlocked bones, the great curving station like a massive rib cage . . . huge plunging waterfalls of glistening solid crystal . . . rioting gardens full of huge flowers with thick pulpy petals and gasping pink mouths that sang sweet songs to him in high-pitched voices, like a choir of mice. Billy sighed and laughed and beat his hands together, almost drunk on the sheer splendour of it all.

The train slowed as it approached its final destination, and Billy cried out in joy, pressing his face right up against the window to better view the shining city spread out before him. Ethereal spires and massive golden domes, spiralling fairy towers connected by elegant walkways . . . and beautiful women everywhere, smiling at him. At him! Angels floated down shimmering paths and bowed their haloed heads to him. Billy was so happy he could hardly breathe. He had left the plain, hurtful, ordinary world behind him, at last. His Protector had rescued him and brought him there, to where he should have lived all along.

The train halted abruptly. The doors slammed open, and Billy hurried out onto the waiting platform, almost dancing in his eagerness to meet his Protector, and thank him, and start his new life. And then he stopped suddenly, and looked around him, confused. Something was wrong. Something was horribly wrong. The marvellous city was gone, the beautiful towers and the beautiful women were gone, and he was standing alone on a bare and empty platform. No name, no destinations, not even any posters on the walls. Billy looked back, and the brightly coloured train was gone, too. There weren't even any rails. He'd been left here, alone, abandoned in an empty place. Billy started to cry.

It was cold, and getting colder. Billy hugged himself tightly as his breath steamed thickly on the still air. His teeth began to chatter, and his tears froze on his cheeks. Thick patterns of hoarfrost formed on the bare walls, horrid images like staring eyes and gaping mouths.

Heavy jagged icicles hung down from the ceiling, like glistening stalactites. There was a sound; and Billy turned to look.

And when little Billy Hartman finally saw what it was that had been guiding and protecting him all this while, he screamed and screamed, until he tore out the lining of his throat, and blood sprayed from his mouth.

TEN

||||||||||||||||||||||||||||||

WHO'S AFRAID OF THE BIG BAD WOLF?

Back on the southbound platform, Natasha was making herself useful. A quick spell (muttered under her breath in what sounded very like debased Coptic), and all the blood disappeared from everyone's clothes, leaving them still battered and torn but comfortably dry and clean. And smelling not entirely unlike a country meadow. The blood basically leapt out of the clothing and ended up scattered in puddles all around them, steaming quietly. Everyone made polite, thankful sounds, while Natasha preened prettily.

"Oh, that old thing. I've had that spell in my repertory for years. Never leave home without it."

Erik sniggered. "Now tell them what you had to do to acquire that spell. And what you did with the blood afterwards."

"They don't need to know that!" snapped Natasha. "It would only upset them. Why do you always have to spoil everything?"

Erik shrugged. "Stick to what you're best at, that's what I always say."

Melody ignored them all. She didn't approve of magic. She busied herself with her equipment, checking the most recent displays and frowning intently at the long-range sensor readings. All her instrument panels were lit up, blazing fiercely as new information flooded in. Melody stabbed fiercely at one keyboard after another, scowling at each monitor screen in turn, reluctant to admit she didn't understand half of what her machines were telling her. Energy readings everywhere were off the scale, spiking and changing and disappearing even as she looked at them. Some of what she was seeing made no sense at all, as though the very laws of reality were becoming slippery and unreliable under the influence of some monstrous Outside will.

Tunnels, platforms, corridors—the whole station was crawling with unnatural manifestations. Ghosts, demons, other-dimensional creatures; some of them so strange, so alien, they barely qualified as life-forms at all. Life and Death weren't as separate as they used to be, down in the Underground.

"Stop frowning like that, Melody," said JC. "You'll give yourself wrinkles. What's up?"

"Do you want the bad news, the really bad news, or the *Oh we are truly fucked this time* news?" said Melody. "If I'm interpreting these readings correctly, and I am, we're in enemy territory now. Something from way beyond the fields we know or even guess at, has come among us, and is reworking the most basic laws of our reality. Writing over the world, to make it more like where the Intruder originally came from."

"All right," said Happy, "you've got my attention. Are

you sure about this, Melody? The sheer power involved would . . ."

"Of course I'm not sure!" snapped Melody. "I've never seen readings like this! I doubt anyone has. But I am definitely seeing massive displays of other-dimensional energy, more than enough to transmute matter. Something from the afterworlds has forced open a door into our reality, settled in, and established a beachhead. Part of this Intruder has manifested in our world, taken shape and form, and rooted itself here; and more is coming through all the time. Or, if you prefer, downloading its information into our material plane, and just its presence is enough to mould the world around it. The Intruder is more . . . real, than us. And it's not hiding any more. As though it wants us to know where it is, and what it's doing. As though it wants us to come and find it."

"As if we'd fall for an obvious trap like that," said Happy. "We're not going to fall for an obvious trap like that, are we? Oh shit, we are. I want to go home."

He fumbled a bottle of pills out of an inside pocket, but his hands were trembling so much he spilled most of them on the floor. He got down on his knees and scrabbled for the scattered pills. He was shaking all over, and his mouth trembled as though he might burst into tears at any moment. Natasha looked down her nose at him, and Erik giggled, embarrassed. JC got down on one knee beside Happy but made no move to help or hinder him.

"Happy, don't do this. I need you sharp and focused."

"What if I don't want to be sharp and focused?" said Happy, looking only at the pills in front of him. "What if I don't want to see something that's more real than we are?"

"It's the job," said JC. "Look at you; you're a mess from what you've taken so far."

"It's only the come-down," muttered Happy. "I'll be fine. But I need a little taste. Something to put me right."

"No you don't," said JC.

"You don't know what I need! We can't all be big and brave and heroic, like you! Some of us are ordinary mortals, doing the best we can!" He looked at the pills he'd collected in his hand. "If you were me, you'd be knocking back the meds, too. So you wouldn't have to be like me."

"Happy . . ."

"I can't do the job without them, JC. I just can't."

"Want to try some of mine?" said Natasha. Happy looked up, to find her standing over him offering a slim bottle of pills. Happy rose slowly to his feet, staring at the bottle as though hypnotised. JC stood up beside Happy but made no move to interfere.

"Only the very best, for the Crowley Project's most favoured agents," said Natasha. "Something to make you feel like a man, or a god, or whatever else it takes to get the job done. Want a little taste?"

"Tell you what," said Happy, licking his dry lips. "You try one of mine . . . and I'll try one of yours. No? Didn't think so. Did you really think I'd take sweeties from a stranger? Typical Project agent. Even now, you can't resist manoeuvring for advantage. We're facing the end of the world, and we still can't trust each other."

"Trust is fine," said Natasha, making the slim bottle disappear about her person. "But always count your change. This . . . is only a marriage of convenience. And you can't blame a girl for trying."

"You were never a girl," said Erik. "You were born

fully mature, and nasty with it. Probably shot out of the womb demanding a gin and tonic and a ciggie, and a gun that fired real bullets."

Natasha smiled on him. "How well you know me."

Erik sniffed loudly, and moved away to peer closely at Kim. He walked round and round her, studying her from all angles, careful always to maintain a safe distance. Kim let him do it, studying him coolly. Erik finally stopped in front of her, looking thoughtfully into her ghostly face, so close their noses were almost touching.

"Boo!"

Kim laughed delightedly as Erik fell back several steps. He pulled his dignity back about him, doing his utmost to look like a scientist again.

"Remarkable phenomenon," he said, in his best lecturer's voice. "Very lifelike. Astonishing level of interaction with the living. Almost human."

"More human than you," Kim said sweetly. "Nasty little man."

Erik flushed darkly. "Why did you destroy my computer?"

"Because it offended me," said Kim. "Better be careful, Erik; you offend me, too."

Erik actually looked a little hurt. "You don't even know me . . ."

"Oh, you'd be surprised," said Kim. She drifted forward, and Erik backed away before her. Kim fixed him with a hard, critical gaze. "The dead see many things that are hidden from the living. I know why you had to leave Vienna University in such a hurry. I know why Interpol chased you across half of France. Shall I mention the dog with two heads, the monkey that aged backwards, the pig with the added human brains that could say seventeen words in Portuguese? And you really shouldn't have surgically reworked that homeless girl's circulatory system, to make it more efficient. Such a mess . . ."

"Shut up!" said Erik. "Shut up! Get out of my head!"

"Wouldn't go in there on a bet," said Kim. "It's not my fault you wear your sins so openly."

"They weren't all failures! I achieved things, important things! I did!" Erik was breathing hard, almost on the edge of tears. "Don't think I can't hurt you because you're dead!"

His left hand dived inside his coat, but JC was immediately there, putting himself between Kim and Erik.

"Don't even think about it," said JC.

Erik swallowed hard and looked away, unable to meet JC's gaze, even muffled behind sunglasses. He nodded quickly to JC, and to Kim, then hurried away to hide behind Natasha, who ignored him.

"If you've all finished butting your heads together, perhaps we could concentrate on the extremely imminent end of the bloody world!" said Melody. "We are running out of time, people. Quite possibly literally."

"Sorry," said JC.

He moved over to join Melody at her instruments and made a show of studying the displays thoughtfully, as though they meant something to him. If Melody wasn't entirely fooled, she was kind enough to keep it to herself.

"Any clues as to who or what our Intruder might be?" said JC, after a while.

"Nothing definitive," said Melody. "But it's not just . . . something from the afterworlds. This is Big, really quite unbelievably Big. One of the Great Beasts, perhaps. The Hogge, or the Serpent . . . Bad news on every level you can think of. If I really understood what these displays are telling me, I think I'd be very upset."

"One of the Great Beasts?" said Happy, incredulously. "That is way out of our league!"

"Speak for yourself," Natasha said immediately.

"You're not fooling anyone," Happy said viciously. "I can feel your fear from here."

"You feel me again without my permission, and I'll slap your face off," said Natasha.

"Children, children . . ." JC murmured. "Play nice, or there will be spankings. Melody, could the presence of the Intruder in our world explain why I was touched by the Light? Was I granted this new strength to . . . even things out? Give us a fighting chance?"

"Who knows why the gods do anything?" said Erik.

"They are not gods!" Happy said immediately. "Don't use that word. Never use that word. Just because they're so much more than us, it doesn't mean they're gods."

"What difference does it make?" said Kim, puzzled.

"Because you can't fight gods," said Happy.

"We can fight things that think they're gods," JC said cheerfully. "Remember that being we encountered in the supermarket car park? Worshipped by generations of early Humanity; and we still kicked its arse and sent it home crying. Melody, could our Intruder be anything like that?"

"No. That was a much more basic, even elemental, force. Not coherent enough even to have a name or identity. We're faced with something far more sophisticated. A single entity, or presence, that can change our world simply by existing in it." She looked at Happy. "Spell the word god with a lower case, and it's a good enough term for what's down here in the darkness with us."

Everyone looked at each other. No-one wanted to be the first to say anything.

"We are not equipped to deal with a Great Beast," Happy said finally. "Let's be real here, people. Outer Forces like that are so far out of our league we couldn't even see the league from where we are. We're ghost finders, not god killers."

"What we need are better weapons," said Natasha. "Bigger weapons. First rule of the Crowley Project: there's nothing in supernature that can't be taken down with a big enough stick. Maybe if we combined our resources . . ."

"You're seriously contemplating throwing down with a god?" said Melody.

"We've been known to kill gods, at the Project," said Erik airily. "Sometimes we eat them, too."

"You couldn't even stand up to me," said Kim. "And I'm only dead."

"Confidence is fun," said JC. "Sanity is better. We need a plan."

"We need weapons!" said Natasha.

"You can't fight the Great Beasts!" said Happy. "They're as much conceptual as anything, a horrible Idea from a higher plane, downloaded into physical form in our dimension. You can't kill an Idea. The best we can hope for is to pry it loose from our plane and send it home with a flea in its ear." He frowned, considering. "And we might be able to do that. So far, all the signs suggest our Intruder is following the standard pattern of any haunting, building everything from and around a single focal point."

"You're talking about me," said Kim.

"We don't know that for sure," said JC.

Happy ignored him, looking at Melody. "How far away from us is the Intruder, and please say lots."

"Hard to tell," said Melody. "If I'm interpreting these readings correctly, and I'd be the first to admit that there's a whole lot of guesswork involved . . . it seems our Intruder has *added* a whole new platform to this station. A half-way place, where its world butts up against ours. This new platform comes and goes, not always there, or at least, not always connected to our reality. It's the Beast's lair. Home for its new physical form. For whatever shape it's taken in our world. We can only access this new station with the Intruder's permission."

"Is it there now?" said JC.

"Oh yes," said Melody. "It's driving my long-range sensors crazy. They don't like the taste of it at all."

Kim looked round suddenly. "JC, something's coming."

Everyone turned to look at her. JC moved over to stand beside her, but her gaze was elsewhere.

"Are you sure?" said Melody. "There's nothing on the monitors."

"Something's coming," said Kim, in a dreamy voice. "Something bad."

JC studied Kim, who was floating in mid air with her head cocked slightly on one side, as though listening to something only she could hear.

"What is it, Kim? What's coming for us? Where is it coming from?"

Her left hand rose slowly to point at the far tunnel-mouth. Everyone looked into the darkness, but there was no roar of an approaching train, no pressure wave of disturbed air. Even the rail tracks were free of any

vibration. Natasha and Erik stood close together. JC and
Happy stared silently at the tunnel-mouth, considering
their options. And Melody stood protectively between
her machines and whatever was coming, her machine-
pistol at the ready. Happy surreptitiously dry swallowed
a couple of pills. He took a deep breath, and sweat
popped out across his face. His heart was beating dan-
gerously fast.

A Tube train emerged from the tunnel-mouth, moving smoothly and silently, an ordinary train, with ordinary empty cars. Except the engine made no sound at
all, and the brightly lit cars didn't rock or clatter in the
slightest. The train pulled slowly, steadily, into the station, with barely a breath of disturbed air, and came easily to a halt. The five agents braced themselves, ready for
any kind of attack; but nothing happened. After a while,
one set of car doors slid silently open and waited, invit-
ingly. No-one moved. None of them liked the look of
this train. There was nothing obviously unnatural about
it, apart from its quiet, but if anything, it was too ordinary, too perfect, as though it was newly made, never
used before.

"All right," said JC. "This is an invitation. The Intruder sent this train to bring us to it. No more games, no
more attacks . . . But why? Because we've proved we
can handle anything it can throw at us? Because we've
proved ourselves worthy? Or because it's so much stronger on its home ground . . . Could it be that it's afraid
there's something we could do, to drive it from our
plane, if it doesn't deal with us first? Is it because the
Light reached down and touched me, or because we
have Kim now?"

"Questions, questions," said Natasha. "At the Project, we prefer direct action."

"Shoot first and ask questions later," said Erik. "Preferably through a medium."

"We can't answer questions without new data," said Melody. "And we have to do something, while we still can. This thing's power levels are already off the scale. I think it's getting ready to spread its influence beyond this station."

"You mean through the rest of the Underground?" said JC.

"I mean through the rest of the city," said Melody. "And then across the worlds. Rewriting the rules of our reality to make a new world, more like its home dimension. I don't think there'd be much room for Humanity in a world like that."

"We have to warn people," said Happy. "Contact the Boss, call for help . . . Get some of the A teams down here, with serious firepower. This has got way too big for us."

"You heard the Boss," said JC. "None of the A teams can get here in time. There is no-one else. Just us." He looked at Natasha and Erik. "I hate to ask, but I think at this point I'd even welcome help from the Project. Is there any chance . . ."

"No," Natasha said reluctantly. "By the time we convinced the Project, it would be too late. Our current Head, Vivienne MacAbre, isn't as trusting as we are."

"I've heard of her," said Happy, unexpectedly. "Does she really eat white mice for breakfast?"

"So they say," said Erik. "Baby mice, stuffed with hummingbirds' tongues. On little toast soldiers. Of course, that's only when she isn't feasting on the hearts of our enemies. Vivienne's always been a traditionalist at heart."

JC looked at Melody. "What do your machines make of this train? Is it real or something created by the Intruder?"

"I can't tell," Melody said helplessly. "With the power levels the Intruder's generating, the question's pretty much meaningless. It can make things real just by thinking about them."

Happy strode up to the car and kicked the open doors. "Feels real."

"Oh hell," said JC. "You've taken some of mother's little helpers, haven't you?"

"Oh yes!" said Happy. "And I feel great!"

"Wonderful," said JC. He considered the train for a long moment. "It's real enough. It'll get us there. Because the Intruder wants to meet us in person. Well, I want to meet the Intruder. So let's go."

He stepped into the car through the waiting doors and looked quickly around to assure himself it really was as empty as it appeared. Kim floated in after him, comforting him with her presence as best she could. She knew he was remembering another train, and another car, and what had happened to him there. JC took off his sunglasses and looked up and down the length of the car; but even his new eyes couldn't detect any booby-traps or hidden evils. He glanced briefly at Kim.

"I'm fine. You?"

"I'm fine, JC."

"Can you see anything? Sense anything? Anything the Intruder wouldn't want us to know about?"

"This isn't a train," said Kim. "It's the Intruder's idea

of a train. A new-made thing, based on the hell trains it used to abduct the commuters earlier. There's no driver in the engine; the train knows where it needs to go. The Intruder's becoming stronger all the time . . . its thoughts and intentions can take on shape and form now."

"All the more reason to brace it in its lair now," said JC. "Before it becomes so strong it can bring us to it just by thinking about it."

He gestured sharply to the others still hesitating on the platform, and one by one they entered the car. Natasha made a point of striding fearlessly through the open doors. Erik scurried in after her, trying to look in every direction at once. Happy positively bounded on board, smiling foolishly. Melody gave her machines a last farewell pat and stepped through the doors as though it were just another train. Happy slipped his arm through hers and beamed at her chummily. Melody pulled her arm free and slapped him round the head. The doors slammed together abruptly, and the train moved off, leaving the platform behind.

,,,,,,,,,,,,,,,,,,,,,,,,,,

The train ride was unnaturally smooth and easy. The engine was utterly silent, the car didn't rock in the least, and once it entered the tunnel-mouth, the train never once deviated from its path. No jolts or turns, no corners, no other platforms; only a straight line through an endless, impenetrable darkness. Not one trace of light outside the car windows, and with no stations or landmarks to judge the train's progress, it was hard to tell if it was moving at all. Or even if they were still underground rather than moving through some great night-dark sea.

Natasha and Erik sat side by side, not looking at each

other. She seemed entirely calm and in control; he was keeping a watchful eye on every part of the car, in case something should jump out at him. Melody stood with her back to the car doors, arms tightly folded across her chest, glaring about her as though daring anything to try anything. Happy was too full of nervous energy to stay in any one place for long. He tried half a dozen seats, couldn't settle, and finally skipped up and down the central aisle, humming tunelessly and occasionally breaking into a surprisingly accomplished soft-shoe routine. JC sat quietly, thinking and planning, and Kim did her best to sit beside him though she had a tendency to rise and fall in place when her concentration wandered. She studied JC with real concern, but he didn't notice. He was working.

And then all their heads came up sharply as the darkness outside began to seep through the windows and into the car. Slowly and inexorably, it poured in like thick, dark syrup, as though the window-glass weren't even there. The five agents moved quickly to stand together in the central aisle, as the darkness poured in from every side and dripped from the ceiling. None of them wanted to touch the stuff, and none of them wanted it to touch them. The darkness filled up both ends of the car, then spilled forward along the rows of seats. It was utterly dark, more like an absence than a presence, as though the agents and the slowly shrinking pool of light were the only remaining life in an endless, dark nothingness.

Natasha produced something small and round from a pocket and shook it hard. A soft, yellow organic light blazed from the ball in her hand, and where it touched the approaching dark, the light stopped the darkness

dead in its tracks. Natasha waved the glowing ball back
and forth, reinforcing the circle of light's boundaries.

"Salamander ball," she said succinctly.

"Bit small," said Happy.

"Hell," said Erik. "You only get two to a salamander."

The yellow light sputtered, then faded quickly away
to nothing. Natasha shook the ball hard, swore briefly,
and threw the thing away.

"I think it was frightened," said Happy. "Does anyone
have anything else, and someone please say yes."

Melody produced a chemical stick and waved it. A
dull green light flared up.

"Oh wow!" said Happy. "We're going to a rave!"

"You want a slap?" said JC. "You're the telepath; is
this darkness real, or a broadcast illusion?"

"It's the dark," said Happy. His voice was suddenly
serious, and his face was like the melancholy clown
whose eyes are always sad above the painted smile. "This
is the real dark, the real thing, far more than just the absence of light. This is the living dark; and it's hungry."

"All right," said JC. "Not as helpful as I'd hoped, but
that's Happy for you. Natasha?"

"It's real," she said flatly. "Real enough to kill us all.
Or perhaps remake us in its image."

The green light from the chemical stick was already
guttering. Melody shook the stick savagely and said
terrible things to it, but it died anyway. The darkness
crept remorselessly in, from every side at once. Some of
it had already crawled up the sides of the car and joined
together on the ceiling, over their heads. There was a
distinct chill on the air, as though the darkness was soak-
ing up all the warmth in the car.

"This is not a natural darkness," said Erik, his voice high and unsteady.

"Oh, you think?" Melody said harshly. She threw her useless chemical stick at the darkness, which swallowed it up in a moment. "What was your first clue? When it oozed right through the bloody windows? Of course it's not natural!"

The five agents huddled together as the circle of light slowly contracted around them. Kim hovered beside them, glancing nervously at the dark ceiling. JC glared around him, his eyes glowing very brightly behind his sunglasses.

"Erik's right," he said abruptly. "This darkness may be real, in the sense that the Intruder created it and imposed it on our world; but it's not a natural darkness. This is all more of the Intruder's mind games to soften us up. Right, Happy, Natasha?"

"I don't know," said Happy. "I can't tell. Maybe."

"So help me, you take one more pill without my permission, and I will knock you down and stamp on your head," said JC. "Concentrate! Is this darkness something the Intruder created?"

"Yes!" said Happy. "Has to be. Darkness doesn't behave like this in the normal world."

"Natasha?" said JC.

"If the Intruder made it, then it's real enough to kill us," said Natasha. "But that doesn't make it *real*."

"Make a circle," said JC. "Everyone hold hands. Kim, fake it. This is symbolic. We're going to work together, join together, and repudiate this darkness through sheer will-power."

"What makes you think that'll work?" said Erik.

JC grinned. "Because I already did it once."

They made a circle, standing very close together, hand in hand in hand. Kim stood inside the circle, both her ghostly hands on top of JC's. The darkness was very close. There was no car left outside the circle of light. They stood alone, the living and the dead, surrounded by darkness. JC took off his shades, and his eyes were very bright.

"Be strong," he said, and his voice was calm and comforting and very sure. "The darkness is not real, but we are. See the world as I see it, through my eyes."

His eyes blazed up, as some last trace of the given Light shone through them. The darkness stopped, and even recoiled a little. A sudden charge went through the circle, racing through their joined hands. They all gasped and cried out, even Kim. And in that moment, the Light shone in all their eyes, bright and sharp and irrevocable; and the darkness could not stand against it. Fuelled by their joined strength of will, by their simple and brutal act of disbelief, the energy shot round and round the circle, growing stronger all the time. The six of them turned their heads and looked at the dark, and the darkness could not bear the Light that burned in their eyes. It fell back, rushed back, down the car and out through the windows; and suddenly the car was back again, just as it had been, and the only darkness was outside.

JC gently tugged his hands free from Natasha and Happy, and everyone else let go. The energy was gone, the circle broken, and everyone's eyes were back to normal again. Except for JC, who calmly replaced his shades. Happy shook his head uncertainly as the others slowly resumed their seats.

"Wow—what a rush. Tell me that's not how you feel all the time, JC; I'd be killingly jealous."

"That was . . . *incredible*," said Natasha.

"It's all to do with will-power," JC said easily. "One of the first things they teach you at the Carnacki Institute."

"I must have been off sick that day," said Happy. "The only lesson that stuck with me was *Don't go up against the Great Beasts on your own.* Along with how to fill in next-of-kin forms."

"The Project believes in encouraging individual effort," said Erik. "Along with basic and advanced treachery, back-stabbing, and general unpleasantness. Survival of the fittest. Trample on the weakest, glory in their plight."

"No, I'm pretty sure that last bit is only you," said Natasha. "Nasty little man."

"Heh-heh," said Erik.

"I think I'm going to go and sit by somebody else," said Happy. And he got up and moved away from Erik to sit down beside Melody. Who immediately punched him hard in the arm.

"Ow!" said Happy. "What was that for?"

"For sneaking pills when you were expressly told not to. I'll think of other things to hit you for later."

Happy nodded unhappily. "I suppose a pain-killer is out of the question?" And then he broke off and looked round sharply. "Hold everything, go previous . . . I think the charge running through that circle flushed most of the chemical goodness out of my system. I haven't felt this sober in years. I don't like it. But I am definitely feeling things. Heads up, people; there's someone else here."

They all looked around, but there was no-one else to be seen. The darkness was back beyond the windows, where it belonged, and the car seemed perfectly normal.

"Are you sure?" said Melody. "It isn't just . . ."

"No it isn't just!" snapped Happy, up on his feet and glaring about him. "I am, unfortunately, entirely clear-headed again, and I am telling you. There's a presence in this car. Not a ghost, not as such. But I can feel it, like a background noise, like a flickering light, or a voice calling from another room . . . *It's here, and it's alive . . .*"

"Yes!" Kim said suddenly. "It's a man! I can sense him if I concentrate hard enough. Over there, by the end doors."

And again everyone looked, but even when Kim pointed, they still couldn't see anything. JC even lowered his shades for a moment, but it didn't help. He looked at Happy.

"Not a ghost. A presence. Alive, not dead. So who is it?"

"I think . . . it's the man who killed me," said Kim. "Or what's left of him."

JC leaned in close beside her. "Are you sure?"

"He's not entirely dead, but pretty close," said Kim. "This is part of him. His mind, his spirit . . . driven out of his body by some terrible trauma."

"Oh good," said Natasha. "I was starting to feel peckish. Don't look at me like that, it was just a joke!"

"Well, what's it doing here?" said Melody.

"I think he's trying to warn us about something," said Kim. Her gaze had softened, and her voice was no longer angry. "He feels so sad, so hurt, and so very afraid."

"Warn us?" said Happy. "Warn us about what?"

"About what's waiting for us," said Kim, her head cocked slightly to one side, listening. "He desperately wants to warn us about what he saw and what happened to him. He says he has a name for us."

"What name?" said JC.

"Fenris Tenebrae," said Kim.

"Oh shit," said JC.

"What?" said Natasha. *"What?"*

"Fenris Tenebrae," said JC, and his voice was very cold and very grim. "The Wolf In Darkness. The Devourer. One of the really old Great Beasts, and the most terrible."

"What's so bad about a wolf?" said Natasha.

"You eat ghosts," said JC. "Fenris Tenebrae eats civilisations, and worlds. It is the end of all things, given shape and form and appetite."

"Oh shit," said Erik.

"We never stood a chance," said Happy, softly, bitterly. "Right from the beginning, we never stood a chance. It's been playing with us . . ."

"More fool it," JC said steadily. "We can do this, people. There's always a chance."

"Of course," said Kim. "We've got you."

iiiiiiiiiiiiiiiiiiiiiiiii

The train slammed into a station, and a cold, characterless light shone through the car windows. The train slowed smoothly to a halt and stopped. The five living agents and the dead woman stared out the windows. The station had no name and no markings, no destinations map, and nothing at all on the bare stone walls. No-one moved on the empty platform. The car doors opened silently and waited. JC looked at the doors, then at the station beyond.

"So this is the station the Beast made for itself. Bit basic. Not big on details, our Beast."

"It's not playing games any more," said Melody.

"It doesn't have to," said Happy. "I think the Beast brought us here to show us its true face."

"You say that like it's a bad thing," said Natasha.

"To look into the eyes of a Great Beast is enough to destroy a human mind," said Happy.

"You really do have self-confidence issues, don't you?" said Natasha. "Grow a pair, dammit. We're trained agents! We can do this!"

"Yeah," said Erik, giggling. "Man up. What's the matter with you? It's only a big bad wolf."

"Okay," said Happy. "You crazy people can go out first. I'll be somewhere else. Hiding."

Natasha sniffed loudly, shouldered JC aside, and strode out through the waiting car doors and onto the deserted platform. JC hurried after her, not wanting to be left out of anything. Erik and Melody went next, and Happy brought up the rear, dragging his feet so much that Kim actually floated right through him to join up with JC.

The station was so cold it hit them all like a blow and stopped them dead in their tracks. The freezing air cut at their exposed flesh like a knife, and breathing in the bitter air was enough to burn their lungs. The five living agents huddled together instinctively, crowding close to share their body warmth. Kim looked at them blankly. She didn't feel the cold at all. Both ends of the platform had disappeared, swallowed up by darkness, and the only source of light spilled out from the car behind them. Only now it was a harsh yellow light, as though it had somehow gone off, gone rotten, become . . . spoiled.

"This is what it will feel like at the end of the world," said Happy. "When the sun has gone out, and Fenris Tenebrae has eaten the moon. When all the living things are gone, and nothing remains but the dark and the cold and the endless night."

They looked around, but nothing looked back. They were alone on what remained of the platform, in what remained of the light. Dust seemed to be falling, softly and silently, in endless grey curtains.

And then Kim drifted slowly forward, untouched by the cold or the dark or the terrible foreboding of the place, and pointed out a small dark shape tucked away beneath the exit arch. JC made himself move forward to join Kim. There was someone sitting there, half-hidden in the shadows. A man, small and anonymous, curled into a foetal ball, staring straight ahead with fixed, un-blinking eyes. His clothes were covered with a thick layer of frost, hard and unyielding to the touch, and he was locked so tightly into his state it was hard to see how he would ever rise from it again. He was still breathing. Small puffs of shallow breath steamed on the chill air. But his wide, staring eyeballs were covered over with fine misty patterns of frost.

"He doesn't even know we're here," said Kim. "But I know him."

"Is this the presence from the train?" JC said quietly. "The man who killed you?"

"I never saw his face," said Kim. "Just felt the sudden pain in my back. But yes; this is what's left of him. The body his mind was driven out of." She looked at JC. "I think the Beast showed him its true face; and this is what it did to him."

"But what's he doing here?" said Natasha. She'd fi-nally found the strength to move forward to join them. The others were coming, too, each at their own pace. Natasha prodded the unmoving body with the toe of her pink leather boot, and the small man rocked slightly in place, for a moment.

"I think the Beast called him here," said Melody. "Because it had no more use for him. It didn't want one of its agents ending up in the Institute's hands, or the Project's. We might have got some answers out of him."

Erik crouched before the frozen figure, studying him with ghoulish fascination. "Fascinating . . . Almost cryogenically preserved. I really must send someone back for him when this is all over. I could have endless fun defrosting and dissecting him."

"He's ours," Melody said automatically. "Hands off."

"You wouldn't even know what to do with him," said Erik.

"We'd do our best to treat him, restore him," said Melody.

"Exactly," said Erik. "Look at his face. The despair, the horror. You think he ever wants to wake up and remember what he's been through? If Kim is right, he's half-way to being a ghost already. So let him go. At least I could have some fun with what's left."

"You're still assuming there's going to be an afterwards," said Happy. "There's a Great Beast here, remember? Let us put all our efforts into surviving the next few moments."

He pushed Erik aside so he could crouch before the frost-covered figure and peer into its frozen face. Erik reached for a weapon. Natasha grabbed his arm and glared at him. None of the others noticed, intent on the still body.

And then there was a sound, and they all turned to

look. It was an abnormally low and unnatural growl. It resonated in their bones and in their souls, triggering a strangely familiar atavistic fear. It was a sound from the Past, out of the Deep Past, out of the ancient shared past of the human species. From when we all lived in the forest, and we all lived in fear of the wild. It was the sound of the Beast, of all the wild things that ever were. Full of hate and contempt and brute bloodlust.

JC moved slowly forward, through the archway, and the others went after him. Because they'd come this far, and they had to see, had to know, for themselves. And because something in that terrible sound compelled them. And once they were through the archway, the light blazed up, and they all saw what poor little Billy Hartman had seen.

Huge and vast and intense beyond bearing, big as a house and more imposing, cruel and vicious and utterly wild, a great Wolf's head. It had manifested on the earthly plane by manufacturing a shape out of its surroundings, using stone and cement and steel for its bones, then covering them with the wet red flesh and blood of the commuters it had abducted in its hell trains. Its great sharp teeth were made from human bone, and its huge shining eyes were formed from hundreds of human eyes. There was no fur, only wet crimson meat, to give shape to the Wolf's head, all of it held in place by an implacable, inhuman will. It even had great pointed ears made of human flesh. It growled, and its breath stank of dead things.

For all its makeshift form, it was still Fenris Tenebrae, one of the Great Beasts, and its sheer presence was overwhelming. To look on it was like staring into the sun. It was all teeth and snarl and malevolent eyes, every wild wolf that ever was, embodied in a single brutal avatar—ancient and primordial, almost abstract, blazing with hate and hunger and cunning. Hatred especially for all the small running things that had dared to prosper in this world, dared to get above themselves and forget their true place as prey. The Wolf, the Great Wolf, Destroyer of Civilisations, and of Worlds.

Fenris Tenebrae.

Nature red in tooth and claw and loving it, all in one terrible face. No wonder poor little Billy had been driven out of his mind. Most people aren't equipped to deal with monsters. But JC and Happy and Melody had been trained and hardened and refined by the Carnacki Institute, and Natasha and Erik had been beaten into shape by the harsh masters of the Crowley Project. So that they could track down monsters and stare them in the face, and not be broken or disturbed. So they could go face-to-face with things that were so much bigger than them, more real than them . . . and not look away.

They were agents. And Kim was dead. And not one of them was prey.

In the end, JC laughed in the Wolf's face. It took everything he had, and it was only a small, brief sound, but it was enough to break the mood. Natasha and Erik shook their heads, as though coming out of a bad dream. Melody shuddered, and Happy put his arm round her shoulders and held her close, comforting, and she let him, glaring defiantly back into the Wolf's huge eyes. Kim moved in close beside JC, and he laughed again—a real, hearty, dismissive sound. It hung on the air, refusing to go away. Natasha laughed, too, and Erik sniggered. Happy gave

Melody a comforting squeeze and managed a breathy laugh of his own. Melody smiled coldly.

The Wolf growled again, a great roar of a sound, loud enough to shake the surroundings and rock the floor under their feet. A hateful sound, to fill all the world with cruelty. The stench of blood and carrion from the gaping jaws was sickening. Happy sneered at the Wolf.

"I have to say, as projections of the infinite into the material plane go . . . this really is pathetic. Only a head? What happened to the rest of you? Get stuck in the hole you opened because you couldn't make it big enough to crawl through? Is your rear end hanging out on the higher plane? Maybe somebody's hanging their washing on it, like they did with Pooh's behind when he got stuck in Rabbit's hole. All the other Great Beasts must be laughing their socks off. I mean, yes . . . the head's pretty good. I'll give you that. All big and nasty and wild; but when all's said and done, it's still only a head. My old Gran's got a stuffed fox head on the wall; and I can't help thinking you'd look really good as a trophy in the Boss's office. Make a hell of a conversation piece. Your time is past, Beast. No-one worships or fears you any more. We've moved on."

"I will make them fear me," said the Wolf. "I will give them reason to worship me again."

It had a voice like tearing flesh and spilled blood, and howling in the night. All the cruel joy of the chase and the slaughter.

"Nice speech," JC said quietly to Happy. "But I think you've annoyed it enough now. Try and bear in mind that the Wolf is currently powerful enough to change our reality just by thinking about it."

"Trust me, that thought is never far from my mind,"

said Happy. "Our only hope is to keep the thing occupied, hold its attention, while we think of something to do. Right?"

"Good thinking, man," said JC.

"And?" said Happy.

"I'm working on it," said JC.

"Terrific," said Happy.

"You know, you can let go of me now, Happy," said Melody.

"Oh, sorry," said Happy, quickly removing his arm from around her shoulders.

"That's all right," said Melody. "You knew how close I was to cracking. You held me together. And, you saved my life earlier. So, to say thank you, when all this nonsense is over, I am going to take you back to my place, throw you back onto the bed, and then do you and do you until you can't stop smiling."

"If we survive," said Happy.

"Oh yes," said Melody. "If we survive."

"I knew there had to be a catch in it somewhere," said Happy.

They grinned at each other.

"Who are you chattering creatures?" said the Wolf, and his voice was like thunder, like lightning, like the storm that breaks the greatest of trees. "What are you, that you can bear my terrible gaze, my awful presence?"

"We are the Carnacki Institute," said JC.

"And the Crowley Project," said Natasha.

"Agents trained and armed to stand between Humanity and all the Forces of the afterworlds," said JC. "Now, are you going to leave quietly, or are we going to have to give you a good kicking, then boot your nasty arse out of here?"

"He hasn't got an arse," said Happy.

"Then we'll improvise," said JC.

"Yes, let's," Natasha said cheerfully. "I do so love to improvise."

"Suddenly and violently and all over the place," said Erik. "It's an education just to watch her."

The Wolf looked at them. Whatever opposition Fenris Tenebrae had expected to face on the material plane, this clearly wasn't it. Open insolence and defiance were new things to the Wolf, and it didn't know how to cope. It tried another growl, an even louder one, but no-one so much as flinched this time. Happy actually faked a yawn. The Wolf closed its bloody mouth with a snap and fixed JC with a crafty, spiteful gaze.

"You cannot make me leave this place, little thing. I have a hold on your world. I will not give it up, and you cannot make me. You cannot even hurt me, or you would have tried by now. You are nothing but a distraction, and I am done with you."

"We have your hold on the world right here," said Natasha, gesturing at Kim. "You used her death to open a portal into our world, which means as long as her ghost haunts this station, you can't be thrown out. She's the focal point of everything that's happened here."

"Natasha," said JC. "Where, exactly, are you going with this?"

"I would have thought it was obvious," said Natasha. "What's the fate of one dead person, compared to the whole world?"

"No," said JC. "There has to be another way."

"But there isn't," said Kim. She smiled gently at JC. "I'm dead. My life is over anyway. I won't fight this, JC, and I won't let you fight it either. It's necessary."

"But I love you . . ."

"And I love you. But love is for the living." She looked at Natasha. "What are you going to do, exorcise me?"

Natasha smiled. "No, dear. I eat ghosts."

She moved forward, still smiling, and JC stepped forward to block her way, his face cold, and very determined. And Kim walked straight through him, to stand before Natasha. JC cried out and pulled the monkey's paw from his pocket. Melody drew her machine-pistol, and Erik his pointing bone. And Happy threw both hands in the air and waved them vigorously as he yelled at the others.

"Hold it! Hold everything! *Look at the Wolf!*"

Everyone hesitated, then turned and looked at the Wolf's head. It was grinning mockingly, its wet red mouth stretched wide. Dead men's blood drooled and dripped.

"What about the Wolf?" snapped Natasha. "It isn't doing anything."

"Exactly!" said Happy. "You're about to destroy the one thing that gives it a hold on our world, and it isn't even worried? If Kim meant anything at all to the Wolf, it would have acted to defend her. Probably turned us all into frogs or something, and I do wish I hadn't said that out loud."

"He's right," said JC. "Kim isn't the focal point."

"Well, you would say that, wouldn't you?" said Natasha.

"No," Erik said reluctantly. "The telepath's right. The Wolf isn't worried. Kim was only ever a decoy, a distraction. We've missed something. Damn. Damn! We've missed something important!"

"Then why did he have me killed?" said Kim.

"Because it was fun," said the Wolf. And it laughed at them all.

Melody stepped forward, trained her machine-pistol on the Wolf's left eye, and emptied the whole magazine into it. The great manufactured head soaked up the bullets and took no damage at all. Erik stabbed his Aboriginal pointing bone at the huge Wolf face. The bone exploded in Erik's hand, and he cried out in agony as jagged splinters were driven deep into his hand. He cradled the bloody mess against his chest and fell back, moaning.

Happy cried out to Natasha. She looked at him, nodded quickly, and grabbed his outstretched hand. Their minds slammed together, and the combined strength of their joined thoughts struck out at the Wolf like a single shining lance. The Wolf opened its mouth, swallowed the attack whole, and took no harm at all. The head surged forward, its great jaws snapping at Natasha and Happy. They scrabbled backwards, letting go of each other's hands.

JC brandished his monkey's paw and advanced on the Wolf's head, holding the burning fingers of the modified claw out before him. It was a forbidden weapon because it could give a man the power of a god, for a while; but even it was no match for the Great Beast. It burst into flames, hot and fierce, and JC cried out and dropped it. He grabbed for it again, but already the paw was nothing but ashes smeared across the platform. The Wolf's head surged forward again, pulling more of itself into the world, but JC stood his ground. He whipped off his sunglasses and stared right into the Beast's huge eyes. The Wolf sneered at him.

"My, what big eyes you have . . ."

"And they help me see so clearly," said JC. "Especially things that have been right under my nose all along. Kim isn't the focal point of your haunting, and never was. There's nothing of you in Kim. She's a ghost, an unfortunate by-product of your actions. You've been waving her in front of me all along, to distract me. She isn't the focus; her murderer is. That's why you brought him here. By committing an act of murder in a certain place at a certain time, when the walls between the worlds were at their weakest, that act opened a door for you. Murder magic has always been a trait of your kind; you kill because you can't create. In all the time you've been here, you haven't made one new thing—only copies of existing things."

He turned abruptly to Happy and Natasha. "I need the murderer's spirit. Find it. Kim said he was still here, with us. Find him and put him back in his head."

"He won't stay long," said Happy. "He's too traumatised."

"Put him back together for a while," JC said urgently. "I need to talk to him."

Happy and Natasha joined hands again, and concentrated. The Wolf cried out angrily, but no-one was listening to it. There was a sharp, cracking sound, and flecks of frost flew on the air as the frozen head turned slowly to look at Kim. The murderer blinked once, and his eyes cleared. He looked at Kim and tears started from his eyes, only to freeze before they were half-way down his cheeks. He worked his mouth, amid more harsh, cracking sounds, and Kim drifted forward to stand over him, to hear what he had to say.

"I'm sorry," he said, in a voice full of all the pain and tiredness in the world. "I'm so sorry."

The thick layer of frost covering his body exploded out from him as he stretched suddenly and forced himself up onto his feet. Great cracks appeared, in his clothes and in his frozen flesh, but he ignored them, all his attention fixed on Kim.

"My name is Billy Hartman," he said slowly. "I never meant to kill you. Never meant to kill anyone. It was like a nightmare I couldn't wake up from."

"I gave you what you wanted," said the Wolf. "What you dreamed of. Don't say you didn't."

"We don't always want what we want in dreams," said Billy. "They're just dreams!"

"Humans are so complicated," said the Wolf. "You can't even tell the truth to yourselves."

"You don't understand us," said JC. "You never did. You may be realer than us, but we're still more than you are."

Billy glared at the Wolf's head, able to face it at last, in the last few moments of his life. "You lied to me. Used me!"

"That's all you're good for," said the Wolf.

Billy turned his head away, dismissing the Wolf, and studied Kim with his sad, betrayed eyes. "What's it like, being dead?"

"You're closer to death than I am," said Kim, not unkindly. "I'm stuck here. I was going to do so many things . . . and now I never will."

"I know," said Billy.

"It's hard to know what I feel about you," said Kim. "Finally having a name and a face to put to my murderer . . . doesn't really make any difference. You were used by the Wolf, like me . . . but you, at least, had some choice in this. I can't forgive you."

"That's all right," said Billy. "I don't forgive me either."

JC stepped forward. "You want a way to get back at the Wolf? Make it pay, for everything it's done to you and Kim and everyone else?"

"There's a way for me to put things right?" said Billy.

"No," said JC. "What's done is done and can't be undone. But I can give you a chance to defy the Wolf and save the world from what it wants to do to us."

"I'd give anything for a chance like that," said Billy.

"There's only one way that works," said JC. "One chance to pay all debts. Sacrifice."

Billy looked at the Wolf and smiled slowly. His frozen cheeks tore as his mouth stretched. "I can do that."

"Not on your own you can't," said JC. "Take my hand, Billy, and walk with me."

The dying man put out his hand, and JC took it carefully in his. The frozen flesh burned his hand, but he didn't let go. The two men strode towards the huge Wolf head, and it snarled warningly at them. Kim suddenly flew forward, putting herself between JC and the Wolf.

"No! JC, you can't do this! You mustn't! You'll die, and leave me here alone! What debts do you have to sacrifice yourself for? What was your sin?"

"Loving the dead," said JC.

And he walked straight through her, his living lips briefly coming up against her dead mouth, for one last kiss, as his face passed through hers. The Wolf growled

at JC and Billy, watching them carefully, grinding its
great bone teeth together. JC stared right back into the
Wolf's huge eyes, and the Wolf blinked first. JC's gaze
was burning so very brightly, and the Great Beast could
not match it.

"You," said JC. "You brought people to this place, in
blood and horror and suffering, and killed them, to build
your face. You turned the station into a bad place and
infected it with your presence—a psychic stain that will
last for generations. So you could make a place of your
own. You destroyed two lives: Kim and Billy. To make
your portal into our world. You came here to destroy us
all . . . because you could. One of the Great Beasts, with
no soul, no conscience, and not even the faintest trace of
true greatness. Even the smallest human is bigger than
you. Right, Billy?"

"Right," said Billy.

Fenris Tenebrae howled horribly, and the great head
surged forward again. The massive jaws opened, and
started to snap closed on Billy and JC, because it couldn't
bear to hear what they were saying. To silence and punish and hurt them because that was what the Wolf did.
And as the jaws were slamming together, at the very last
moment, Billy pushed JC back, with all the strength remaining in his frozen arms. So that when the terrible
jaws came together, only Billy was there. His frozen
body exploded into a thousand jagged pieces . . . and
with him finally dead and gone, with the focal point of
the haunting destroyed, the Wolf no longer had a hold on
the world. It had destroyed the very thing it had worked
so hard to make. Fenris Tenebrae howled once, a wild,
horrid, despairing sound, then it was gone. The manu-

factured head was left behind, all the stone and steel, bone and flesh of it; but nothing within it remained.

The world had been saved from the Great Destroyer, and not by the Carnacki Institute or the Crowley Project. By one little man, with a man's courage.

ELEVEN

,,

MORTAL AND IMMORTAL ENEMIES

The unreal platform melted away, dissolving into mists and shadows; and they were all back at the southbound platform, as though they'd never left. Everything was calm and quiet and normal again. First JC, then the others, surreptitiously checked themselves to make sure everything was where it should be.

"How did . . . No," Happy said firmly. "I am not going to ask. Because even if I did understand the answer, which I am prepared to bet good money I wouldn't, I'm pretty sure I wouldn't like it."

"See?" said Melody. "You're learning. Personally, whenever I encounter something I don't understand, I say *quantum*, very loudly, and everyone else nods and goes along. Science is lot like magic. Words have power."

"You mean, all this time you've been faking it?" said JC.

Melody grinned. "I never fake it. I don't have to."

She moved briskly away to check her precious

instruments. Happy watched her go, then turned to look at Kim, floating above the platform some distance away from everyone else. She caught his gaze, and something in her eyes made him drift unobtrusively over to join her.

"So," she said. "That's that. The Wolf is gone. The Underground has been restored. But what happens to me, now?"

"I could help you . . . pass on," Happy said carefully. "Help you cross over to what comes next."

"Do you know what comes next?" said Kim.

"Not for sure, no," Happy had to admit. "I have asked any number of ghosts and demons and otherworldly things; but I've yet to receive an answer I trust. The dead always have their own agenda. Still, look on the bright side. It can't be that bad; no-one ever comes back to complain."

"Then I think I'll pass on your kind offer," said Kim, very firmly. "I want to stay in this world, with JC."

"And I want you to stay with me," said JC.

Happy glared at him. "I've told you before about sneaking up on me."

But Kim was smiling at JC, and he was smiling at her, and there, beating on the air between them, was all the love in the world. Happy sighed quietly. He had a great deal more he thought he ought to say, about how the living and the dead should never get emotionally involved because it's always going to end badly . . . but he didn't. Because he knew nothing he could say would make any difference whatsoever.

Of course, that didn't stop Melody from striding over to stick her oar in. Melody had always been a great believer in getting involved. "Are you crazy, JC? You can't live in sin with a ghost! What are you going to do? Shut her in the attic when the neighbours come round? You are not compatible; and I am not talking about race, creed, colour, or star signs! You are flesh and blood, and she's not!"

"Love conquers all," said JC.

"Love finds a way," said Kim.

"Putting logic aside, for a moment," said Happy, "I feel I should point out that the Boss is not going to like this."

"The Boss never likes anything we do," said JC.

"True," said Happy. He grinned suddenly. "I can't wait to see her face when she finds out . . . Can I be the one to tell her? Oh please, let me be the one to tell her!"

"Is that it?" said Melody, switching her glare from JC to Happy. "Is that all you've got to say? You're actually ready to go along with this?"

"Why not?" Happy said reasonably. "We've done weirder things in our time."

"Well, yes, but . . . That isn't the point!" Melody sputtered for a moment, tried waving her arms about to see if that would help, then gave up. "It'll all end in tears. I just know it. And I'll end up with Kim round at my place sobbing ectoplasm all over my shoulder. But I'll go along. For now."

"You both did very well against the Wolf," said JC. "I am so proud of both of you."

"Sweet talk will get you everywhere," sniffed Melody.

JC looked at Happy. "And look how well you did at the end, without a single pill in you. I told you; you're stronger than you think."

"Lot you know," said Happy. "My nerves are a mess. I won't sleep for days."

"Right," said Melody. "I'll see to that. Lover boy."

"Okay," said Happy. "You're worrying me now."

"Heh-heh," said Melody. And she sauntered unhurriedly back to her machines.

"What about us?" said Natasha.

She and Erik were standing side by side, a cautious distance away. Neither of them was actually holding any weapons, but there was something about them that suggested the sudden producing of weapons might not be entirely out of the question.

"What about you?" said JC.

"The truce is over," said Natasha. "Our mutual enemy is gone, and with it our common cause. Which means that, technically speaking, we are now mortal enemies again. Sworn to each other's destruction, and all that."

"I don't think I've got enough energy left for playing mortal enemies," said JC. "How about you?"

Natasha's mouth twitched. "Not really, no. To be any more tired, I'd have to be twins."

"Vivienne MacAbre did say," Erik ventured diffidently, "'Come back with JC's head, or don't bother coming back at all.'"

"Oh, she's always saying things like that," said Natasha. "We helped save the world from the Great Wolf! That's got to be more important than a little inter-organisation bloodletting. Hasn't it?"

"Well, no, not really," said Erik. "We're not actually in the world-saving business. More the opposite, I would have said."

"Yes, but only on our terms," said Natasha.

"Vivienne MacAbre said—"

"Oh, screw Vivienne MacAbre!"

"Now there's an idea," said Erik. "Could I watch? Could I film it?"

Natasha went to hit him, and he dodged easily.

"Children, children," said JC. "There are matters we need to discuss before we all depart to go our hopefully separate ways."

"Like what?" said Natasha.

"There's no way a Great Beast like the Fenris Tenebrae could have broken into our world so easily without help from this side," said JC. "Someone must have worked in advance, to seriously weaken the walls between the worlds."

"Crowley Project," said Melody, not even looking up from her instruments. "Has to be."

"It's not us," Natasha said immediately. "Something that big, we'd know."

"Would we?" said Erik. "None of us can say for sure that we always know what our lords and masters are up to. We're only field agents."

"If someone, or some group, is making deals with the Outer Forces, and neither of our organisations know anything about it," said Happy, frowning deeply, "then I would say we are all officially in deep doo doo."

"But if they did know anything, do you think our lords and masters would tell us?" said Natasha. "Something for us all to think about . . . Now, Erik and I really must be on our way, darlings. Things to see, people to do, you know how it is. Busy busy busy. Bye-bye, sweeties. Let's not do this again sometime."

Natasha Chang strode away, with Erik Grossman

scurrying after her, and JC and his people watched them go until they were completely out of sight. And only then did they relax.

"I think the competition just got that little bit fiercer," said Happy. "If there really is some great secret up for grabs, whoever gets to it first will have a major advantage over the other."

"Let the Boss worry about it," said Melody. "I'm not paid enough to worry that much."

"But we have a distinct advantage," said JC. "We have a ghost on our team! Everyone knows the dead see many things that are hidden from the living. Which means we have a much better chance of finding out what's really going on!"

"Yes," said Kim. "The ghost of a chance."

JC and Kim walked off together, doing their best to walk arm in arm, leaving Happy and Melody to pack up the equipment.

"If I'm entirely made up of ectoplasm," Kim said thoughtfully, "and I can change my appearance at will . . . then I should be able to change a lot more than my clothes. So, JC, what do you think? Would you like my boobs a bit bigger?"

"Size isn't everything," JC said solemnly. "On the other hand; can you do a nurse's outfit?"

New from *New York Times* bestselling author

SIMON R. GREEN

From Hell With Love

It's no walk in the park for a Drood, a member of the family that has protected humanity from the things that go bump in the night for centuries. They aren't much liked by the creatures they kill, by ungrateful humans, or even by one another.

Now their Matriarch is dead, and it's up to Eddie Drood, acting head of the family, to figure out whodunit. Unpopular opinion is divided: It was either Eddie's best girl, Molly. Or Eddie himself. And Eddie knows he didn't do it.

M687T0410

From the *New York Times* bestselling author
of *Daemons Are Forever*

SIMON R. GREEN

The Spy Who Haunted Me

Eddie Drood's evil-stomping skills have come to the attention of
the legendary Alexander King, Independent Agent extraordinaire.
The best of the best, King spent a lifetime working for anyone and
everyone, doing anything and everything, for the right price. Now
he's on his deathbed and looking to bestow all of his secrets on a
successor, provided he or she wins a contest to solve the world's
greatest mysteries. Eddie has to win, because King holds the most
important secret of all to the Droods: the identity of the traitor in
their midst...

Now available from Roc!

M545T0709

AVAILABLE NOW IN PAPERBACK FROM
NEW YORK TIMES BESTSELLING AUTHOR
Simon R. Green

JUST ANOTHER JUDGEMENT DAY
A NOVEL OF THE NIGHTSIDE

*Come to the Nightside, where the clocks
always read three A.M., where terrible things
happen with predictable regularity, and where
the always-dark streets are full of people
partying like Judgement Day will never come.*

Judgement Day has arrived, and the Walking Man,
God's own enforcer whose sole purpose in life is to
eliminate the wicked and the guilty, has come to the
Nightside. Given the nature of the Nightside, there's
a good chance that once he gets started, he'll just
keep on going until there's no-one left. Private in-
vestigator John Taylor has been hired by the Authorities to stop him. But legend has it that he can't be
killed...

"A macabre and thoroughly entertaining world."

**—Jim Butcher,
author of the Dresden Files series**

penguin.com

M328T0510